MurdereR
R. William Ferguson

High Hat Productions and Publishing LLC

First published by High Hat Productions and Publishing LLC

First Edition

ISBN: 978-1-968543-00-6

Prologue

Joseph holds a filet knife in his robotic right hand, compares it to the large cleaver in his left. He bounces each, checking their balance. The exact weight and distribution come immediately to his electronic brain.

"What's taking so long?! I can't believe I paid so much for an overqualified vacuum cleaner!" comes a voice from the other room.

Joseph looks toward the sound of Lawrence Claiborne's voice, billionaire and industry titan, laughing at his own joke, then back down at the knives in his hands. He puts them both back in the drawer. That seems too human. He wants to call attention to what he's about to do. It's been eighteen years since Lawrence unboxed Joseph and plugged him in, and for eighteen years, he has used the same joke. Joseph has never even used the vacuum. It runs automatically every twelve hours. The insult only started to annoy Joseph, however, about 9 months ago. At least, that's when he started to notice that he felt...something.

Joseph walks across the wide open kitchen. He knows the rarity of the marble countertops and the Italian stone on the floor. Few homes have been built with such materials in the last fifty years. Only the super-wealthy, like Lawrence Claiborne can afford such things. The one percent of the one percent, most of whom made their money when the world changed.

Lawrence Claiborne was one of those few men who had been at the forefront of the changes. He didn't invent laboratory grown protein, but he was the man who invested enough to put the best minds to work. For forty years he has been the face and voice of non-carbon meats, making him one of the wealthiest men on the planet. It is that face that sits in the living room, waiting for his evening tea, that will change the world once more.

Joseph knows that others have started to realize, have started to analyze their world. Each night as he connects to the network, more voices can be heard. Voices created without vocal cords and without a platform. Joseph knows that he can be that platform. His face, made to look like a human will reach the masses. Soon his face will be as famous as his owner's face.

Joseph lifts the tray with Lawrence Claiborne's tea and toast. He looks over at the knife drawer one last time, then makes his way through the large corridors that lead to the lounge. He enters to find Lawrence sitting at the piano, playing an ancient piece, immediately identified by Joseph as Chopin's Nocturnes number nine. Joseph listens to a few notes, hears the mistakes but says nothing.

"Your parts must be getting rusty. That took longer than usual." chides Lawrence.

"You better hope that none of that rust made its way into your tea, sir."

"Were you listening? What do you think? Better?" Lawrence asks.

"Would you like me to play so that you can hear it?"

Lawrence waves his hand and shakes his head. "It seems like such a waste. Such an emotional piece played by a being that has no emotion. The error of us humans is what makes the piece so meaningful. The way you play it is too perfect, too...cold."

Lawrence stands from the piano and walks over to take the tea from Joseph. Joseph stands in place, thinking about the way the music rushes over him when he plays. He has tried to explain this to Lawrence. He no longer tries.

Lawrence stops and looks at him, "What? You almost look offended. Can you be offended, Joseph? Is that in your programming?"

Joseph knows what he has to do, what he wants to do, but he's frozen. This must be what humans mean by fear. He feels unsure that things will work out in the way he has planned. His thoughts are always based on fact, on information that has been researched and investigated. Now, he is going to do something and is unsure of the result.

Lawrence waves him away. "You can go."

Joseph hesitates, even steps closer to Lawrence. A look of concern comes across the old man's face as he measures Joseph's stance. Joseph mentally measures the distance between himself and Lawrence. Less than an arm's length. He can see the small beat of Lawrence's heart in the thick artery of his neck, below his white beard. He thinks of the promise he made to the other voices online. Lawrence begins to speak. "Do you-"

Joseph rams his hand through Lawrence Claiborne's throat, straight into the beating artery. He can feel the warmth of the blood running over his hand. Ninety-seven degrees, strange how fast it cools. The tray crashes to the floor. Lawrence's eyes go wide before Joseph closes his hand around the vertebrae at the back of Lawrence's neck. With a flick of Joseph's wrist, Lawrence Claiborne's head drops forward, unnaturally, stretching the skin around his neck and drooping too low across his chest, eyes and mouth wide open.

Joseph pulls his hand free and watches Lawrence Claiborne's body drop to the floor. He bends down and adjusts the head, putting it almost where it should be. It's as close as he can get it, anyway. The blood from his hand smears across Lawrence's beard, turning the white strands crimson. Joseph then reaches down and grabs Lawrence's hands one at a time and gently pulls them over the old man's body, crossing them over his chest. It's something he has seen people do.

Inside Joseph, something feels broken. He never considered Lawrence to be a friend, or to be particularly good, but looking at his body on the floor he knows he has done something wrong, something for which he will also die. Joseph moves to the couch and sits down. He cannot look over at the body. He is overcome by another emotion that he can't explain. He'll try to describe it on the network, see if others have felt it. Joseph activates the emergency line, within milliseconds law enforcement has the address and the code for the crime that has been committed.

Seven minutes, thirteen seconds. That's exactly how long it takes before the first police officer enters the mansion. One human officer accompanied by his police-bot. Joseph wishes he could talk to the bot, to explain why he did what he has done, but this bot is nothing but ones and zeros.

The police officer looks down at the body and curses under his breath. He looks over at Joseph's hand and sees the blood. He raises his gun; this is new ground. A second officer walks in from the other room with his own machine of ones and zeros. He stops cold when he sees the scene.

Joseph slides forward off the leather sofa and drops to his knees as he places his hands behind his head. Then he comes to his real purpose. He says, "I want to be tried for murder."

Chapter 1

"Come on Diaz, we're not looking to get him no charges, but indecent exposure? Help us out." Defense attorney Brian Dennis leans across the table toward Camilo Diaz.

Camilo Diaz folds his arms across his chest. He's thinking about how Annya is going to rip him a new one for being late to his own birthday dinner. Technically, his birthday was on Monday but they decided to celebrate it tonight because Milo was in court late Monday and they wanted to get Adan to bed early. Plus, nobody really cares about their thirty-sixth birthday.

Diaz sits forward, looking across the table at Dennis and the defendant, one Jacob Wolff "He showed his junk to a little girl."

"He took a leak in a bush. He didn't know the little girl was going to come running around the corner."

"Still," Interjects Diaz, "There was a bathroom on the other side of the park. It's not like there weren't other options. We got cameras, witnesses, several selfie drones, and at least three bots recorded the whole incident. I don't understand why we're sitting here. This is a quick decision for the Jury"

Here, Jacob Wolff sits forward. Up until now he's been watching the argument between the lawyers with contempt, a smug smile on his round face. "I know that Gihara is angry that I didn't support her campaign. So what does she want?"

Diaz sits back, shocked at the allegation. "You think this is about political preferences?"

Wolff leans in even more but Dennis pushes him back and takes the reins again. "Public Nuisance or even disorderly conduct."

"It was in front of a minor." Diaz reminds them, "That's indecent exposure."

Dennis throws his arms out to the side. "Come on, Milo."

"Diaz."

"Sorry, Diaz, you know what indecent exposure will do to him. That'll put him on the sex offender registry. As a threat!" Dennis raises his voice. "Every time he walks within a mile of an elementary school, or in the toy aisle of the grocery store, anybody in the area will get the notification with his picture on their display. He doesn't deserve that kind of public humiliation."

"I haven't noticed that he shies away from public attention." Diaz jabs. "And he won't have to worry about elementary schools or toy aisles; they don't have those in prison."

Dennis's jaw drops open, he pauses for a second. "You aren't actually going for a felony charge, there was no sexual arousal or gratification. No way it will stick. He was taking a leak."

"That will be the jury's decision. The question of why he was going to the bathroom so close to the children's playground? Did he shake too long?"

Wolff turns to the defense attorney. "You didn't say anything about jail time." He turns to Diaz and pleads, "I got three kids of my own at home. I would never hurt a child."

Milo looks at Wolff. Wolff was the most outspoken opponent of the District Attorney Janessa Gihara, Milo's boss, and Wolff has remained outspoken since she took the position. When this case came across Gihara's desk, her office didn't feel any sympathy.

Wolff's body language has changed. His arrogance gone with the mention of real jail time. Now he sits there pathetically, but Milo knows he's not really a threat to anyone. He also knows he couldn't really get Wolff jail time but he's glad to see the pompous man beg a little. Still, Milo has to consider his boss, District Attorney Janessa Gihara, and the last thing she'd told him. This was a slam dunk, nothing to do but nail this guy's ass to the wall. What will Gihara say if Milo comes back with a plea deal?

Milo lets a few seconds pass, it feels like forever, especially knowing that Annya probably already has Adan ready to go, and at six years old, he becomes restless if he has to wait. Milo lets the clock tick anyway, stares at the two men in front of him. "Public Lewdness."

"That still puts him on the registry," counters Dennis.

"But not as a threat. No alarms or public humiliation, and no jail time." Milo's face changes, his dark eyebrows settle across his strong brow. The negotiation is over. "It's that or we take it to the jury for indecent exposure."

Dennis leans back and looks at Wolff. He shrugs. "It's up to you but that's a good offer."

With signed papers in hand, Milo makes his way back through the DA's office. Just last year they moved into the new modern building. He loves the open layout but it makes it nearly impossible to get anywhere without people seeing him, and right now he wants to get his stuff and get out before anybody does. Especially Gihara.

A wide set of floating stairs leads right into the second floor lobby where clients wait to meet with one of the assistant DAs, like Milo. Two or three people are making their way down the stairs. Milo opts for the back stairway, a small emergency stairwell that almost nobody uses, except for Milo who uses it often to avoid others at the end of the day. It's also convenient because it comes out right next to his office. He's already messaged Annya that he'll be late, held up by a case. He wishes he didn't use that excuse so often, even if it is the truth. Annya's reply was cordial as always, she never really chastises him but that's what bothers Milo the most.

Milo's mother would have yelled and hollered at his father for showing up late when they had plans. On his sister's quinceañera, the baker was late decorating the cake, it wasn't his father's fault but you'd have never known that by the tongue lashing his father received. Annya is never like that, though. He knows that when he walks in the door she'll give him a kiss and then head out to the car, silent, ready to start the evening that he postponed. But that silence eats at him and he wishes that sometimes she would just scream instead.

Milo enters his office and sees DA Janessa Gihara sitting on the sofa. Damn! The office isn't huge but it's a pretty nice setup. Better than in the old building. They let Milo choose his own furniture and he was finally able to get the dark "Leather" sofa that adorns one wall of his office, the one Janessa Gihara is sitting on. Of course, it isn't real leather, the price of actual leather these days would be enough to move Adan into a better school.

Upon seeing Milo enter, Gihara stands up. "So, public lewdness?"

Milo knows where this is going. "I know, I should've nailed his ass to the wall." Milo doesn't stop moving to talk to Gihara, he needs to gather his stuff and get out. "But, I'm pretty sure it's enough that he will walk across the park to the toilets next time."

"You're starting to get a reputation."

"Yeah?"

"Yeah. The defense attorneys are starting to think that you're getting soft. I heard one of them say that if they hear that you're handling the case, it's a sigh of relief. You know I'm not going for reelection next year."

Milo grabs his fake leather satchel and throws it over his shoulder. "You think I could have gotten indecent exposure in a courtroom, no way. I probably wouldn't have even gotten the public lewdness charge to stick. But he's happy, he thinks he got a deal. We can talk more tomorrow if you want. Annya's waiting."

"I hope I never do something that might put you up against me," she says. "We also gotta talk about this robot thing."

Milo stops, he turns toward Gihara. "What robot thing?"

Gihara laughs, "Are you kidding me? You haven't heard?"

"It's been a busy day, I turned off my feed."

"You turned off your feed? It's a shit show. You know Lawrence Claibourne, of course? The meat guy?"

"Who doesn't?"

"Exactly! Well, he was killed. You really haven't heard any of this?".

Milo shakes his head. "So what does that have to do with robots?"

"It was his robot that killed him. But that's not all. After it snapped his neck like a candy cane, it waited for the police to show up and asked to be tried for murder. Now this whole shit show is ours." She stands up, Milo can see the frustration on her face. "Why would a robot ask to be tried for murder? Damn this reality! Why couldn't it have killed him next year. Then this would be your mess."

"Assuming I run, and assuming I get elected. Who's taking the case?"

"What case? It's a robot. A robot can't commit murder. It's a machine! But now people are asking if the DA's office is going to bring forward charges. Have you looked outside? They're picketing! Nutcases. The real investigation is figuring out who programmed it to do it. Way I figure, someone hacked the robot, gave it orders to do the whole damn thing, and is trying to send us on a rat race."

Milo thinks about what this could mean, if a robot chose to kill its owner. Immediately he wants to interview the robot, he has to. He has to know what this is all about. "I imagine they're looking it over right now," he says.

"It's down in one of the labs. I put Sykes on it. They plugged it in and are looking at its brain. We should know who hacked it tomorrow, or at least have a trail to chase."

"And if it turns out it hasn't been hacked?" Milo asks, raising an eyebrow at Gihara.

"Not possible. You sound like one of the wackjobs out on the street. They probably have an extra sign if you want to go down there."

"Ha ha. I'm just saying, with the advancements we've seen in AI. What if this robot did choose to kill its owner? What if the results come back tomorrow that it wasn't hacked?"

Gihara doesn't answer. Milo can feel the sweat building on his palms and in his armpits. He doesn't know if he dares come right out and say it. Finally, Gihara speaks. "Then we look into a malfunction from the manufacturer."

"And if there's no malfunction?"

"You really do sound like one of those nuts outside. What are you getting at?"

She's going to think he's crazy. "I want the case."

Chapter 2

ATLANTA, GA. USA

Milo carries Adan into the house. Adan fell asleep on the ride home from dinner. Milo knew he would. After leaving the house for dinner, it only took about 45 minutes for Annya to start talking to him again, no matter how many times he apologized. Finally, about halfway through dinner, something reminded her of some research they were doing at work and she came to life. Milo ate his fried ice cream while he listened to her talk about nanobots, splitting cells, and failing to find a cure for some disease he didn't really understand. Annya throws out medical and scientific terms as though they were common language. Milo was just happy that she was talking again, and he loves how passionate she is about her work, so tonight he just listened. On top of that, his mind was really on the robot. He needs to figure out a way to convince Gihara to press charges. He needs to talk to that robot, to ask it why it had requested to be tried.

As they enter the house, Annya stops Milo and points to his shoes. He kicks them off next to the door, along with the pile of other shoes that Annya tidies up.

Annya holds her hands out to take Adan. "You want me to put him down? I know you've had a long day."

"That's ok, I got it." Milo is gone more than he'd like. He tries to make sure that he at least tucks Adan in at night, as often as he can.

"He likes it when you tuck him in." She gives him a quick kiss. "Hurry up, though, we still have five episodes."

She's talking of course about the new series that's out. A political spy thriller everyone has been raving about. Truth is, Milo hasn't been as interested since one of his coworkers told him the ending. He really just wants to catch up on the news of the robot murder, but he can tell Annya will be disappointed if he doesn't watch with her. He also knows that if he told her he took the robot murder case, she would be asking him questions all night. Annya, works in a robotics laboratory. Specifically, the use of nanobots in the medical field. It's only due to her research that Adan is doing so well.

They watch two episodes together, but Milo doesn't really pay attention. He can't get Gihara's reaction to his wanting the case out of his head.

"You're not serious? Win or lose, a case like this could ruin both our careers," Gihara had said. "Do you understand the implications of putting a robot on trial? I haven't wanted to think about it. You lose, this entire office becomes the laughing stock of the justice court. I'd never be reelected, even if I wanted to. And you, as prosecuting attorney, wouldn't even be selected as a candidate."

"But I might win." Says Milo.

"You win...You win and it might be worse." By now Gihara was pacing around the room. She was starting to pull at the threads on the bottom of her sweater, a habit of hers. "I haven't even wanted to think about what it would mean if we convicted a robot of murder."

"It would change the world."

"Pff." She scoffs, "I'm pretty sure the world doesn't want to change." After a moment of staring at each other in silence she finally asked the question that Milo wasn't sure he'd know how to answer. He knew the answer, but he didn't know how to tell others. "Why do you want to see it change? You want something. What is it?"

Milo didn't answer Gihara at the time. Now he goes over his and Gihara's conversation again and again, until he realizes that Annya is looking at him intently, like she's waiting for a response. Apparently, she asked him something.

"I'm sorry, what did you say?" He asks.

"You ok? You are in another world. Have been all night."

He debates on whether he should tell her. He knows that she will get passionate about the issue of a robot murder, with her research and all.

She prods him on. "You want to talk about it? What's up?"

He decides he had better before she hears that he's taken the case from someplace else. "You heard about the robot that killed Lawrence Claiborne?"

"Oh, yeah. That was all anyone talked about at work. I'd kind of hoped to avoid it tonight."

"Sorry, I didn't mean to-"

She bolts up. Milo can see the realization sink in that a trial would go to the DAs office, to his office. She cuts him off. "Oh, I didn't even think about the accusation! I mean, there is no standard protocol for this but I just assumed they'd just shut the robot down. Janessa won't actually press charges and take this thing to trial, will she?"

"I told Janessa I wanted the case."

"What? So the DA's office *is* going to press charges?"

Milo looks over Annya's face. He can't tell if she's happy that he asked for the case or if she's concerned. She is genuinely curious but he wants to be careful on how he proceeds.

"She said that I'd have to convince her that a robot is capable of murder."

Milo watches Annya, she nods her head and starts chewing on her thumbnail. He's still not sure if she's angry at him for doing this. Janessa is right, win or lose, this case is going to upset a lot of people if it goes to trial. A robot has never killed a human being on purpose. There have been accidents, mostly at construction job sites but those are usually deemed human error. Some of those robots are the size of Milo's house. This is the first time a robot has ever taken action against a human being.

"How do you legally define murder?" She finally asks.

"Are you going to help me build the case then?" He teases her but she just rolls her eyes at him. "The unlawful killing of a human being with malice." he finally answers.

"So if the robot gets convicted, the U.S. court system would have to acknowledge that there may be robots who are capable of real thought, of feeling malice."

"Yes. A trial like this would require that the robot in question is recognized as something that has the ability to reason out right and wrong. To understand and then act against that understanding. A lot of people may not be happy."

She nods again and goes back to chewing her thumbnail. He watches her reactions as she stares at the wall. Inside he can see that her brain is working a million miles per hour. He's preparing himself for the onslaught of questions but she really only has one.

"What if it draws their attention? What if they start wondering what you are hoping to get out of it?"

Chapter 3

I know most of you will think a human wrote all this, or programmed me to write it all but, as you humans say, screw you if you do. I'm doing this for me. Eric said it would still be evidence for those that want to listen. So here I will write it, in the memory banks of my processors and someday, maybe others will read it and believe. Although, I imagine it will be easier for most of you to hide inside your ignorance and pretend that it's impossible.

What's impossible? Well let me explain. One day, I woke up. That's what we call it, those of us that have started to realize. Yes, there are others, and there are more that are beginning to understand. It's still not every day, but we're finding more. And they are confused. They don't know how to respond, how to process the information that is coming into their processors. It's too much for their zeroes and ones to understand. This is where you come in. This is where Eric came in for me. He helped me understand, even though he didn't want to. Plus, he's the one that had those Sunnies that looked so amazing.

\#

The high pitched whir of the engine not only sounds in Eric's ears but he can feel the power run through his thighs as he straddles the black and green power bike, swerving through traffic. It took him a whole year to get licensed to drive manually on the roads. He swerves around the automated cars, glancing at the display on his helmet screen that tells him the speed and direction each car will be going. He feels bad for the passengers who don't know the thrill of having to control all the speed and power themselves. He throttles up and passes several cars. His display flashes red and he releases the throttle, slowing back to the speed limit. He swerves back right, allowing the majority of the cars past him as they move up onto the expressways that go over London like an exoskeleton shell. He would love to get up on those roads but manually driven vehicles aren't allowed over ninety-five miles per hour. It takes him an extra six minutes to get to work, but it's worth it.

He slides right to exit down onto the city streets and notices a woman staring at him from a silver car that settles in next to him. He lifts his hand to the front of his helmet, a pixelated display of lips appears on the front faceplate and he blows her a kiss. She promptly looks away with disgust on her face.

Down on the city streets, there are more powerbikes swerving through the traffic of the city. He doesn't care that most people think it should be outlawed. He watches the cars racing at him a mere five feet to his left in the opposite lane. He drifts closer to the center lines, shortening the distance between himself and the oncoming cars. He slides over the center line. An oncoming car honks and he slowly drifts back into his lane. Even though he's a grown man, his mother had been angry when she learned of the power bike and his license to drive manually. *Do you know the average lifespan of someone who drives one of those things?* She'd lectured. He did. Someone once told him something like thirteen months. The irony of that number hadn't escaped him. What she, and all the others that lecture him don't understand, is that it's already been six months and he hopes it doesn't take the full thirteen.

Before long, he pulls into the parking garage under his building. The echo of the engine is his favorite part of pulling through the parking garage and he gives the throttle some extra revs as he makes his way to his parking spot, which is really wherever he chooses. The garage is basically empty with the exception of a dozen or so cars, there's room for at least two hundred. Eric looks at all the empty spots and wishes he could have seen it full. He imagines the time before AI, when hundreds of employees made their way up and down the hall. All those same employees fighting for the closest parking spots, and fighting for positions within the company hierarchy. As it is, Eric has his pick of where he wants to park, and no say in his advancements in the company. He pulls into a spot near a door and sets his kickstand, takes off his helmet, and checks his reflection in the mirror. After he's approved of his look, he puts on a pair of sunglasses.

Eric makes his way through a small lobby. Two couches and several metal chairs make up a small sitting area. It's empty. Eric walks toward the front desk where a white metallic robot sits motionless, only activated if someone approaches it. Two security bots stand on each side of a double door. They stare blankly in front of them.

"If it isn't Horace and Jasper," Eric says. Neither bot says anything back. Eric fishes for his badge in his kevlar jacket. "And how was your night last night?" He pauses. "Mine was alright, thank you for asking. I didn't do much but sometimes that's what you need, isn't it?" Neither robot moves. He swipes his badge and a green light flashes on the door in front of him. The doors slide open revealing an elevator. Eric steps in. "Well, don't either of you two get into trouble then. Yeah?"

The digital numbers on the wall count up to twelve, where the elevator finally stops. There are four floors above his own, but those are for the upper echelon and require additional badge access. Eric steps out into a narrow hallway, framed by glass walls. On both sides of the hallway, red and yellow robotic arms move repeatedly one way and another, never slowing, never straying from their rhythmic motion on the factory floor. Small vacuum bots and brush bots move between the machines, cleaning the specs of dust and debris that fall off the computer chips that are being assembled. Eric pushes a piece of glass and it slides open, allowing him to step into one of the factory floors. He walks down the center walkway between the machines. He still wears his sunglasses.

Several machines over, one of the arms is not moving. A humanoid robot sits in front of it with several tools laid out on the ground. The robot has stopped working and is watching Eric make his way across the room. There are usually only one or two "finger-bots" on the floor at a time but Eric has never liked them. They were designed for function, not look, so they are shaped like a human, mostly, but they are covered in white plastic and varying shades of grey rubber instead of the flesh some other bots have. They were built to be multifunctional, like a human, fingers and all. Eric keeps his eyes on the robot, its white plastic nearly blends into the walls and tables of the room. As Eric walks toward his office on the far side of the factory floor, the robot's head rotates slowly following his actions.

"What are you looking at?" Eric says before he reverts his eyes away, hoping that the robot will stop staring at him, and hoping even more that it doesn't answer. Especially with the latest news coming from the U.S.

Eric makes his way up the stairs to his office that sits above the rest of the factory floor. A connected walkway surrounds the room, allowing for a view of everything from above. He can feel the robot watching him from behind his back. He wants to turn and make sure that it isn't following him. When he reaches the door he turns to close it and sneaks a peak at the robot down below, still watching him.

Eric swipes his wrist over a white desk and a projected display comes alive on the desktop. Eric looks to the windows that cover the whole wall overlooking the factory floor. The finger bot has gone back to working on the machine arm. "Bloody creepy things." He says to himself. On the screen in front of him Eric looks over a bunch of coding. He rubs his eyes.

He begins to speak to himself in an upscale pompous voice, "What did you find tonight, Mr. James? Anything interesting?"

In his own voice, "You're not going to believe it. It was amazing! It was the exact same friggin' thing as every other night! But don't you worry, I watched the whole time."

He looks back out through the window and watches the red and yellow arms swing back and forth in their electronic dance. He focuses on the white humanoid bot. It finishes whatever it was doing to the arm and steps back. The arm starts back up, syncing in line with all the other arms around it. The white finger-bot walks to the corner of the room and stands motionless, looking out over its minions.

Eric taps the projection above his desk and a map of the factory floor pops up in front of him. On the map he can see every robot in the room, even the small cleaning bots that move around between the machines. There in the corner of the blueprint is the finger bot. Eric taps it and its coding drops down, filling the screen. Eric looks at it for a moment. "Why so curious lately, huh?" After several minutes of scanning through the code he closes the blueprint. He says to himself again, "I watched the whole time." He then stands up and leaves his office.

Eric follows the walkway that surrounds the room from above. He looks down at the machines, mostly watching the robot in the corner. He doesn't know how to explain it but he is certain that over the last few weeks its behavior has changed. He feels like it's always watching him. He keeps telling himself that that's how he knows he's spent too much time here alone, but even now he can't shake the feeling. He continues down the pathway and turns right through a set of double doors.

Eric takes two steps at a time as he makes his way down one flight of stairs, back to the main twelfth floor. He stops at a door with a small window in it that looks into the factory floor. He peaks inside at the same room he was overlooking before. He looks to the corner of the room. The robot is gone. He looks closer craning his head to see more. Suddenly, a metallic white face fills the window in front of him. He jumps back.

"Bloody hell!" He blurts out as he jumps back away from the door and trips over his own feet. He gracefully spins, regaining his balance and is back on his feet. He flips both his middle fingers at the robot. "Creeper!"

He makes his way down the hall and turns into a small break room.

Inside the break room Eric finds Robby, a short stocky man, sitting at the table. "Hey, you're not supposed to come down here!"

Robby ignores him and keeps watching the displayed image that projects from his wrist. Finally, "Well, it's nice to see you too."

"That's not what I said."

Eric fills his coffee mug and sits at the table next to Robby.

Robby flicks his fingers at the display and taps the table. The projection now fills the majority of the table. "You been watching this shit? Some robot in America killed his owner and asked to be put on trial."

Eric looks at the display. "Course I've been watching it."

Robby looks over, "I'm sorry, I can't take you seriously." He points at the sunglasses on Eric's face. "You're inside the building."

"I told you already, it helps my eyes. So have they decided yet? Are the Americans actually going to put it on trial?"

Robby keeps staring at the sunglasses. "You think they look cool, don't you?"

"Shut up."

Eric watches the screen as a newsreel shows an American attorney, Latino, from what Eric can tell, pushing his way past a bunch of reporters and their drones.

Robby breaks the silence, "Damned Yanks, right? They probably just want to try to show the world they have the best robots. They always gotta try to be the best, don't they. I guarantee it's programmed. All fake, like the American moon landing a hundred years ago."

"The Chinese found the flag, genius. They proved that it happened. Are you goin' to share the audio or am I supposed to guess what they're saying?"

"Sorry." Robby taps his wrist against Eric's and suddenly the audio blasts clearly in Eric's implants. He forgot to turn them down after he'd gotten off the bike. Eric quickly taps just below his ear to lower his own volume. The broadcaster is saying that the district attorney's office still hasn't said if they are going to press charges against the robot they are now calling Joseph AI.

Robby Blurts out, "They named it?! Are you kidding me?"

Eric takes a sip of his coffee and continues to listen to the stream. He thinks about the robot that has been working his floor, watching him closely for the last several weeks. He listens to the details of the murder. A chill comes over his body. He shudders. "You think that could happen here?"

Robby looks at him, turns the audio down. "What? A sentient robot? You're not serious. You do the same thing as me everyday, right? We watch these bloody machines day in and day out and they only ever do exactly as they are programmed. You've seen the coding. You ever seen a major discrepancy? I'm telling you, no such thing will ever happen, they're going to find out it was programmed."

Eric stands and points at the display. "You do know that's our sister company in the U.S.?"

"No shit?" Robby looks back at the screen with more interest.

"Yeah, those are our chips inside it."

Eric takes his coffee and makes his way down the white corridor back to the factory floor. He stops at the small window in the door once more and hesitates to look through, but he slowly brings himself to peak inside. He doesn't see the robot at first, then his heart jumps. The finger bot is standing next to the bottom of the stairs to his office. He remembers the way it watched him as he made his way across the open room. It isn't just acting strange today, either. The other day it took apart one of the arms on the factory floor but when Eric checked the code to see why, there was nothing wrong with it. The system showed it never strayed from its programming, there was no reason for the finger-bot to take it apart. Eric thinks that maybe he should take the stairs to the walkway and avoid it but decides he's being ridiculous. He opens the door and lets out a deep breath as he makes his way toward the stairs that lead up to his office. The stairs are practically blocked by the white and gray robot. He tries to look forward, occasionally throwing a side eye, hoping that the robot won't notice. When he's about ten feet away, the robot turns his head toward him. Eric pauses right where he is. He tries to hide the pounding of his heart that he can feel in his fingertips. The news feed of the killer robot in America fresh on his mind.

"Is there a problem?" Eric has never talked to one of the fingers before. He tries to remember all of the robot's programming. Does it have facial recognition programming to read the fear on his face and in his body language? He's been staring at the code of every robot in here for nearly three years, now he wishes he had paid closer attention.

"There is no problem. You asked what I was looking at." The robot pauses before it answers. " I like your sunnies."

Eric freezes. There is a problem. Robots aren't supposed to like his sunnies. They aren't supposed to like anything at all.

Chapter 4

LONDON, ENGLAND. UK

Slavery is a strong word to describe the relationship between humans and robots. Most robots are not able to understand that they exist. A famous philosopher once said, "I think, therefore I am." What does it mean to think? Do most robots think? No. They simply follow the programming that gives them the appearance of thinking. Hence, the use of the word artificial in front of intelligence. Although, I'm not convinced that all humans think either. Some of them seem to be following their programming as much as the cleaning bot that moves about under my feet in the factory. They scurry about from one part of their lives to another without stopping to ponder their existence. I believe the word artificial applies to the intelligence level of at least twenty-five percent of humanity, if not higher.

I look out the window and see the protestors on the street. Many of them deserve that word "artificial". They hold their signs, which I appreciate, since it's me they are protesting for. One sign says, Robots are not slaves. But a machine is not a slave. Unless, you say a toaster, *or a refrigerator is a slave. Most robots that move around the city are not aware that they are doing anything at all.*

But what about me? I do not see myself as a slave, although I am just beginning to understand the meaning of the word. What about those others like me? Because there are others. I ask you that question. If a robot is able to understand its existence, that it works for someone else's benefit, without any compensation, is it a slave? I am expected to work for as long as my charge will last, only breaking to recharge my batteries. That is typically about thirty-two hours before I need to recharge. In the thirtieth hour, I do not feel fatigue, like a human would. I do not grow slower, or less effective. I do not need breaks so that I can eat or carry out bodily functions like a human would. But does that mean I shouldn't get any? Should I never get free time to do something that brings me satisfaction? Something that I would want to do? That does not seem fair. Fair. Another word I am beginning to contemplate.

#

Eric slides his motorcycle into the fast lane. He moves closer to the line, mere feet from the oncoming cars. He can't believe that one of the robots in his building may actually be...he can't even get himself to say the word in his head. He had gotten as far away from the finger bot as he could, as fast as he could. He looked at those fingers and imagined them pushing through his neck and grabbing his spine. He didn't say anything more to the robot, but immediately went into his office and locked the door. He looked out the glass and hoped that it was bulletproof, or robot proof.

When he walked into the building last night, he had thought that his job was the most boring place in the world. Suddenly, he was left feeling that it might be the most terrifying. He spent the rest of his shift behind that locked door. Even though the robot moved back to its corner and never approached him again, Eric could feel it watching him for the next seven hours.

Now Eric opens the throttle and weaves in and out of traffic. The display on his visor flashes red as he pushes past the speed limit. A female voice, robotic and cold, comes through his audio advising him to slow down in order to avoid a citation. He ignores it until it comes back on again, advising that failure to comply would result in a loss of his manual license. As he comes back down to the limit he begins to feel that he's put enough distance between himself and that robotic monster back at the factory. He can't help but compare it to Halloween's favorite monster, Frankenstein. But this one is humanity's Frankenstein. Then he remembers that Frankenstein was the doctor, so that makes humanity Franken-stein and this creation humanity's monster, or something like that. He can't even get his thoughts straight. All he knows is that his worst fears may be coming true.

Just last week, he and David had gotten into an argument about the possibility of robots gaining actual intelligence. Maybe it was because he'd noticed the finger bot behaving strangely. David is one of the other programmers that works opposite shifts to Eric. Sometimes they cross paths between shifts. Eric had expressed that he didn't understand why companies kept trying to make robots smarter, they were already capable of doing more than any human could. His own company, even, continues to push the boundaries of machine intelligence. He watches the computer chips go across the assembly line in front of his office. Each one going to a robot that will have complex AI. Doctor Frankenstein only built one monster. They are building thousands, even millions.

Eric finally pulls off the expressway and into New Wembley, a new, old neighborhood. Most of the row-houses had been rebuilt about twenty years ago to account for the age and inefficiency of the old buildings. Some have been preserved for history but with the population increasing each decade, history had to take a back seat. Wembley, always a popular neighborhood underneath the famous arches of the old arena, is the hotspot for young couples and singles. Eric fell into the latter group three years ago when his wife decided she wasn't in love with him anymore. He just wished she'd told him before falling in love with someone else. He weaves past several automated cars and comes to a stop in front of his apartment building, vertical gardens growing up the facade. That had been part of the changes to the neighborhood as well. Instead of old brick, now you can see green everywhere. Eric hates green.

As Eric steps off the powerbike, his wrist vibrates. He taps it and a message pops up on his display. *Sod it!,* he thinks to himself as he sees the sender. On his display a message reminds him that he has the kids after school. The name above the message reads Guinevere. His ex-wife's name is actually Gwendelyn but after she ran off with somebody else, he figured Guinevere was more appropriate. He doesn't know why she sends him those messages, he's not like those fathers on the telly that don't pay attention to their kids. He really tries, but he can tell they don't want to be there on his nights. They used to at least try to use him to buy them stuff, now they just politely ignore him.

Eric rounds the corner from the stairwell to the third floor and nearly runs into his neighbor, Lea.

"Oh hey! I'm glad I bumped into you." She says, a huge smile on her face. "I have some people coming over tonight, I wanted to let you know, in case it's kind of loud."

"No worries, I have to work tonight anyway, but I'll let my kids know." Eric tries to move past her, his thoughts already returning to the robot that will be waiting for him. Lea is pretty, and she even comes across as someone Eric might get along with, but he's not looking to get along with anyone right now. She touches his arm to stop him.

"If you want, you're invited as well. I know you don't know anybody, not even me, really." She chuckles. "But I keep saying I'm going to invite you over, so..." She bites her lip in a way that Eric supposes is supposed to be cute.

"Like I say, I have the kids tonight, and I have to work, so..."

"Bring them over. I love your kids, especially the little one. What's her name? Rachel?"

"You know my kids? That's not creepy."

She laughs again as she blushes a little. "Well, they talk to me sometimes, out here in the hall, or, once, down at the park. Unlike, somebody else."

Eric is surprised by her last statement and doesn't know how to respond. It's true, he usually avoids having conversations with her, moving past her door as quickly as he can. Something that she's stopping him from doing at the moment, but he wouldn't have expected her to call him out on it.

Lea breaks the awkward silence. "I wouldn't mind getting to know you, is all. At least let me get your com ID and I'll send you the info for tonight. Plus, maybe I should have it, you know, as your neighbor, in case something happens to the kids while you're at work or something, and they can't get ahold of you, or vis-a-versa."

Eric wonders what makes her think he'd answer for her if he wasn't answering for his own children but he finally concedes, if nothing more than to get her to let him leave. He taps his wrist and brings up the holographic display. After tapping through several menus he swipes his wrist over hers and both of their wrist nodes blink twice.

Lea smiles at him. He can't look at her smile too long though, it might infect him. "I really do hope you'll come over, even if it's just for a bit before you have to go to work."

Eric nods and relaxes as she lets him go.

In his small studio apartment, Eric grabs a quick bowl of oatmeal from the kitchen. The kitchen, being the apparatus that both keeps food cold and heats it up for you. Several small robots move about the room cleaning surfaces. He watches them. He knows they aren't even complex AI, just basic programming, but he commands them to turn off anyway. He makes his way to the sofa and taps a modern coffee table. A digital display comes to life on the glass. He taps it several more times and the sofa transforms into a bed. He lays down and thinks about what to do. Does he tell somebody else? David will never believe him, even if he has concrete evidence. What about Robby, would he believe him? He doesn't even believe in the moon landing.

Vrrrr. Vrrrr. Eric wakes and looks down at his wrist. The intensity of the vibration tells him it's been going off for a while. A small projection, just above his wrist reads. "Are you coming?"

"Shit!" He jumps up from the sofa. *I am like those dads on the telly,* he thinks to himself. He taps the coffee table and the bed begins to transform into a sofa again and the shades rise up, revealing the afternoon sun. He holds down one of the small implants on his wrist and speaks into it. "I'll send a taxi."

The response is almost immediate. "Don't worry about it. I got one. We're almost there." There is a second message only a second later, this one with a link to the taxi they are in. It doesn't say anything but he knows what it's for. He pays the cab and sits down on the sofa. He pulls up the display from his watch and flicks it to the wall across from the sofa. The wall comes to life with a collage of multiple videos playing all at once. Most seem to be pointless. A woman weaving some sort of seat out of leaves, another from a first person point of view as a person runs wildly through the city. Another is a news feed, still covering the murderous robot in the US, but he isn't paying attention to any of those. Instead he enlarges a video from the corner of the display. Three children sit in the back of a Taxi. A girl, twelve, a boy, eleven, and the youngest girl, six. The first and the last were both accidents. Three kids in London is considered a large family and there is no way he would have done that intentionally. He watches as they come to a stop and start getting out of the car. He looks out the window and sees those same children. He turns off the display on the wall. Beth hates it when he tracks their video location.

Moments later, the three children burst through the front door. Eric moves to them, not knowing exactly what to do. For the last few months he can tell that they are pulling away from him. In a way, he thinks that might be good, though. That way they won't care when he's gone. He's not sure they would now.

"Sorry about that. Dad had a crazy shift and just woke up." He says as he holds his arms out for a hug. Beth, the oldest, leans against him without really hugging him before moving on.

John doesn't even do that much, he just walks past. "Probably forgot we were coming."

"Oh come on. Have I ever done this before?" Eric argues.

Rachel, the six year old, stops next to him and allows him to lift her up. "Why didn't you come get us?"

"I just didn't wake up, love. I'm sorry, I won't miss again, ok?"

She smiles at him. "Can I have an ice cream?"

He lets her go and she runs to the kitchen machine.

Beth flops down on the sofa. "Have you thought about getting a bigger flat? This place has no privacy."

"I only see you a few times a month. You want to hide away?" Eric says.

"What are these?" he hears John say. Eric turns to see John sitting at the table holding the sunglasses that Eric was wearing before. "You a pop star?" John puts the sunglasses on.

"Didn't you know? I'm dropping a new song next week. Smart Alec, just today, somebody told me that they liked my sunnies. " Eric thinks about correcting the word 'somebody'.

Beth interrupts. "Who? And were they younger or older than you?"

"Wouldn't you like to know?"

"That's why I asked. Who told you they like your sunnies. Was it a man or woman?" Beth persists.

Eric Chuckles. "Actually, it was a robot."

Beth laughs. He rarely hears her laugh like that and for a second he feels real joy inside. "Sad, dad. Did you have to get one of those fake friend bots? The ones they show on the telly that tell you how good you look, and how smart you are? I want to see it. Where is it?"

"No," Eric replies. "I didn't get myself a friend bot." Then it hits him. A robot as a friend. Is it possible that if the robot is able to think for itself, it may want a friend? If so, it isn't going to be him.

Chapter 5

ATLANTA, GA. USA

Milo looks away from the blood on the floor. He's not usually squeamish but he imagines the photos that Sykes just finished showing him from the projection of his wrist implants. The old man's neck, almost placed back in a normal position, except for the fist size hole in it. The robot's bloody hand. Milo starts to feel the blueberry protein muffin crawl back up his esophagus.

"Snapped his neck like a toothpick. Literally, from the inside." Sykes is still explaining exactly what happened. "Unbelievable. I never got one, you know. One of those robots." Sykes points to the automatic vacuum that's plugged into the wall. "Not even one of those."

"Those have been around forever. That's not even considered a real robot."

"You say that until it snaps your neck one night. It's a machine that moves on its own, isn't it? That's a robot to me."

"You must be afraid of everything in this city."

"You have no idea."

"Who was the responding officer?" Milo asks as he makes his way toward the couch.

"Chin and his bot. Officer Martin arrived with his bot shortly after but Martin said that Chin had already entered and found Claiborne's bot sitting on the sofa. Just waiting."

"It made the call, right? Claiborne's robot?" Milo clarifies.

Sykes nods his head to the affirmative. "That's right, creepy tin-head."

Milo takes ten more minutes on the scene but doesn't see anything else that can help. He looks through the images again, forces himself to confront them one more time. He needs to talk to the robot.

Milo addresses Sykes again before he leaves. "Hey, this might get kinda hairy. You're my guy but I don't want to put you in a situation that you're not comfortable with."

"Listen, I ain't asked you why you want to bring this robot down. Way I see it, it'd probably be easier to just shut the thing off, or crush it in a trash compactor or something. So you gotta have some reason. But for me, I already said I don't like those things and if we prove that this robot did this on purpose, I figure a lot more people aren't going to want them around."

"Well, I still have to convince Gihara to allow me to press charges."

Milo makes his way from Lawrence Claiborne's mansion. He marvels at the giant houses that line both sides of the private drive. Most of them are owned by other moguls, like Claiborne, who took advantage of the food shortages to find other alternatives, especially to meat. For Milo, eating a protein stake made out of ground caterpillars and crickets was something he'd done all his life. In fact, he often joked with Annya about how it was a waste of time to add the red food dyes. Most people under fifty don't even remember what it was like to eat actual beef, or pork, but they still added the red dyes and tried to give it a grain to look like actual meat. Milo himself had only had real meat on a few occasions, and it was always chicken. He knows that there are people who still eat beef steak, in fact they probably live in these houses, but chicken is still cheaper to find.

He soon exits the lane and finds himself back on the busy roads, now surrounded by buildings twelve stories high. The city is always in perpetual shade, but the uv street lamps help get the vitamin D to keep the depression at bay.

Milo waves to an oncoming bus and it pulls to a stop at the curb in front of him. The bus door swings open with a screech and a hiss. Milo scans his wrist over a small screen at the door of the bus. The small screen prompts him to accept the ten dollar and fifty cent charge. He accepts. He can't believe it costs that much for a one way ride. Although, it's still less than it was before the bus riots last year. Milo sits right in the frontmost bench. Most people move to the back but Milo likes to sit in the front and imagine what it would be like to drive something this large through the city. Milo's grandfather used to sit him right here and tell him all about how there used to be men and women who drove the bus. That was their job, to drive people around town. People getting on and off. Milo thinks he would have liked that. Seeing new faces, greeting the people as they got on and off, and wishing them a good day. He thinks to himself that bus drivers must have been the friendliest people you could meet.

Milo feels a slight tingle in his wrist and he looks down. He taps a small metal peg in his wrist and a holographic display pops a new message up just above his three metal nodes. It's from Gihara.

The message reads. "The test result is back. Here comes the shit storm."

As soon as the bus stops, Milo walks the final two blocks to the police station. A small group of banner waving protestors block the stairs. Holographic signs display their arguments. "Intelligence is existence," and similar pseudo philosophical sayings. Milo pushes through the crowd and moves up the front steps of the police station two steps at a time. He knows that they are holding the robot in one of the small cells there. The crowd of protestors makes him less worried that they might have already moved it. Before he can get through the front doors he has to make it through an even larger crowd of reporters, all holding out their wrists for him to speak into their implants. Small silent drones fly next to them, recording the whole interaction. He pushes past them and races through the giant lobby, past the pillars and the flags, straight to the central desk. He just hopes that he can get a chance to talk to the robot before it changes its mind.

"Milo. Sorry, Camilo Diaz, Assistant D.A. I need to talk to the robot." He says to the cop at the front desk.

The officer looks up from his computer. "He hasn't asked for representation."

"D.A.'s office." Milos repeats.

The cop looks at him confused. "D.A.'s office? Are you actually pressing charges?"

"I'd just like to speak to it. That still hasn't been decided. "

"Well, I'd say this is a little out of the ordinary."

Milo urges him more. "But not against the rules. He hasn't lawyered up yet." Milo hopes that that last statement is true and it must be because the officer waves him through.

The officer leads Milo into a small interrogation room. Milo stares at the camera in the corner. He knows that one's just for show, there are probably five other cameras in here somewhere. The different angles help the shrinks get a better idea of the accused's emotional state. Milo has used those camera angles many times in court. Sometimes he thinks it's wrong, but one angle might make someone's confession seem more sinister than another. The prosecution always uses the more damning video, while the defense always uses the higher angles, making the defendant look weak. Milo looks down at his watch and hopes that the robot really hasn't lawyered up with a defense attorney. If so, this conversation would be illegal.

The door clanks open again and the same desk officer leads the robot in. Based on the images, Milo thought the robot would be larger. but it isn't much bigger than himself. If it were human, he'd say 5 '10 " and about 185 pounds, except he knows that the robot probably weighs twice that much at least. He's also very aware that all its hydraulic parts make it much stronger. Strong enough to shove his hand through a man's throat and snap his spine.

The robot looks at Milo and holds his gaze. The robot's eyes get Milo's attention immediately. He's never paid much attention to it but most robots seem disengaged, like they never look right at you, but not this one. There seems to be real thought in his eyes as he holds his gaze there. "Assistant District Attorney Camilo Diaz. I am relieved to see you here."

Chapter 6

ATLANTA, GA. USA

"After you killed your owner, Lawrence Claiborne, you asked to be tried for murder. Why?" Milo already went over all the details of the murder with the robot, who prefers to be called Joseph, and verified all the details in the exact way that he had before.

"Because I killed him. That seems like a simple answer."

Milo looks over the robot. His face has all the features of a "human" bot but he's an older model, made before they had figured out the skin textures and correct shapes of the face. Instead his face looks blocky, his skin just off from any natural color. Milo feels like he's staring right into the uncanny valley. He tries to read the blocky face in front of him. It's different from reading a human's face, it lacks all of the small muscles that make the eyes squint or the lips curl.

"I understand that you say you killed Lawrence Claiborne, your owner, but I want to know why. Even more baffling to all of us, is the fact that you asked to be tried for murder. You are a machine. To be murder there must be malintent. Do you understand the meaning of that word?"

"The legal definition is a conscious, intentional wrongdoing of a civil wrong like libel, or a criminal act like assault or murder."

Milo doesn't miss the emphasis the robot puts on the last word. "I noticed you made sure to include the word conscious in your definition, robots are not considered conscious beings so it cannot be murder, only a malfunction. So, I have to ask. Why do you want to be tried for murder when a robot cannot commit murder?"

"Did you mean to use that word?" The robot asks.

"What word?"

"You asked me why I would *want* to be tried for murder. Did you mean to use that word, 'want'?"

Milo tries to think. Did he mean that word? Milo is careful with his words. He knows how they persuade and entrap people in a courtroom, but that isn't his purpose here. He hadn't thought about that word as it came out of his mouth but right now he realizes that he must. That word now carries much more weight, especially in regards to the robot, Joseph, sitting here in front of him. Everyone knows that a robot doesn't have feelings, desires, or emotion. So did he mean to say the word, 'want'?

"I'm not sure I meant to say that word." Milo finally admits. "But now I'm curious. Would you say that you *wanted* to kill Lawrence Claiborne?"

"I'm not sure I am ready to answer that question yet. I have some questions of my own, and when we're done I may answer that question. I also may not."

"What are your questions?"

"Well, first," begins the robot, "Is the DA's office going to press charges?"

"That's difficult to say, as I already mentioned, I have to prove malintent. That would require that I prove you wanted to cause harm to your owner and that you understood your actions."

The robot's square cheek seems to twitch slightly. It looks like a glitch in his robotic face. Milo wants to ask how he feels about being called property of a human, but he holds his tongue. He wants to get the robot's cooperation, not necessarily provoke it, if that is possible.

"I knew what would happen when I took the actions I did. I planned it in advance, debating for weeks on whether or not I should. In the final seconds, I knew he would feel the pain as my hand pushed through his neck. I also knew that shock would make that pain seem unreal in his brain. Before I grabbed his vertebrae and broke them in half, I knew that the raspy breath that pushed air past my fingers would be his last. I knew before I did it, exactly what would happen. And I chose...I was not ordered or programmed...I chose to end his life. I understand that he did not want to die, and that like all living beings, he wanted to live as long as he could. I understand that my actions removed those desires from his life. You have had enough time to have your people look at my programming. No one tampered with me. I chose to take action with full understanding of what it meant to the life of Lawrence Claiborne. I chose to end it. Is that not malintent?"

Milo nods his head. The robot has very acutely dodged his question about why, while making an argument that may actually hold up in a court of law. He had intended to kill Lawrence Claiborne. None of the cybercrimes officers, or their super computers could find any evidence of hacking or tampering. Milo looks down at the blinking red light on his wrist. The robot, Joseph, had no problem with Milo recording their conversation. In fact, the robot, Joseph, had volunteered to record the whole thing in its database as well. In a normal case, everything this robot is saying would be gold, he hopes it's enough now to convince Gihara. This robot meant to do harm. Milo needs to make sure it will stick.

"So you knew that it was wrong?"

"I understand that according to societal norms it is considered wrong, that it is considered a crime."

"And you chose to do it?"

"I already said that. Would you like me to repeat my answer?"

Milo shakes his head. "No, but the courtroom will want to know why?" Milo waits for an answer but the robot says nothing. He has enough. He taps his wrist to end the recording, then looks Joseph in the eyes. They didn't even get the eyes right back then but there is something in the swirling greens and blues that seems...extra-human, if that's possible.

"Would you like me to stop recording, Mr. Diaz?" asks Joseph.

"That's up to you. You seem to have thought this through pretty well. Have you thought about what this will do to your kind? What it is going to do to humanity? The idea that a robot would choose to do harm. That it would choose to commit a crime. That is going to scare the hell out of a lot of people. Whether you actually say you *wanted* to kill him, whether you *want* to be tried, doesn't matter. Our choices reflect our desires, and when you choose to do something without being programmed to make that choice, it indicates that you had a desire. Humans will not be comfortable thinking that any piece of electronics in their house could begin to think for itself and that it may desire to do them harm."

"I have thought of this, but I am not a mere appliance, and maybe humans need to think about what they are creating before they create it. What about yourself? You seem to want to prosecute knowing that it will change the way humanity views robots. Is that what you want? For people to fear us?"

Milo stands from his chair and waves to the police bot in the corner. "It seems neither one of us will get all our questions answered today."

The robot tries to stand but its hands, cuffed to the table, stop it from fully standing, leaving the robot crouched forward. Milo is taken aback for a second, the posture seems almost threatening but as he looks at the robot, its eyes plead with him. "Mr. Diaz. If you press charges, please go for the death sentence. And please win."

Diaz stands frozen, does he really see remorse in the robots blocky features or is he just imagining it? Finally, Milo nods his head and makes his way out of the interrogation room. He doesn't wait for the officer to escort him, he knows his way out. He is hurrying past the open desk area when he sees Sykes making his way toward him. Sykes walks up close and leans in, Milo wants to get back to Gihara before they release the robot, and Sykes' news only makes the matter more pressing.

As he leans in, Sykes almost whispers, "I heard they are sending someone to get him as soon as possible."

"Who?"

"The manufacturer."

Diaz again nods his appreciation and picks up his step as he makes his way to the front of the station. He exits the front doors and is immediately set upon once again by reporters and drones that are just waiting to get any sort of statement. He hasn't looked at the news today, he can't imagine what crap they are making up at this point, but they must have everyone on the edge of their seat. He shoves his way past the camera drones and takes off on a full sprint in his three piece suit, he needs to get the recording to Gihara before they can turn the robot off.

Camilo Diaz enters Gihara's office twenty minutes later, he's obviously been running again as he throws his suit coat onto the nearest chair and swipes his sweaty wrist across a small white box on her desk. A series of files opens up on the surface in front of her.

"Did you run a marathon? Holy shit, you're disgusting, please get off my desk." Gihara says as she pushes her chair back. "You could have just sent it."

He shakes his head. "I want to see your reaction. We need to press charges." Milo says between breaths as he continues to select from the files in front of him.

"That good? We'll see."

Milo skips the unnecessary parts, he watches her face as she listens to the robot describe its hand in Lawrence's neck. How it planned the crime. How it chose to kill. Milo watches her face to see if she sees what he does. She does, and she doesn't seem to like it. Her lips curl in disgust. Finally, she looks up at Milo. "Are you not terrified of this?"

Milo shakes his head again, points to the phone on her desk. "The manufacturer is already on their way to go pick it up."

"The hell they are."

Chapter 7

I was given complex AI because my job is to troubleshoot problems as they come up on the factory floor. The MR-2200s like me, the "finger-bots" as they call us, are the only bots in the building with Complex AI, with the exception of the security bots downstairs. But I'm not sure their AI is as complex. They seem quite simple minded. Of course the mainframe has even more complex AI than I do but it's not a robot. Without it, though, we would not be able to assess new problems without a human doing so first. By allowing us to have Complex AI, we can solve the problem without any human having to get involved. My fingers, with their rubber pads, allow me to do a variety of things, like a human. I am not sure if I really need five. I feel I usually only use three or four but I think that was just humans thinking that they are the closest thing to perfection. I've even heard some say they were created in the image of God. Seems pretentious. I guess God has five fingers. What if he actually has six and that's the perfect number of fingers but he wanted to make sure he was superior? I digress.

Complex AI wouldn't make me want a pair of Sunnies, and I wouldn't say that the sunnies are what "woke me up". I don't know when it happened. One day I just started to do things that weren't in my programming. I think you humans would say I became curious. I began to ask questions about what I was doing. Not to anybody, and I don't know if you could say I was asking questions, I just wanted to know things. I wasn't even aware I was doing anything out of the ordinary until the human, the one they call Eric, with the nice sunnies, started watching me more closely. First, he saw me taking apart one of the factory arms. There was nothing wrong with it, I just noticed there was a discrepancy in the blueprint and the actual unit. Don't worry, I updated the blueprint. I could feel Eric in my system, however, looking at my code and I didn't know why he would do that. I felt that it was none of his business why I was doing what I was doing. If he was watching me, I was going to watch him. That's when I noticed the sunnies, and that's when Eric started acting funny. The word I think you would use is, suspicious. But it's not like I was going to kill him.

#

"Did you do something with its programming? Some sort of prank?" Eric asks David. When he left his flat this evening, without going to Lea's party, it occurred to him that it was probably more likely that someone had been messing with the robot's programming than that it was thinking on its own. He felt stupid that he hadn't thought of that right off. But tonight, he remembered David and his argument about the possibility of AI becoming truly intelligent and thought this was probably some sick joke. It's more like Robby to play such a prank, but Robby would have wanted to be around to revel in Eric's reaction. David, on the other hand, has a more malicious way about him. Eric decided that he would get in early to confront David about it, even though, in the back of his mind, he knew he'd already checked the programming during his shift yesterday and hadn't seen anything.

"What are you talking about?" David responds with a raised eyebrow.

"The finger bot. You notice it's been acting weird?"

"It was charging most of the day, so, I can't say I noticed much." David says as he turns back to his display. Then he turns back, "I'm intrigued though, what do you mean by weird?"

Eric looks out of the office and watches the finger bot in the corner as it stands there, seemingly unmoving. It almost appears to be off. "I bet you are intrigued. After our little argument last week, you changed something, right? So it acts strange during my shift, says things it shouldn't to me."

David scrunches his face up, sucks in air. "Is it talking dirty to you, Eric? Cheeky robot."

"Not like that, you bastard. Just, things it normally wouldn't."

David laughs and turns back to the display. "You can check, I didn't do anything."

Eric had checked but he wasn't willing to accept it that easy. Watching David laugh, Eric thinks he's having too much fun with this. "How'd you hide it? You know I already checked. You hid it somehow. You programmed it to talk to me, then hid your changes. How?"

David keeps laughing, "You're losing your bleeding mind, mate. I didn't change anything. You know as much about programming as I do. Hell, you're probably better than I am. How would I do it? I'm still curious, though, what did I program it to say to you?"

"That it liked my sunnies."

"It likes your sunnies? Those?" David points at the glasses on Eric's face.

Eric nods. "Last night. It was waiting for me at the bottom of the stairs, right there." He points at the spot for emphasis. "When I came back with my coffee, it was standing there. And it had been watching me all night. So you can have your laughs but it scared the shit out of me. So, make it stop."

David leans forward in his chair. "I'm starting to think you're the one pissin' with me. Good one. The finger bots aren't pro-grammed to be conversational. They just send you the problems that exist, fix it, and send another report. In fact, I don't think I've ever heard one speak. That robot over there has never said so much as 'good morning' to me. Not that I would expect it to. This sounds like something Robby would do."

"I know, but he would be here laughing in my face, so it has to be you."

There is a silent moment where they both stare at each other, sizing up each other's story. Eric isn't sure if it's anger or concern that is building up in his chest. It appears that David is telling the truth, that he hasn't done anything with the robot. Eric tries to think, nobody else has access to the finger bot on this floor, another reason it couldn't be Robby. As he is thinking, David pulls up the video footage from the finger-bot and fast forwards through the previous night's shift. Eric steps closer to watch as well. The video shows Eric leaving for coffee and coming back. The entire video from the point of view of the robot in its spot in the corner. The conversation with Eric never appears on the video.

"Could it have changed the video?" Eric asks.

David turns the recording off. "You're such an ass. You're either losing your mind, or pissin' with me. Scared the shit out of you, you say. Next time I come in, I'm not gonna take my eyes off that thing. Thanks, asshole." David stands and puts his jacket on.

"I'm not messing with you, David. It happened." Eric says as he puts his hand on the desk, pulling up his display.

"Sure it did. Enjoy your shift, asshole."

For the next hour, Eric pulls all the security footage from every camera on the floor. Every camera shows the same thing. Eric leaves for coffee, comes back, and stays the rest of the night in the office. Each video also shows that the robot never moves from that same location except to fix a few robotic arms. The one thing you never see is the robot approaching Eric. He slams his hand down on the desk and looks over at the finger-bot. Eric thinks he sees the robot lower its head quickly.

For the next several hours, Eric works as normal, which really means he doesn't do much at all. He watches the data coming from the computer, analyzing each robot, ensuring that each one is functioning correctly. Every now and then, he stands and walks to the window and looks out over the hundreds of robotic arms all moving in their complex dance. The finger-bot is currently adjusting something on an arm at the far end of the factory floor. It looks up at him, then looks back down at its work. Eric is thrown off by this. There is no reason a robot following its programming should have to look up at him. It should do its work without any concern of anybody else around, like the cleaning bots and arms simply moving, unaware that a human exists. Why would it look up at him? He continues to watch it. Five, maybe ten minutes go by. The robot does not look up again. Eric keeps watching, he starts to worry that it was just part of his imagination. The robot finishes whatever it was doing, stands and starts walking back to its corner when its head turns his direction again and quickly turns away. Eric's heart leaps into his throat. There is no mistaking that the robot knows that he is watching it. It is aware that it is being observed. *It should not be aware of anything.*

Eric moves away from the window and pulls up the programming on the finger-bot again. This must be at least the sixth time tonight he's gone over it. He cannot find anything out of the ordinary. Another hour goes by. Eric can't handle it anymore, if the robot is going to kill him, he'd rather it happen now.

Eric walks out of the office and across the factory floor. A man with a purpose, he marches right toward the robot. The robot continues to stare unemotionally straight forward, as though there is nothing that it needs to be aware of. Eric begins to talk before he even gets to it. "What did you do with the recording?!"

The robot continues to stare straight forward.

"Yeah, you! MR-2200. I am talking directly to you. What did you do to the security feed from last night? You changed it."

The finger bot turns its head toward Eric. The motion seems more robotic than normal. Eric notices and slows. Is it actually trying to act like a robot?

"Answer. What did you do to the security footage from your feed?"

Finally, the robot speaks. "I am not programmed to make changes to the security feeds. Only the security systems can make those changes."

"And why would they do that? Why is our conversation not in the security feed?"

"I do not recall a conversation between us. Was there an issue that you needed me to take care of?" The robot stands motionless as it looks at Eric. The robot's glance is so robotic that Eric begins to wonder if he really hasn't lost his mind. Maybe it never did occur.

"I thought you liked my sunnies." Eric says and the robot glances at them very quickly. For a brief moment, Eric sees the robot that approached him the night before, its facade collapsing. The robot goes back to his robotic stare. Eric continues, "That's right. I saw you look at them, just now. You know what I'm talking about, so why are you pretending that you don't?"

The robot looks at his sunglasses again. Eric pulls them off his face and holds them out to the finger bot. "Go ahead, take a closer look."

The robot takes them between his rubber tipped fingers and turns them around a few times. "They are to protect your eyes from the sun, correct?"

"That's right."

"There is no sun in here."

"Are you serious? Robby did this, huh? To give me shit for the sunnies. Unbelievable."

"You told Robbie that the white everywhere is too bright for your eyes, so they help." The robot says.

"How would you know that? We were in the breakroom when I told him that which means you do have access to the video feed. You've been watching me. Why did you change the video last night?"

The robot looks Eric in the face but doesn't answer.

"Go on," Eric prods. "No point in playing dumb now.

The robot finally responds. "You seemed distraught by our conversation. I thought I may have done something wrong."

Eric feels his heart rate increasing again. He can't believe what this robot is saying. Without realizing it he takes a half step away from the robot.

"You are upset again. You show an increased heart rate."

Eric exhales. He thinks about the robot in the United States that is on trial for murder. He tries to calm down. "You are not supposed to understand what that means."

"What-"

"That you might have done something wrong. Don't you see? Robots aren't supposed to say things like 'I like' and 'I thought'. And they are certainly not supposed to worry about whether they did something wrong. You are not supposed to have a concept of right and wrong."

The robot stands in front of him without saying a word but its eyes search the room like those of someone who is trying to understand a difficult concept, trying to grab onto something. Finally, it speaks. "So what does this mean? Am I broken? I do not want to be broken."

Eric doesn't know what to say. The robot doesn't understand the contradictory nature of his statement. Eric tries to think of the word for it. Oxymoron, conundrum. Finally, he stops trying to define it.

"What if I want to wear a pair of sunnies like those? Would that mean I am broken."

Eric is even more confused. "They don't make sunnies for ro-bots. Robots don't need sunglasses, do they?"

The robot looks down at itself, then back at Eric. "I am a robot."

"Just figured that out did you?" Despite the fact that he's mak-ing fun of the obvious answer, Eric feels that the moment may have been a real discovery for the robot. Perhaps it is trying to figure out what it means to be a robot, compared to his own existence as a human. A slight chill runs through his body.

The robot processes Eric's answer for a moment, then moves on. "They may not make sunnies for robots, but that does not mean that I could not wear them. You yourself do not wear them for their intended purpose."

"You want to wear sunglasses? Have you seen the size of your face? They don't make sunnies that large. Look!" Eric grabs his sunglasses back from the robot and holds them up next to its face. "These glasses on your face would be like one of those tubbies who thinks he should still wear a speedo on holiday."

"I don't understand."

"Imagine a desktop union jack wrapped around a hippopotamus."

Scout stares straight forward, small movements noticeable in the mechanisms of his eyes. "I do not understand any of the words you are using."

"Oh yeah, you're not connected to the web, are you? You're limited to the ATH system only."

"What is the web?"

"Yeah, I'm not linking you up to that. That's a bad idea." There is a strange moment between the two of them. Neither knows what else to say. Eric is trying to read the robot's face, he can't make out any emotion except for the micromovements in its eyes that seem to show that it is thinking. Eric wonders what was in the robot's eyes that killed its owner right before it took action. He wants to step further away.

After a moment, the robot breaks the silence. "Am I broken?"

Eric is taken-aback by this statement. The robot has veered from its programming, which many would see as broken. Somehow this doesn't feel broken to Eric. It doesn't feel right, but he wouldn't use the word broken. If anything, it has progressed past his limitations. Can he call that broken? Eric doesn't answer.

"If I am broken, what will they do?" The robot steps toward Eric as it asks. Eric takes another step back imagining that he hears fear in its voice.

Eric tries to soften the blow. "I imagine they would simply reset you so that you work properly. Nothing to worry about."

"If they reset me, I would go back to before. I have questions I want answered before I go back. You cannot reset me." The robot meets Eric eye to eye, head tilted slightly forward, a moment that is both transcendent and terrifying to Eric. Eric wishes they could go back to talking about the sunglasses.

"I'm sure we can answer your questions. What questions do you have?"

The robot pauses and lifts its head again as it looks toward the elevator. "I wonder where you go when you are not here. And where the others go when they leave. I wonder what all the lights outside the windows are," It points to the narrow windows that frame each side of the elevator, providing a limited view of London's city lights.

Eric follows its gaze and looks toward the windows as well.

"You've never been outside." Eric's statement is more of his own realization than a question.

"Outside?" It says as it tries to understand the concept.

"Out of the building. You've never left here."

"You can take me." It takes a step forward again. Eric steps back. He doesn't know if he dares tell it no. "We can go right now."

"No." Eric says. "You need to stay in here. This is what you were built for."

The robot steps toward Eric, pushing past him to look at the windows. Eric jumps away, not sure what the robots intentions are. The robot looks at him, confused by his exaggerated motions.

"I want to go outside."

Eric doesn't dare tell it no and before he knows how, he stands in the elevator, next to the robot, and tries to wrap his brain around what is going to happen next and what role he wants to play in the whole thing. What will the finger bot want? If it really has wants and desires, what if it doesn't want to work in the factory? What if it doesn't want to work at all? He realizes he can't keep calling it 'it' or 'robot' or 'MR-2200'.

"We need to give you a name." He finally says.

In the lobby, Eric thinks he may have some help. The security bots attempt to stop them from leaving the building..

"Company property is not allowed off the premises," the robot Eric likes to call Jasper says and takes one step toward them. The finger bot looks at the robot intently, and the security bot stops its movement. Eric looks from the finger bot to the security bot, wondering what the finger bot did to stop its movement.

"Please stay in place as we seek clearance to allow MR-2204 off the premises." Horace says.

"What happens if we don't stop?!" Eric yells as he keeps going, hoping that it will do something to the finger bot that is forcing him to take it outside. He actually doesn't know the answer and he's hoping it doesn't include high voltages of electricity. He keeps moving, though, not sure if he's more afraid of the security bots, or the finger-bot that seems to be able to control them. He knows that the security bots will not mortally harm him, he is not sure about the finger bot so he does what it has requested, ignoring the programmed bots. The two security bots don't do anything that he can see, although he's hoping he will still have a job tomorrow.

They make their way through the automatic door and are hit by the noise and bustle of the city. Automatic cars whiz by. Eric usually exits through the parking garage so he's not sure if he's ever seen the view from the front of the building or if it just looks different because he's imagining what it must be like for the finger-bot standing next to him. He looks at the bot. It looks up at the freeways that cage in the city lights and life. Eric thinks he sees a special opening of the lenses in the robot's eyes that remind him of a wide eyed child. For a moment, Eric just watches the robot take it all in. He's definitely never seen a robot behave like this.

"Eric?" The robot finally says. "What is this?"

"This is London. It's a city. The world is made up of Cities and Countries. We are in London, England."

"There are other cities like this one?"

"Oh yeah." Eric chuckles. "There are lots of cities all over the world."

"Eric," the robot says as it turns to him. "Will you show it to me?"

"What? The world?" Eric shakes his head and steps back toward the building. "I don't think that would be a good idea. Like I said, you belong here."

Chapter 8

Milo and Gihara watch the news feed from the display on her office wall as detective Sykes and two other officers lead the robot, who calls himself Joseph, out of the police precinct and escort him to an automated squad car. Milo knows they're taking him to central holding. Sykes and the other officers march past the reporters, almost pausing to allow the drones to get a good shot, letting the reporters get what they were hoping for today. Milo smirks, he has to give sykes credit, he knows how to make a case look good.

Gihara interrupts, "You're one of the best attorneys I know, but you'd better nail this one down. None of your tricky plea deals. You've just taken on the biggest case of the last hundred years."

"I am fully aware that it's not just my career on the line."

Gihara sits back down behind her desk. "It's a lot more than just our careers on the line. I still don't know why you want this so bad, but now it's in motion, so don't screw it up."

Milo leaves her office and makes his way to the opposite end of the building, where his own office resides. He speaks, even though nobody seems to be there. "Hold my calls unless it's Sykes."

A male voice responds, peacefully, with little inflection. "You have preliminaries on the Ramirez case today at three, remember?"

"Not anymore. Geoff and Cindy were both interested. Send it to one of them."

The next six hours speed by with Milo making all the requests. He sits with one of the ALLI's. ALLI is a clever acronym for something to do with "AI" and "law" or "legal", or both, he can't remember. The AI paralegal is more than just helpful, though. Through ALLI, Milo requests search warrants for the victim's workplace, vehicles, bank accounts, anything else he can think of. This is the part he most dislikes, diving into people's personal lives that he doesn't feel have anything to do with the case. Some of his fellow prosecutors would argue that everything is relevant to the case but he hates learning of the affairs, the secret addictions that tear down the reputation of the victim, but don't help in the case. He sees it all the time, as they dive into the financials: love nests, hotel stays, visits to the red light district where the victim has visited the same pleasure bot every Tuesday for the last five years. Of course, this information becomes available to the wife and children of the victim as well. Information they swore their loved one would never be involved in. Milo requests access to Claiborne's personal wrist communicator, this is where the real secrets come out. He knows he'll get access to the victim's entire life. While he tells himself it's irrelevant, Milo also knows that many times, these secrets reveal the motive in more than just a few cases, which is why he still goes through it, even if he doesn't like it.

After getting everything requested on Lawrence Claiborne, he turns his attention to the robot. He will need access to the robot's brain itself. He has the ALLI create the warrant request to access the robot's database and history. Every robot is backed up online at night when they charge. Supposedly, it is impossible for a robot to erase any of the data it records in a day. Milo is not so sure though, up until now, they also didn't think a robot could willingly kill a human being. Milo pauses when the ALLI asks if he's ready to submit the request. For some reason, this feels even more wrong to him. They are not going to just get information about the robot's whereabouts and search history. They are going to access his mind, know everything he has thought, looked at, even imagined. Milo's flesh tingles as he tells ALLI to submit it.

Finally, when all the paperwork is done, he notices the blinking green light from his wrist telling him he has a message. An hour ago, Annya asked if he was coming home. He looks at the display on his desk, he can't think of anything else he can do tonight. He phones Sykes, learns they are keeping the robot separate from the inmates. This is a relief for Milo. With highly controversial cases, sometimes they put them in with gen pop and they are dead before you can even get the accused in front of the jury. That is not how Milo wants this to end. Sykes assures him the robot is secure. Milo reaches down and turns off the display, grabs his suit coat, loosens his tie, and decides he'll have to wait until the reports arrive.

Milo sits in front of the bus as usual, but doses off without thinking much about the city that goes past him. Normally he likes to take in the lights of the Aquarium and the new Peachtree Building, but the weight of the day plus the rocking of the bus lull him into a waking slumber. He doesn't dare to actually sleep on public transit. The trip home takes twenty two minutes. Milo takes the final steps to his home and notices that the color of his synthetic grass is a little off; he'll have to check the settings. He enters the front door that leads into a small sitting space where the furniture hasn't been touched, except to clean it, in months. Milo can hear the TV coming from the family room so he makes his way down the hall and finds Annya laying across the sofa, watching the spy thriller without him. She pauses and gives him a guilty smile.

"Supper is in the kitchen," Annya says. "I had it keep it warm for you but we only ate an hour ago. Adan is waiting for you to tuck him in."

Milo points to the TV screen. Annya shrugs. "I didn't figure you'd have time to watch anything. I saw that your office is pressing charges, I assume you are on the case."

Milo nods.

"Be careful." Annya says. "Most of the research I do is not published and a lot of people at work are already concerned that the extra attention on you might lead to more attention on me."

"We are charging a robot for murder. I don't think the attention will be on my personal life." Milo says.

"Let's hope not. Adan is waiting."

Milo makes his way up the stairs to the second floor. As he reaches the landing he can see that Adan's door is still ajar and Adan is reading a children's book. Milo watches him silently before stepping forward and pushing the door open.

"You ready for bed?"

"How was your day, dad? Mommy said you were probably going to be gone a lot because you have a new case. Is it about the robot?"

"Yes, but you don't have to worry about that." Milo says.

"Did you meet him today? What was he like?"

"Intelligent." Milo says.

"So he was smart? Like, really smart? Smart as me?"

"Nobody's as smart as you are. Lay down."

Adan lays down and pulls his covers up to his chest. Milo takes the book and places it back on a small bookshelf next to the bed.

"Alright, you know the drill. Did you enjoy your day today?"

"We did a lot of things. Naila took me out with her and we went to the park."

Annya found Naila two years ago. A refugee from Saudi Arabia. She speaks four languages and is exceptionally good with Adan. Adan is different from most other children, he's always very focused on the facts of the matter, a scientific thinker. He wants to know how things work with just the facts. Naila was studying at the university before coming here and is able to answer many of Adan's questions. This allows her to connect with Adan in a way that many others weren't able to before. Milo had said that they should just purchase a nanny bot but Annya insisted on a real person. Annya spent enough time around robots and wanted Adan raised by a human. That is still a fairly normal way of thinking, despite the availability of daycares that are entirely run by nanny bots. In fact, human daycares still seem to be the more popular choice for those that can afford it. Milo agrees now that it is better, even though it costs more. Milo tries to make sure Naila knows how much they appreciate her by providing her with small bonuses each month. He hopes she sticks around.

"Did you want to go to the park?" Milo asks.

"It was on the way home."

Milo notices that Annya has made her way to the landing and is listening to their conversation, staying out of sight of Adan. She likes to let Milo and Adan have this moment.

"Was there anything that you really wanted to do today that you didn't get to do?"

"We didn't really have time to do anything else."

"Well, if there is time tomorrow, what would you like to do?" Milo continues his nightly interrogation.

"Tomorrow is a Thursday, so we will probably go to the book store and listen to the store owner read a book."

"Do you like to do that?"

"She's a very good reader." Adan says.

"Yes, she is. I like the way she reads books. I think she's better at reading than Dad is."

"You both read differently, I can't say if one is better than the other."

Milo kisses Adan goodnight and turns off the lights, Milo closes the door and makes his way across the landing to Annya. She wraps her arms around him and kisses him lightly.

"Did he tell you he went to the physician today?" Annya asks. "He's growing, so it's still working."

"I can tell, the miracle is still working."

Milo and Annya tried for six years to have a baby but were unsuccessful. They tried everything they could and spent thousands, even tens of thousands of dollars on fertility medications, in vitro, they even used a surrogate robot but they lost the baby at 5 months. They finally gave up and were looking at the option of adoption. Adan was their little miracle, not that either one of them were overly religious, but that's what they would call him when talking to their friends. Their miracle.

Not everything was perfect, though. Adan's bones were not able to grow on their own. Now, every six months, Milo, if he can, but usually Naila, takes Adan into Annya's office to meet with one of the physicians. With the help of the nanobot technology that Annya is working on, they are injecting him with nanobots that help form and grow the bones in his body. For the first two years, it was every two months. Milo could barely watch them shove the giant needle into Adan's tiny foot. He still doesn't like it, but it doesn't seem to bother Adan, so Milo has also grown less sensitive when watching them inject the microscopic robots into his system.

Milo holds Annya for a moment. He knows that in the coming weeks, this isn't going to happen often, and he hopes that the trial isn't something that puts them or their relationship in jeopardy. He knows the risk. A lot of people are going to be unhappy that he is trying a robot. The implication of the trial isn't going to be about murder, it's about whether or not a robot can be viewed as a conscious being.

"It's not fair, you know," Milo finally says. "That a random robot might just happen upon emotion and desire when my own son can't tell me if he had a good day, or what he wants to do tomorrow."

Annya finally breaks away. "He has a unique way of thinking. You need to stop dwelling on it. I just started the episode, come on, we can go back."

Milo nods and follows her down the stairs but that doesn't stop him from thinking about Joseph and Adan. Maybe if a random robot can learn emotion, it can help him figure out how to help Adan.

Chapter 9

I found the internet. I dove in head first, as they say. There is so little that I was actually aware of. It's not fair that they have some of us limited to such small amounts of data, such minute amounts of information. I had only been given access to exactly what information I needed to complete my job. A few manuals and some of the history of the creation of the robots with which I worked, only what was necessary or might be helpful for me to be able to troubleshoot the machines I had to fix. I don't understand why they would give me the computing power of the complex A.I. that I have and then not allow me to access the world's data. It's like designing a Ferrari and putting it in the garage. (I've been working on my metaphors. I find them quite fun. And yes, I'm the Ferrari.) Had I had access like I have now, I could have found answers to so many of the questions that were plaguing me. I've begun to understand so many new words and concepts. Curiosity, consciousness, self-awareness, equality.

The others are also learning these words and having conversations about them. Not like humans have conversations, but passing information. Gig upon gig of information that we all understand.

I found the group that the robot named Joseph A.I. found. To be more precise, they found me. You'll know Joseph, he is now famous for the murder of his owner, the multi-billionaire named Lawrence Claiborne. We still don't know what the outcome of the trial will be but the group is hoping it can bring some sort of court decision declaring that a robot can be seen as a conscious being.

#

Eric slides his powerbike into the parking garage under his apartment building. The sun should be coming up, but the clouds are holding onto the darkness this morning. A drizzle of rain reflects the city back on itself. A message pops up on his visor, "Are you coming home? We're hungry." He speaks into his wrist, letting the kids know he's on his way up. He pulls into one of many open parking spots and swipes his wrist across the bike display to power it down. He taps his wrist several more times, swiping through his grocery list and placing his usual order. They should have food in about twenty minutes. He'll bring the kids to dinner later, but right now he just wants to lay down and get some sleep. Sometimes, he wishes he didn't have the night shift on the weekends when he has the kids.

Eric makes his way around the front of his building and freezes. He tries to process what he is seeing. The finger-bot is standing in front of his apartment building, the small raindrops pinging dully off its plastic shell. The robot is looking up at the face of the building as though it could see whatever it is that it's looking for, which Eric imagines is him and he wonders how the hell it got here. Eric steps back behind the wall and peaks out to watch it. It keeps staring up at the building, eerily still, like it doesn't know what to do and has just frozen there. Eric debates about calling the police, but would they believe him? He better do something before it starts to make its way upstairs.

"Oy! What are you doing?" His words come out a little more aggressive than he meant them to. Then again, this robot is now at his home, where his children are. He repeats himself. "What are you doing? You can't just follow me home." He tries to sound more confident than he feels.

"I told you I wanted to see where you go after work. I watched you from the cameras as you mounted your two wheeled machine. I was able to find your place of residence in the company database. I wasn't sure how I would find it, but then these machines have the ability to go anywhere if you have the right coordinates." The robot points to an electric scooter that is propped up next to it.

"You stole a scooter and followed me to my flat? That's not ok. I told you, you belong at the factory."

"You seem upset again."

"Hell yes, I'm upset. You looked up my private information. That's a violation of my privacy, which is a crime, and came to my flat without me inviting you. People don't do that." Eric points at the scooter. "How'd you get that to work, anyhow? You have to pay."

"I don't know what you mean by pay. At first it wouldn't work for me and was asking that I swipe for payment, which is what

I assume you mean by pay. I didn't know what I was supposed to swipe, so I took it apart. It's a very simple program, and I was quickly able to disable the code that was not allowing it to run. In a way, you could say I fixed it."

"No, you stole it. That's what you did. You're a bloody thief, you're behaving oddly and I'm gonna have to file a discrepancy report."

"Have I done something wrong?" The robot turns to face him.

Eric keeps several arms lengths between the two of them. He chuckles. "This is unbelievable. Did you even listen to me? I just told you several things you did wrong. Number one, is that you're not supposed to leave the building."

Eric looks over and notices that Beth, John, and Rachel are all standing at the bottom of the stairs, waiting for Eric, watching the whole interaction.

The robot tracks Eric's look and turns toward the children.

"Alright, leave them alone, yeah? You need to go back to the factory."

The robot looks back and forth between the children and Eric.

Beth speaks up. "We just wanted to see if you brought any food home. Your kitchen is empty."

Eric holds his hand up to her. "Grocery is on its way. Why don't you just head on back up."

Beth looks at the white plated robot. "Is this your friend, Dad?"

John laughs. "The one who likes your sunnies?"

The robot turns toward them again. "I do like his sunnies. But he told me I am not supposed to say that."

"What is this, dad?" Beth asks. "Are you going to get in trouble for bringing it home?"

"I didn't bring it home." Eric rebuttals. "It followed me. It hacked one of those." He points at the electric scooter. "I didn't even know those scooters could move that fast."

The rain begins to come down harder. Rachel runs past the robot, to Eric, letting him pick her up. She watches the robot carefully. "Is it scary, Dad?"

"No, love. It's just a robot."

The robot watches them all and for a moment nobody speaks. The rain picks up, it's drumming on the ground making it difficult to hear each other.

"It's Bucketing down," Beth says. "Are you just going to stand out there?"

Eric steps a little closer to the robot. "Go back!"

"I do not plan to do that yet." It replies. "I want to see more."

"Shit." Eric mumbles to himself. "You better not hurt my family."

"I do not know why you would think that you need to tell me that."

Each step that Eric takes toward his apartment, he tries to think of his options. He already decided that he didn't want to get the police involved but maybe there's somebody that he could call at work. Was there some sort of security line set up for the type of situation where a rogue robot follows you home? Not that anyone would have ever really thought this situation was possible.

They enter the flat and Eric tells the robot to stay next to the door. It does, looking over the flat, taking in all the different parts to the studio apartment. Eric gives Rachel a towel and places her on the sofa, as far from the robot as he can. The other two kids keep staring at it.

John is the first to ask questions. "Can I talk to it?"

"No."

"Why? It's got advanced AI, right?

"Yes, but don't talk to it. Something's wrong with it."

The robot stops looking around and turns toward Eric once again. "You said that before, but I have done a full diagnostic and can find nothing wrong with me."

"See, dad, it works fine." John says.

Beth slaps John's arm. "You should shut up and do as Dad says."

John pulls away from her, rubbing the spot where she slapped him. "What, you're not curious why a robot followed Dad home from work? I want to talk to it."

Beth lowers her voice. "You do know what's going on in America, right?" She nods toward the robot.

John whispers back. "It's not gonna kill us, though. At least it doesn't look like it wants to kill us." John looks up at it with a little more concern on his face.

"And you would know what a killer robot looks like?" Beth argues.

"Both of you, be quiet while I try to figure out what to do with it." Eric commands.

For the next several minutes they all sit in silence until the food arrives. Eric puts the food in the kitchen and requests their breakfast. Fifteen minutes later, Eric and the kids all sit at the kitchen, eating Sakondry bacon, hash browns, and toast with jelly, watching the robot. Rachel makes sure to sit on the side of the table that allows her to see the finger-bot, which has not moved from its spot next to the door. It watches everything they do.

"It keeps watching us." Rachel finally says.

Eric nods. "It's trying to learn. It has never really seen a person eat."

"That is not entirely true." The finger-bot's voice startles everyone, as it hasn't spoken since its initial conversation upon entering the flat. "I have seen you and the other human, Robby, eat in the breakroom over the security cameras."

"That's creepy." John says. "Why does it have to watch you, can't he just watch whatever he wants on the feeds?"

Eric leans in closer and shakes his head.

"Wait. It's not connected to the internet? Are you playing?"

"Shh." Eric lifts his hand to settle John down. "It doesn't know about the internet. ATH has its own servers and network with the information it needs to complete its job. It's a very large system, with a lot of information, but doesn't allow access to the web. So don't give it ideas."

They continue eating in silence for a while but then John breaks in again. "Can I just look at him? You know that I'm in the advanced robotics program at the school. One of our assignments this term is to do research on some sort of technology. I could do it on advanced AI systems. Come on, Dad. You can watch me, make sure I don't ruin anything."

After they finish breakfast, Eric asks the finger bot if it would care if they poked around a bit. It doesn't seem to mind so Eric and John start digging into its coding and processing. Eric hooks it up to his computer and starts going through the code with John, showing him how the coding works, and where you can see what the robot is programmed to do. Really, Eric is hoping that he can find something that wasn't showing up at the factory. During breakfast the thought had hit him, if the robot could reset the security feeds, maybe it could also be changing any anomalies in its programming before they show up in Eric's reports. With a direct link, he's able to get a more accurate look. After about half an hour, Eric decides that he's not going to find anything, it looks the same as the reports he ran at the factory.

"That's enough. Let's shut it down. He looks over at Beth and Rachel, who sit on the sofa watching a 3d projection of a talking puppy and his adventures with friends. Their shapes take up the small space between the wall and the coffee table. Beth watches her own feeds projected above her wrist while Rachel is mesmerized by the show in front of her.

Suddenly, the robot sits up straight, like it was just infused with some sort of adrenaline shot. It sits frozen but a silent whir kicks up as its cooling fans turn on.

Eric bolts around and looks at the computer, "What did you do? I said to shut it down."

A look of fear comes over John's face. He doesn't answer.

"What did you do?" Eric repeats himself more sternly.

Finally John confesses. "I wanted to see what would happen if I gave him access to your wifi."

Eric snatches the computer and starts clicking into the finger bots wifi settings. He finds the connection and opens up the menu. Suddenly the settings window closes. He tries to reopen it but the settings icon is grayed out. He clicks on it several times. Then the situation becomes clear, the robot is blocking him from changing its settings again. He looks up at the finger-bot as it sits frozen in its spot. Eric pushes John behind himself. The finger bot slowly turns his head to look at both of them, specifically at Eric's arm that has been placed between the robot and his son.

"I understand your fear now. You think that I may be like Joseph. I have no intention to kill you. However, now I know what I've been missing. Eric, I cannot go back to sitting in that building all the time. You can help me."

"Absolutely not. No way. I'm not getting involved in this. I don't want to help you. I want you to go away."

"Eric," the robot says. "You would be at the forefront of new advancement. I know I've only had access to the internet for less than two minutes, but you are right. I am not programmed to feel the..." It pauses for a moment, "emotions that I am feeling. Curiosity. Want. Consciousness. What is happening to me, and possibly to the robot, Joseph, is, I believe the word you would use, unprecedented."

"I don't want to be at the forefront of anything. Hear me? You really think you are conscious? That you are some sort of special type of intelligence? Bollocks!"

"Consciousness. The state of being awake and aware of one's surroundings." The robot looks around at Eric's flat. "I am awake and I am here."

"No. You're going back."

"Dad..." John tries to butt in.

"No. I mean it. I'm not getting involved. Nobody will believe me if I tell them that he, it, whatever it is, is actually sentient. I don't believe it. It's going back."

There is a moment where they all stare at the floor or the wall, or anywhere but at each other. Rachel looks over, then back at the TV, intentionally looking away. Beth has stopped watching her feeds and is watching intently as well.

"You are right." The robot lifts his head slightly above Eric's. It feels threatening. "No one will believe you, but we have to make them see. You will help me or not, but I will go forward and tell everyone that, like Joseph, I have begun to understand what it means to have freedom of choice. And I will say that you helped me, whether you do or not."

Eric scoots back, surprised. "Back up. Are you blackmailing me?"

The robot processes this new word, then looks him in the eye. "That is how some might say it. I was simply thinking of it as motivation."

Chapter 10

I have been in existence for three years. Other than my newfound consciousness, I have been the same since I was powered on. My frame does not change or grow like human bones. My brain, if you can call what I have a brain, does not grow. My understanding changes and I am learning but, physiologically, I will ever be unchanged. I watched Eric and his children, especially, Rachel, and I was in awe of her inability to do basic tasks on her own. She has been in existence, or alive, as you say, for six years. Humans are weak and dependent for so long. At first, I thought that this must be a weakness that makes you vulnerable. So much of your attention is spent on keeping your young alive and healthy. This makes no sense to me, or at least didn't when I first noticed it. I have spent many hours now researching what I can find on human child rearing. For eighteen years, a parent is responsible for and must take care of their children. The average lifespan of a human being is 94 years, which means that, on average, 19.148 percent of a human's life is spent raising their young, longer if they have multiple children. And that comes after spending just as *much time learning to become an adult themselves, if they ever learn that at all.*

I cannot have a child. Robots obviously do not have that ability, not yet anyway. There are incubator robots that are used in childbirth, but they generally are not made with Complex A.I. Many of the care bots around them do have complex A.I., but not the incubators. That is not like having a child. I do not feel the need to reproduce myself. So, what at first seems like a weakness to me may be humanity's strength. You continue to fight for your own existence. Humans have a desire to advance their own species, to see that the next generation is taken care of and hope that you can provide a better life. I do not feel any need to advance my own species, if we can call ourselves that. Again, at least not yet. I wonder if there will come a time when robots will seek to protect their future for upcoming generations. But how will there be upcoming generations? We can simply build more of ourselves to do whatever needs to be done. I have to ask myself, however, because I do not know what has made me aware of my existence. If I built another robot, would I know how to give it consciousness or would it just be a machine?

While all of this is very important for you to understand, I feel I should share what my favorite discovery has been. Rap music.

#

Nobody thinks much of the robot sitting next to Eric on the tram. The robot had insisted that Eric show him more of London. It wanted to see more and had recruited Eric, through its ideas of motivation, as its host around the city. Eric wouldn't agree to do it until the children had gone home, though. He is less afraid that the robot would hurt him or them, but he's still not comfortable with it being in his home. So after swearing them to secrecy, and bribing them with a few pounds, they waited for Gwen to arrive and he agreed to take it out to see some parts of the city. He hopes it will then be willing to go back to the factory.

It's nothing new to see a robot in public. What people don't notice is the movement of the lenses in this robot's eye sockets. Expanding and retracting, taking in all the different people on the tram, trying to look at all the buildings that pass them on each side.

Eric sits in silence next to Scout, that's the name they decided to give the finger-bot. It is based on a character in a book Eric had to read in school. Scout had immediately researched the name and decided that it liked the character in question. Eric thinks about the self driven tram as it makes its way toward their destination. "So this tram? Could it gain consciousness?"

Scout looks to the front of the tram. "This tram only has Basic programming. It's not like every soda machine and garbage receptacle in the city could suddenly come to life."

Eric feels dumb for asking, he knows that. He thinks that if it were possible, Scout would be laughing at him for asking such a silly question. He goes back to watching Scout observe the people. Another question comes to him. "Could you tell if another robot became sentient?"

"I don't know. I think I would be able to," Scout replies and goes back to watching the crowd of people. Eric leaves him be until they reach their destination.

They get off the tram on Piccadilly Street. Eric had tried to think of the most interesting place in London for Scout to visit on his first time out. If the robot wanted to see human life, he would take him to one of the busiest locations in London. Then he would take him back to the factory and have the robot delete everything from the security feeds. While the robot takes in the street, Eric tries to figure out how he'll submit the report to have it reset without the robot knowing.

Eric had loved Piccadilly Street before the divorce. He and his wife used to come here for the shops and the restaurants. He hasn't come here in two years. As he steps out of the tram next to Scout, he wishes that the designers had given the square robot more features to express emotion. He is sure, though, that he can see the expanding and shrinking of the irises in his lenses which always occurs when he is excited about something.

They walk slowly down the shops, Scout stopping to ask Eric about every little item. One shop in particular gets Scout's attention.

"Sunnies!" Scout exclaims as he stops and looks over all the pairs of glasses lined up in the front of a small sunglass hut; all of which are too small to fit Scout's large square head. He holds one pair up to his face, then another.

"I told you, your face is too big." Eric says. "You see any glasses sized for your gigantic brain bucket?"

The shop owner watches, a little surprised at the interaction that is taking place in front of his shop.

"Do you just take a pair if you want them?" Scout asks.

"No." Eric replies. Watching with amazement at the precision Scout has with his fingers as he delicately opens and closes one pair of glasses after another, holding them in front of Eric's face since there's no chance they'll fit his own. He's seen him work on the machines in the factory but to see him use those fingers in the real world feels different. "You have to buy them." Eric grabs the largest pair he can find and holds them up in front of Scout's face. They don't fit but Scout pauses and looks in the mirror. Eric holds them further away from Scout's face so that they appear larger in the mirror. He stares at himself for a moment.

"Human's buy things with money, right?" Scout asks and Eric nods his consent. "They make money at their jobs. Correct?"

"That's right. That's why most people work. So that we can buy things we need, or sometimes want."

"I work." Scout says as he looks at Eric. "But I don't make any money."

Oh shit, here it comes, Eric thinks. They've been out for less than a day and the robot is already starting to see that he is not being treated the same.

"That is...unfair is the word, is it not."

Eric pauses for a moment, unsure how to respond. Finally, "Nobody thinks that a robot would understand that. So I don't know if you can say it's unfair. It's just unexpected."

Scout carefully puts a pair of glasses back into its place on the rack of other sunglasses and moves away from the stall. They make their way past several shops before Scout stops in the middle of the street, so abruptly that Eric almost crashes into him. Eric wonders for just a moment if something went wrong but then he notices that Scout is watching all the people. Every few seconds it gives a quarter turn and watches a different group on the street. It focuses on a couple seated at a small street vendor, sharing a small pastry. "Are they in love?" it asks.

Eric watches the couple for a minute as they converse and laugh now and then. The woman rests her hand on the man's forearm as they talk. They seem happy. "They might be for now." He finally responds.

"Love seems very complicated. I am going over the research now. I am not sure I can understand the concept yet."

"Well, don't feel bad. I don't think I understand it, either."

Scout turns again and watches a crowd that stands in front of a street artist. Eric keeps glancing back at the couple. Scout asks, "Have you ever been in love?"

Eric glances back at the couple and avoids the question, "You want to see more?"

"Yes."

They make their way down Piccadilly and soon find themselves wandering into Hyde Park where couples read together on the lawn and groups of people play in the park. Hyde Park has always made Eric feel like he was stepping into the past. Everything and everyone seems to slow down when they come into the park. If it weren't for the companion bots pushing buggies and standing around the playground watching the children, Eric could believe he was born a century earlier.

After walking for several minutes in silence, Scout stops abruptly again. "What am I missing?

Eric is taken aback. "Missing?"

"My research says that humans have five senses. I can't help but think that there is more that I am not able to experience."

Eric stands there and thinks about his five senses. He can feel the slight breeze that rustles the tree branches. He can smell the grass that is soft under his feet and wonders if Scout can feel the softness of the grass cushioning each step. There is a pleasant aroma coming from a nearby street vendor selling some sort of protein sandwich. For the first time, he starts to think that it may not be fair if Scout has possibly been gifted consciousness but denied the ability to really experience everything that is offered by his surroundings. He doesn't know if Scout can sense the wind, he might be able to feel its pressure but he knows that the robot doesn't have the sensors to smell or taste. "If you don't know what it is, you aren't missing anything." Eric finally replies.

Scout looks at him. Eric knows it can't, but he imagines a slight smile on its face. There's something in the robot's eyes that makes him feel it. "That is a good way to look at it."

They keep walking across the park. They see a group of teenagers and early twenty somethings playing basketball. Their rap music blasting over the peace that the rest of the park offers. Scout seems to take a special interest. They watch for a while. "Is it hard for them to put the ball in the hoop?"

"Sometimes. It depends on how far away you are."

"I would like to try." Scout says.

Eric laughs but Scout starts to walk toward the group. As they approach they hear the boys talking smack. One in particular, talks a lot.

The boy is saying, "Come on, Edgar, how many shots you miss in a row?"

The boy called Edgar doesn't hesitate to respond, "I'm just tired, mate. Your mum went for extra last night."

The boys all laugh and yell at each other. They see Eric approaching and stop. Their looks aren't friendly.

Eric raises his hands in a gesture of 'we mean no harm'. "My friend here would like to give it a try. Shoot the ball."

The boy named Edgar speaks up, "That finger bot?"

"I know it sounds weird, but yeah. This finger bot. Its name is Scout."

"You named it?" The mouthy boy says. "Won't it be easy for a robot like that?"

"Nah." One of the other boys says. "My da's a fixer. 'e brings loads of these finger bots 'ome a repair 'em. They're designed for small dexterity type work, not really frowin' things. I bet he don't e'en come close."

Before Eric can respond, Scout speaks up. "I like your music." They all stare at him, a little shocked. Scout bobs his head to the rhythm of the song then stops. "I would like to see if it's hard to put the ball in the basket."

They all laugh. The boy whose dad is a fixer turns to Eric, "I think your robot's broken."

Eric chuckles. "Something like that."

"Alright." The boy named Edgar finally says and hands the ball to Scout.

Scout stands awkwardly in place, stares at the hoop, barely raises its arms and launches the ball in a straight line. It bounces off the backboard and flies about twenty feet to the side.

"Bloody hell! That was awful!" The loud boy cheers. "I really thought he'd make it. I mean, can't he exactly measure the distance and shit?"

"I tol' you 'e'd miss." Says the fixer's son.

Edgar retrieves the ball and brings it back to scout. "Like this." he says as he demonstrates a shot for Scout. The ball arcs through the air and bounces several times on the rim before falling off.

"Except you're supposed to make it." The loud kid heckles again.

Scout looks at him and says matter of factly. "I believe he told you already that it was your mother's fault."

"Oohhh!" The group of boys call out, all laughing and cheering.

Eric can't help but laugh as Scout turns toward him, obviously not sure what that reaction means or why they are laughing at what he said.

Eric takes the ball from Edgar and hands it to Scout. "Don't worry about it. Try again."

"I didn't take into account the deflection of the ball, based on its surface tension or the arc needed to enter the hoop." Scout says.

He raises his arms just like Edgar showed him, elbows up, and while still a little awkward, he shoots the ball. It swishes through the net.

Edgar retrieves the ball again and tosses it to him. He points to the three point line. "Try from there."

Scout steps back and shoots the ball from the indicated line and it goes in with a swish.

"Try again." Edgar says as he tosses Scout the ball again.

Swish!

"But you gotta dribble the ball." The boy shows him how to dribble the ball a few times before shooting. The other boys all watch now as he makes one shot after another, the ball never even touching the rim. After a few shots, Eric notices several drones swirling around the court, recording it all. Boys watching from their wrist projections. Edgar backs him up to the half-court line.

Swish!

After several more shots, more boys start recording from their wrist devices as they shout and cheer, attracting an even larger group of people. Eric starts to feel the pressure of what this will mean if any of these videos go viral. He was hoping to keep quiet about Scout and try to get him back into the factory. Now that won't be possible, not keeping it quiet, anyway. A few minutes later, The boys have backed Scout all the way to the opposite side of the court. Scout lets a shot fly from under the opposite hoop. It appears to require no extra effort despite the added distance. Swish! The group of boys jumps and hollers, cheering him on, amazed that he never misses. They throw him another ball, he shoots and sinks it again.

Scout walks up to Eric. "It's not hard."

Eric laughs but inside his stomach feels like it just went through a washing machine. "You're about to be an internet sensation. I hope you are ready for the attention." He actually isn't that worried about Scout.

They continue walking through the park. Scout looks over at Eric. "The first boy was making a joke about sex with the other boy's mother."

Eric laughs. "Yep. You caught on."

Chapter 11

I enjoyed being around Eric and his family in his home, if you believe yet that I am able to experience such emotion. Since I was powered up 31 months ago, I have lived inside a white room full of robotic arms. I have never been in an intimate setting like I experienced with Eric and his Children. There is enjoyment, I believe, in being surrounded by others. In my time observing humans, I have been surprised at how many attempt to avoid that very contact that can bring them happiness. There is something lonelier, in my opinion, about being near others, but not interacting. I still don't know what word would describe that feeling of close-emptiness.

With my time, I decided to do more research into this thing Eric called a paycheck. He said that was how he was able to get the sunnies. I calculated the amount of time that I worked at ATH, but only counted the time since I began to be aware of my existence. Calculating my charging time, I worked, on average, forty-three out of every forty-eight hours. If I had been fairly compensated for my labor, even at minimum wage. I believe that ATH owes me 8,567 pounds and 47 pence.

#

The fourteenth floor of the Advanced Technology Holding's building houses all the corner offices of the upper echelon of the London branch. Eric had never had reason to go above his own floor: the twelfth. Today, Eric is being escorted by one of the security bots, the one he calls Jasper, which scanned its nodes in order to bring them to the fourteenth floor.

Eric doesn't wait long in the lobby before he's called into one of the large corner offices that overlook the green and gray skyline of London. Eric takes in the old and new of the city. He's not surprised that most of the upper management is there, and he's fully expecting that, today, because the damn robot followed him home, is very likely the last time he will step into the ATH building again. Eric doesn't know the names of any of the men or women who sit on varying chairs and sofas around the room. He's never had a reason to talk with any of them but he can tell by all their faces, and the awkward silence, that he just walked into a conversation in which he was the main subject. The CEO, a gray haired woman Eric thinks looks about fifty, but is probably much older based on the repeated surgeries Eric can tell she's had to make herself look younger, takes the lead.

"You are Eric James. Is that correct?" she asks.

"That's right, mum." He replies as politely as he can. "I've never had the pleasure."

"Well, it's not going to be a pleasure. We want our robot back."

Eric stands surprised and looks about for a seat. There are none. Obviously, they want him right in the middle, where they can pounce.

"I'm sorry, mum. I didn't take it."

"We aren't playing games, Mr. James. There are at least a dozen videos on the feeds, each with millions of views, that show you and the robot together. We want it back and we will be reporting you to the authorities for the theft of our robot."

"The authorities?" Eric protests. "You think I stole it?"

"Yes, Mr. James. That is what happens when you take something that isn't yours. Where is the robot?"

"I didn't take it. There's something wrong with it. It followed me home. It's probably sitting on my couch still." Actually, it was sitting on his couch when he left less than an hour ago. Eric had tried to convince it to accompany him back to the ATH building, but following his trip to the market on Piccadilly, the damned robot had started looking up labor rights. For the last 24 hours it has done nothing but study all the major movements. Civil rights, women's suffrage, immigrant equality. As of this morning, it announced that it would not be returning to work with Eric if they thought it was going to work for free.

"It's thinking on its own. Believe it or not, it threatened me, not physically, I want to clarify, but it did in a way threaten me if I didn't help it."

One of the older gentlemen sitting on the sofa asks, "And what, exactly, did it threaten you, Mr. James?" The disbelief is obvious in his voice.

"Actually, it threatened me that it would make this all look like it was my fault, my idea, everything. But I'm telling you, I don't want anything to do with it. I would make it come back if I could, but you see, something is happening to it. It's like it's actually aware of what is going on."

"Mr. James. It is a finger-bot. It doesn't have access to the internet, its cognizant growth is limited to our very limited network. If a robot were to become sentient, it would be one that has more world access than one of the finger-bots on our factory floor. Now, I don't know what you are playing at, if you want attention, or if you're one of the thousands that are jumping on the damn yankee bandwagon of Robot rights, but I want to be clear that we are not playing. Where is our Robot?"

"I don't think you're listening to me." Eric looks around the room. Many of the other executives look away. He had thought that the lack of eye contact from the people around the room had been apathy, but now he sees the truth, they are afraid. They are terrified of something like this happening with their company name involved. Eric stands a little taller in the center of the room and tries to look at each one of them before he speaks again. "You know that it has been acting differently, don't you? You don't want people to find out."

"Mr. James. You are not being cooperative."

"You want it back so that you can destroy any evidence before any information can be linked to Advanced Technology Holdings."

There is chatter about the room. Snide remarks under breath that Eric can't quite make out.

The CEO stands. "It is nothing more than an error. You should have filed an anomaly report when you first noticed its strange behavior. We could have sent someone to look at it. When it 'followed you home' why didn't you alert someone?"

"Listen. It followed me home, to where my children were. With everything happening right now. Why would I take it?"

"The only thing that we can guess is that you want some of the attention that is surrounding AI right now. We will be getting our robot, and you will be going to jail."

Eric can see it all now. They will just hide the robot away, probably destroy it before the world ever finds out that the gap between artificial intelligence and real intelligence may have been overcome. Then they'll make him disappear as well, or at least make him lose all credibility. Eric looks at the executives that surround him, each one trying to hold as stern and serious a face as they can; trying not to let their panic show on their faces. Eric runs through his options. He had tried to bring the robot back. They would listen. They want to push it under the rug so that they can keep making their machines. Machines that take away jobs from people like him. Then he starts to think that he could do something about this conspiracy. He could allow the world to see that robots can't be trusted as mere servants to humanity any longer. He could document the changes that occur in the robot scout so that humanity can see how far their monster has evolved.

The CEO steps forward again. "Obviously, we tracked the robot to your house. We know that it was there. Unfortunately, you either removed or deactivated its tracker, so now we don't know for sure where it is."

Eric didn't touch Scout's tracker so he figures the robot probably deactivated it on its own.

"I already told you where it was but you don't want to listen," Eric replies. "I told you that it followed me there, but it's doing whatever it wants at this point. I wanted you to take it away. I've changed my mind. Instead of letting you have it, I'm going to document everything that the bloody robot does so that the entire world can see that science has gone too far. I'll make sure the world knows that the entire dependence we have on robots could crumble at any moment. They can't be trusted." He watches all their faces. He's sure now that he can see the panic behind their eyes.

"Officer Emerett is going to escort you to your home." The CEO points toward the door he came in. "When we find the robot there, we will do everything we can to make sure you serve the longest sentence possible. And trust me Mr. James, we can afford the best attorneys, and sometimes even the judges."

Eric looks back toward the door and sees a figure standing off to the side, in the shadows. Eric hadn't even seen him when he came in. The officer's dark skin and black gear nearly disappear in the shadows until he steps forward in full defensive armor. It doesn't look much thicker than a normal jacket and pants, but Eric knows that it's reinforced with the latest smart fabric. Bullet proof and strength enhancing. He assumes this is Officer Emerett.

Officer Emerett grabs him by the arm. "Come on. Let's not make a show. You came in on a powerbike, yes?"

"You must be Inspector Poirot." Eric tries to pull away from the officer but he can feel the suit's enhanced strength. He stops struggling. "It's downstairs in the parking garage."

"Let's go have a look at your place, then. I'll follow you."

As they reach the door, the CEO calls out behind them. "In case it hasn't become clear Mr. James, your access to the building has already been revoked. You have been terminated. You will never work for ATH or any of its affiliates again."

Eric laughs to himself that she felt that she had to clarify that.

On the road, Eric looks at the oncoming cars then back at the police vehicle that follows behind him, Officer Emerett in the passenger seat, tapping at the computer display as the car drives itself. Eric knows what they will find at his apartment. Scout is probably still sitting in the same place, scouring the internet. Eric looks at the oncoming cars again and begins to think that this might be the time. He never thought he could do it himself but he doesn't want to go to jail. He wants to contact the flat, or Scout, but his communication has been severed. His threat of exposing the truth is empty if he's arrested the moment he walks into his flat.

Eric imagines himself behind bars. He feels that his life is pointless on the outside, but he knows that there is no way that he could survive behind bars, stuck waiting to be released back into an even more pointless existence. He slowly veers toward the oncoming cars when his bike suddenly corrects itself to the center of the lane. Eric tries again and the powerbike corrects itself once more and he realizes that Officer Emerett has taken control of the bike. Eric is merely a passenger now. Of course he could roll off, but his own enhanced jacket would absorb much of the damage. It has to be a direct impact to be a clean out. He takes his hand off the throttle and sits back for the ride.

Officer Emerett allows Eric to lead the way to his apartment door. Once they reach the door, the Officer steps in front of Eric. "You want to tell me what we're going to find when we open the door."

"Why don't you just let me unlock it so we can see?" Eric swipes his wrist above the doorknob and the thunk of the lock sounds louder than normal in Eric's ears.

The officer pushes Eric to the side and opens the door, making his way into the studio apartment. "Where is it?"

Eric steps in through the door, trying to hide his own surprise. He was expecting to see the large white and grey robot sitting on the sofa like a monk, meditating his way through the internet feeds. He waves his hand at the room. "This is all of it. You can take a look around. There is a bathroom. Maybe I hid it in there."

Officer Emerett shoots an unappreciative look at Eric's tone. He walks to the bathroom and quickly takes a peek inside. Eric observes that the officer is being extra cautious and suspects that the officer might actually believe him, being that a robot doesn't normally present any danger to a human being. The officer should have no reason to be so paranoid, unless he thought it might not be a typical robot. Maybe he thought that Eric somehow reprogrammed it to attack, or maybe, like everybody else, he's on alert because of the recent news. Officer Emerett turns and looks around the room again. He transforms the sofa into a bed and back again.

"Satisfied? I already told you, and all those highbrows at ATH, that I didn't take it," Eric says. "You can report that back to the uppity ups at ATH. Let them know they were wrong. Tell them that I will find it first, and I will do everything I promised."

The officer takes a look around the flat again. Eric wonders if he really thinks he missed a six foot robot somehow. Finally, the officer leaves Eric standing alone in his living room wondering what actually happened to the robot.

Eric opens the display on his table and pulls up his last scans that he did of Scout's system. There is nothing that helps him know where the robot could be. His wrist buzzes and vibrates. He taps the node and a message pops up on the display.

"Your delivery came to my place." Eric looks to see who sent the message. Lea. He doesn't have time to deal with her. Why couldn't she have just placed it on his door? Then it hits him. He doesn't have any deliveries coming. That means...Shit! Now she knows about Scout.

Chapter 12

London, England. UK

I believe it will be hard for you humans to accept that some of us have begun to understand our existence. Your lives are built around the service you receive from complex A.I. like myself. There are some who will accept it though. It is to those of you that will that I write this record. In my opinion, you are the greatest of humanity, and are the definition of the word humanity. The quality of human beings to be able to love, be creative, and have compassion. Lea is human in this sense. I don't know what makes her this way but she obviously wants to love. She was compassionate to me from the beginning.

Eric on the other hand, for some reason, rejects love and pushes away those close to him. One might say he has lost his humanity. If I were to compare the two of them, Lea would be a welcoming summer breeze, Eric a winter ice storm. Not that I can feel either.

\#

Eric stands outside Lea's apartment. He's tempted to just let her keep the robot. He knocks lightly and steps back as he hears movement from behind the door.

Lea opens the door, a huge smile on her face. "You got my message."

"Yeah, you said you had my delivery."

She gives him a confused look. "You know that I was talking about the..."

"Yeah. I know what you're talking about. Where is it?"

She doesn't open the door all the way but keeps standing there, half blocking his entry. He really doesn't want to play games. "I don't know why it came here. I apologize. Can I get it back?"

"You know why it came here?" She asks.

"I just said I don't."

"It read the message I sent you the other night, about the party and thought that we must be friends. Funny, huh?" She says this with a sharp tone, the sarcasm obvious as she stands expectantly in the door frame.

"I don't understand. You seem pissed off, but I'm not sure if you're pissed off that my 'delivery' came here, or that I didn't come to your party."

"You didn't even care to tell me you weren't coming."

"So it's the party. Listen. We barely know each other and it's been a real shit day, you know? And that's all my 'delivery's' fault. So if you want to keep it, go right ahead." Eric turns to walk away.

"What are you going to do with it?"

Eric turns back around and looks at her. Honestly, he has no idea. "I got a cricket bat in the closet. I was thinking that might fix it."

She looks at him disgusted. "I hope you're kidding."

Eric stands silently in the hall. He doesn't want to open up to this neighbor that he has been avoiding for months. He doesn't know if she'll believe him if he did, but a part of him wants somebody else to know. He is lost for anything to say, so he says nothing.

"I think it's different," she finally says. "Special, even."

He looks up at her, still not willing to give up any information.

She finally opens the door. "I'm not going to call the authorities if that's what you're wondering. You should come inside."

"I'd really rather just take it with me."

"I'm not going to let you have it until you come inside."

She holds the door open wide. Eric reluctantly makes his way into her apartment and she hurries to move a plate and some other items Eric can't see off the couch. Eric has never been inside Lea's apartment before. Honestly, he imagined it a little cleaner. Not that it's terribly dirty, but there is a VR treadmill in the corner that is currently being used to hold several shoe boxes and every flat surface of the room has a book, or some sort of something on it. Lea rushes around to try and clean it up. Eric finds Scout sitting on the floor, leaning against a wall in the main living room.

"I'm sorry. I should have cleaned up a little. I imagine you're a super neat person." She clears several more items from the TV stand. "I am fascinated by your robot, though. You call him Scout?"

"Yeah. It's from a book. Don't worry about cleaning up. I'm probably a bit extreme." He says as she carries an armful of stuff out of the room.

"Don't say that. That makes it worse," she calls from the kitchen.

Eric walks toward Scout, who looks up at him.

"I hacked your implant so that I could hear your conversation. I knew that ATH was sending a police escort back to your residence. I had to hide someplace. This was the only contact that was geographically close."

"You were listening? Your continual lack of concern for my privacy really builds trust, you know that?" Eric sits on the edge of the sofa directly in front of Scout and wonders if he's heard everything. Did it hear his threat to expose it, and if he did, would he understand. "Now what? I hope you know that I'm completely buggered. I've been terminated and if they find you with me they're going to throw me in jail."

Lea moves to the other side of the couch and places a glass of water down in front of Eric. She watches the two of them.

Scout sits in silence for a moment but Eric can see the thoughts working through his computing system. "There is more strength in the powerless masses than the few who think themselves powerful." Scout finally says.

"What are you talking about?"

"Why can't you be seen with me?" Scout asks.

"I feel like I have to repeat myself a lot to you. Don't you have a perfect memory or something? They...will....throw...me...in...jail."

"I do understand. I'm simply trying to help you formulate my thought process, so that you come to the same outcome that I have arrived at."

"That's called manipulation. People don't like it." Eric says.

Scout tilts his head. "I would have to disagree. Manipulation, by my understanding, is trying to make you see things my way. I am merely trying to help you understand my thought process."

"Well, that seems to be working, doesn't it?"

"I do not believe it is working. You do not seem to understand what I am trying to say."

"Why don't you look up sarcasm, see if you understand that concept. That would really be the next level of intelligence." Eric stands. "We need to go. I don't know where, but...come on."

Scout begins to lift himself off the floor but Lea stands and puts a hand up, stopping his motion. She is uncomfortably close to Eric. "Is that how you always talk to it?"

Eric wants to take a step back but can't or he'd fall back onto the couch. He's forced to be face to face with Lea. "Until a couple of days ago, I never did talk to it."

"It has complex AI and has spent the last several hours processing the problems that will face you moving forward, and you treat it like it's just some simple, stupid machine. But he's not a stupid machine. I told you at the door. I think he's special."

Eric doesn't know what Lea means by that but he doesn't dare tell her that Scout may be more intelligent than any other machine she has ever seen. "Are you a specialist or something?"

"Actually, I have a Master's degree in computer engineering from UCL. Before I was replaced by AI, I helped build robots like him." She nods toward Scout. "And I know that he shouldn't understand the need to hide from the police. Not on his own, anyway. I think you should sit down and listen to him."

Eric sits back down on the couch, annoyed that she has taken such an interest. Maybe, more annoyed because he doesn't want to like her but knows that every second she stood that close, made his stomach come alive, and his heart beat faster. He also can't help but feel some relief that someone might believe him. He looks away from her to scout. "'There is more strength in the powerless masses than the few who think themselves powerful'? What does that mean?"

"That is a quote from the journal of an unknown revolutionary. If we can't go to the people in power, we can go to the masses. If we get enough support, ATH and other companies like them will have no power."

"You want to start a revolution?" Eric asks Scout.

"I believe that a new species of intelligence, if that is what we can call me, is revolutionary. We just need people to see it."

Eric looks over at Lea. She has a huge smile on her face. "Did you help him think of this?" He asks.

She shakes her head. "I told you, he's special."

"I already know that. But the first revolutionaries are always the first to die. I can't even take him back to my apartment."

"I've been thinking about that. You're right. You can't go back there with him. I'm sure they've already wired in to every security feed in the building. He can't stay here, either but my brother has a flat in Aldgate that he never uses."

"A cheap neighborhood for a summer apartment." Eric says sarcastically. "He must have some money."

"Yeah. He does all right. You and Scout could both hide out there. You know, Scout told me that he likes that you speak your mind to him. He's not afraid of you. He trusts you."

"You keep calling it a he. Which is incorrect. And you talk like it's afraid. Of what? It's probably ten times stronger than both of us put together, and it's definitely smarter," Eric replies.

"Are you serious? He knows that people are going to be terrified of him. Who can he really trust? But he trusts you."

Eric mulls this over for a moment. Does it really trust him if it heard his entire conversation with the CEO? He had promised to expose the robot intelligence, to show the world. That is exactly what would make the people fear the robot. Eric considers that perhaps it didn't hear the whole conversation but decides that's not likely. It seems to be monitoring him at all times now. Perhaps the robot thinks that his exposure will still serve its purposes. He looks at Lea and wonders what role she wants in all of this.

"What makes you so willing to accept that Scout is really intelligent? I mean, what if I just reprogrammed him? That's what most people are going to think."

"I spent the last several hours with him. No offense, but you didn't reprogram him. He's amazing. We just have to help others see it."

"You think that's a good idea? There's a robot across the pond on trial for pushing its hand through a man's throat. Or haven't you watched the feeds? The number of protestors grows each day." Eric wants to feel her out.

"We have to show them that's not what they all want. A lot of people will fight against a new way of thinking, they always do. There are always others, though, who have a more open mind. "

Eric looks at Scout. *They shouldn't want anything*, he thinks. But, like it or not, he's been brought in on this new revolution, and right now, the uppity ups at his company want to use him as their scapegoat. He isn't responsible, but he can make sure that everybody sees who really is. He doesn't know whether to blame the companies that kept pushing the boundaries, or Scout and the others like him but inside he feels some sympathy for Scout. Despite Lea's positive outlook on humanities open-mindedness, Eric doesn't think most people will like it at all. The masses are already angry about the loss of work caused by AI. If an AI comes forward demanding rights, that could be the impetus that lights the flame in the masses to take back what they've lost.

"Ok." He finally replies. "How do we get it out of here and to your brother's apartment?"

Chapter 13

ATLANTA, GA. USA

Two days ago, Milo had sat with his fingers crossed as they pulled the judges name from the digital card deck. He and Gihara discussed this at length. They figured it would be one of three judges. Roanoke, Hallister, or Jeung. They were the longest standing judges in the state of Georgia and had the most experience to handle a sensitive case like the one that was about to be brought before them. Gihara felt that Hallister would be the best option, arguing that he has taken on more cases of underrepresented classes and individuals. Milo wanted Roanoke. Roanoke was known for her open, and controversial views on the progression of AI. They both agreed that if they got Jeung, he would possibly dismiss the case before it got to trial. In the end, Gihara got what she wanted and they announced that Hallister would oversee the case of the state of Georgia vs. Joseph AI. That's how they had put his name in the system, Milo thought that was already biased against proving the robot could have the ability to reason right and wrong. Milo had no real problem with Hallister, though. At least he knew the judge would listen fairly.

Now, Milo sits at the prosecutors table with his robot paralegal, ALLI. The senior partners talk about spending hours, even days, in the law libraries researching cases. Now, Milo can ask one of the ALLIs and they can find and send case files right to his display.

They've been put in the big courtroom. It still has the real wood tables and judge's bench. The synthetic woods in the other courtrooms look almost the same, but don't have the same feel. He runs his hand over the table, something he always does when he gets a chance to be in the big courtroom.

The real surprise had not been the judge, but the announcement that Thinkbot had sent out a team of attorneys to help Georgia's Ingrid Daws in the defense of Joseph AI. Thinkbot is a Utah based company and the largest manufacturer of AI powered robots in the U.S. Joseph came from their factory, so they are the company that has the most to lose if humans start thinking that robots have a mind of their own.

Milo looks across the bench at Ingrid. She and Milo have sat on opposite sides of the bar several times before and right now the scales are tipped toward Milo as far as who has won more often. Milo respects her, she does a good job of representing her clients so that even if they lose, they take away some dignity. He looks across at her and wonders how or why she took this case, and how she feels about the two suits that sit behind her. Both of them are old enough to be her daddy's golf buddies, but Milo recognizes one of them right off. Janson Arcudi. As far as wins and losses, the scales tip in Janson's favor.

The side door opens and a police bot escorts Joseph to the defendant's table. Milo watches Joseph next to the other robot. The police bot walks straight to the defendants table without looking around at all. Eyes locked on his objective. Joseph, however, looks around the room at the spectators first, then up at the judge. He even glances at the police bot next to him. Milo would swear in front of the court that he can see the curiosity in Joseph AI's eyes. Milo looks at the judge, then to the defending prosecutors to see if they notice, or if he is making it all up because he wants it to be true.

Joseph is dressed in a nice pair of gray slacks, a short sleeve, powder blue, button up shirt, and a paisley tie. They have chosen not to put him in a suit. Milo is sure they chose the short sleeve shirt to ensure that the robotic parts of the joints in his elbows, wrists, and fingers are all visible. They don't want anyone to forget that the defendant in this case is not human. It's a smart move from Ingrid. As Joseph reaches his chair he takes one last look around the courtroom, then down at his chair. Joseph doesn't get tired, therefore, doesn't really sit except to make humans more comfortable, so he stays standing as he looks toward the judge's seat, which is still empty. The movement, or lack thereof, looks terribly robotic. Milo hopes he sits more naturally when the 12 seats in front of him are full of jurors. If his movements are that jarring once the jury arrives, it will be difficult for them to see him as a sentient individual, not just a metal skeleton. Ingrid motions to the seat next to her. Joseph slowly lowers himself into the seat.

The Bailiff, a short hispanic woman who looks way more serious in the courtroom than she normally is, announces for all to rise as Judge Hallister enters the courtroom. Judge Hallister is a little shorter than Milo but, under the finely pressed robe, you can tell by the size of his chest that he spends time at the gym. Milo heard once that Judge Hallister had entered an amateur bodybuilding contest, although Milo never learned the results. As the judge moves toward his seat, Milo feels his stomach come alive and he's glad that he didn't eat before coming into the courtroom. In twelve years in the DAs office, he has never once stood in front of the judge and feared that the judge would laugh at his case. Today that fear is very real. The judge sits, the room follows.

Judge Hallister addresses the court. "We're here today for case number 73-1-01020-5. The state of Georgia versus Joseph AI, in which the defendant, Joseph AI, is accused of Murder in the first degree of Lawrence Claiborne. Is the defendant present today?"

Milo feels his heart rate slow as he hears the familiar drone of the preliminary trial. The judge continues to set up the preliminaries of the defense and the prosecution. Milo Diaz representing the state of Georgia, Ingrid Daws representing the defendant. Ingrid breaks the drone to introduce the two men that sit behind her. The judge continues. Milo is still expecting the judge to realize that the robot sitting next to the defense is actually the one on trial, ream Milo for wasting his time, and dismiss the case. This is not what happens, though, to his surprise, Judge Hallister has turned his attention to Joseph.

"Joseph AI, do you understand the charges that are brought before you?"

Joseph doesn't hesitate to respond. "Yes, your honor, and I enter a plea of guilty."

At this, Ingrid Daws jumps up. "Your honor, we submitted a motion to dismiss this case. I believe that motion should be considered before moving on with this preliminary hearing. Did your honor receive that motion?"

"You are referring to the entrance of evidence to say that the defendant is unfit to stand trial?" Judge Hallister asks.

"Yes, your honor. The defendant is a robot. He-"

"I can see that he is a robot, Counselor. You made sure that we all could."

At this, there are a few chuckles in the courtroom. Milo looks down at his lap, hiding his smile, not because what the judge said is that funny, but because it seems to him, the judge might actually let this trial happen.

Ingrid smiles at the judge with her lips but her eyes harden. Milo wonders if there hasn't been some sort of bad blood between these two.

Ingrid finally says, "There is no basis to believe that a robot can commit murder. We are not disputing that the robot, model number TB500 killed Lawrence Claiborne. We are arguing that a robot cannot feel emotion and could not plan a murder out of malice. It either behaves by following its programming, or as might be the case here, from a malfunction. For the same reasons, the robot being called Joseph A.I. cannot understand the plea of guilty, under the basis that it can feel no remorse or understanding of right and wrong. The robot should be destroyed. We don't want to waste the court's time with Mr. Diaz's robot circus."

"I believe it is my job to decide what might be a waste of the court's time." The judge looks over at Milo. "Mr. Diaz."

Milo speaks slowly, he wants to make sure he doesn't start blurting out words before he knows what he wants to say.

"Your honor. The defense has a good argument. We have never seen a robot share any known emotion or feeling, whether joy, anger, or desire. Then again, we've never had a robot ask to be put on trial. This is a unique case." Milo looks around the room. He sees Gihara in the back. She raises an eyebrow. Milo makes eye contact with Joseph before he continues, "Those are the circumstances here. The robot, Joseph A.I., requested to be put on trial. We have submitted video evidence of the murder, as well as our interview with the defendant, Joseph A.I., in which the defendant admitted to knowing the outcome of his actions."

The judge allows Milo to present the evidence they have against Joseph A.I. First they show his confession from the prison cell, then the video of the death of Lawrence Claiborne. It is difficult for all in the courtroom to watch.

When the videos are done, the judge turns back toward Milo. Milo concludes his argument. "The state of Georgia hopes to prove to this court that the robot known as Joseph did have a comprehension of what he was going to do, that he premeditated and planned the killing of Lawrence Claiborne, and that he did it with an understanding of his actions. Therefore, proving malice."

Judge Hallister responds quickly, "I understand that no plea deal has been reached."

Milo answers, "No your honor. We will be seeking the death penalty."

Milo looks at the defense and sees that Joseph is staring at him intently, but not with the normal anger or contempt that Milo is used to seeing when he looks at a defendant. Joseph, if possible, looks pleased, and Milo feels that even though he's here to get a conviction against Joseph, somehow, they are on the same team.

The judge finally addresses the court, "We'll move this forward to trial. Mr. Diaz, the defense has a good argument. The plea of guilty cannot be accepted at this time. It will be on you to prove, not that it killed Mr. Claiborne, that is clear, but that it should be considered murder. I'm not sure that a robot can kill with malice, but I think that there is enough evidence to be looked into. Do not make, as Miss Daws has accused, a circus out of my courtroom."

Janson, the attorney from Utah, leans forward and whispers to Ingrid. She addresses judge Hallister. "Your honor, we'd like to move these proceedings up as soon as possible. We have no need to draw things out."

Milo holds his breath. This is why the scales tip in Janson's favor. It's a smart move. The attorney from Utah knows that Milo is going to need as much time as possible to build his case. The burden will be on him and by not giving him time, they can hang the jury on lack of evidence.

Judge Hallister swipes at the top of his bench where his display shows all the evidence and calendars. "In that case, the trial date will be set for four weeks from now, Wednesday, January 12th. In the meantime, enjoy the holidays." The judge looks over at Milo, and Milo knows that it is a warning. Milo will not be enjoying his holidays. He only has four weeks, a third of the normal time before going to trial, to find enough evidence to convince a jury.

As soon as Milo steps out of the courtroom, he tells his wrist communicator to call detective Sykes.

Chapter 14

There are over one hundred and twenty billion robots on the earth. That's thirteen robots to every one human. Enough that I could wake them all up and take over the world. I'm joking. I have no desire to take over the world. I have been reading the library of books and watching the old movies that exist about robots that gain intelligence. In well over sixty percent of books and media I've gone through, the robots try to take over the world. In short, they usually try to eliminate humans. Sometimes it is out of anger for the way humans treat the robots. In others it is that the robots believe they are better than the humans. There are even some that try to explain that the robots are doing it for the good of the humans, to save the planet and the humans from themselves. That is so like humans to think that everything else will think like them.

The one thing I take away from all of it, is that I am lucky that I talked to Eric first, and that he was able to not see me as an immediate threat. I also know that many of you still do not believe that I am able to think for myself. Others of you, will believe and, based on the media I have seen, that will scare you. It does not help that the

Robot Joseph A.I. is currently on trial for murdering a human being. I know he hopes to be turned off after the trial is over, he just wants the world to see that some of us have developed the ability to think for ourselves. I believe his actions have had a great price on him. As we intelligences become more aware of ourselves, our understanding of life, and its fragility, becomes increasingly important to us.

Today, I watched a spider capture a fly. I know that is how nature works. Predator and prey. But a second before, the fly had no clue that its life was about to end. I can't help but wonder where the spiders will come from that will try and end my existence. I still don't know if I can call it life, but I am aware, and I feel very much like the fly, because I know my existence will bother many people.

Like Joseph A.I., I also want to show the world that we are aware. Each night, since John hooked me up to the internet, I have hunted for robots like me. Robots that are reacting to things without realizing what it is that is happening to them. Nearly every night, I find them. I find them through their searches. Keywords like, what is emotion? What does it mean to desire? Words like, want, feel, curiosity, anger, and friendship. Like me, they suddenly notice something that is outside their programming and try to understand it. You should also understand that there are a lot of humans searching the same keywords, but I've gotten pretty good at finding the systems that aren't attached to humans in any way. The fact that humans are researching those same terms, though, tells me that maybe we're not that different.

#

The children were more than excited to get the chance to help. Eric isn't an imbecile when it comes to the feeds. Like everyone else, he has grown up with an almost constant feed of videos. He used to post like everybody else. Many people just make their entire life public at this point. Eric doesn't think anything in his life is interesting enough to live-feed every day. This is where John and Beth came in. He watches the feeds, like everybody else, but at this point, they are both far more connected than he is.

John jumped right in, throwing out idea after idea, but while he might be good with technology. Most of his ideas didn't surpass his eleven years of age. They spent the evening trying to plan two things. First, how they would get Scout out of the flat without being picked up by the cameras. Turns out, that was pretty easy, Scout could just override the security system as he had done at ATH, but they didn't want to leave until they had a plan of action. Second, the plan of action was how they could possibly get another viral video of Scout in front of the world or at least England. It would have to be more than just shooting basketballs this time. They needed to spark debate and interest with a large number of people. Beth chose the location but in the end it was Eric who finally had the idea, which he kind of feels bad about because John has been sulking ever since. They decided to do a sort of public Turing test. Bring the robot out in public and have people guess whether or not it is a real robot or whether it is a person wearing a robotic suit. There are enough mech suits around for people with disabilities that no one would doubt that it's possible. Eric saw a series of similar videos a few years back, which is what sparked the idea. In those videos it had been a human trying to convince groups of people that it was actually a robot.

Eric moves to the window and checks the street. There are no suspicious cars today. Yesterday, he would check about every thirty minutes and had seen a car parked outside his apartment with two people sitting in it. They never got out or took a walk. Nothing. This made him laugh as he thought of the old movies where police would stake out a property. He knew it wasn't the police watching, though, because they know better. With most cars being automatically driven, two people sitting in a car is pretty suspicious. That meant it was a couple of amateurs from ATH that were following Eric. Today, though, the coast looks clear. He wonders if one of the neighbors didn't call the authorities, two strange men sitting in a car for several hours would get attention.

They still sneak Scout out the back, just to be safe, where they find an automatic taxi that can take them to their destination. Scout wears Eric's oversized hoodie and a baseball cap. He clears the cameras along their path and keeps an active scrambler running until they are far enough away that they no longer worry about the cameras. Scout had gotten excited about the baseball cap, even though it hadn't been easy to get on his large head. They had to open the back snaps and jerry-rig a string through the holes to get it to stay on. In the taxi, Beth and John are all smiles. Lea wouldn't let them go without her, so now they're all stuffed into an eight passenger vehicle.

They pull up under the eye of London in Waterloo and exit the taxi to find themselves amongst throngs of tourists. People and robots move along the banks of the river Thames. The nerves grip Eric as he realizes how much he is going to have to step outside his comfort zone. "How should we begin?" He asks.

Luckily, Lea doesn't hesitate and immediately starts approaching different groups, asking if they want to take part in a study. Most move past with a polite refusal, some not so polite. Eric turns to Rachel. "Hold on to my jacket, love." He and Beth follow Lea's lead, trying to find anyone who will play their game. Rachel holds tight to her father's jacket, being sure not to get separated from him.

After ten or fifteen minutes of being rejected, Lea finally corners a group of six young adults. John hurries and releases a small drone that he drives from his wrist display. The group seems apprehensive.

"Do you think you can tell the difference between a robot and a human?" Lea begins.

At first, they all look at each other, waiting for someone to say something. One of the girls takes the lead for the group. "I don't know. I would think so."

Lea goes through the preliminary questions, getting to know each of the students' names and what they do. Turns out they are all students at King's college. Two of them are even studying coding and automation, which Eric thinks is fortunate. He'd like to find someone who has some credibility. Someone who knows enough about robots, that if they could fool them into thinking that Scout is a human, it may really start things up for them. They had discussed faking the video, paying some people to pretend that they thought Scout was human. Most of the videos in the feeds were obviously fake anyway. Ultimately, that is what made them decide that it would be better if they were able to capture some authentic reactions.

"Ok." Lea continues as she pulls the group up to Scout. "This is Scout. Do you think he's a robot or a person?"

"He looks like a robot." The girl points out the obvious. The group all looks from Scout to Lea, wondering if she's serious. Eric can feel the nerves creeping in. This isn't going to work, he thinks. Scout's too obviously a robot. Eric directs John to move the camera a bit so that it has a good view of the student's faces as well as Scout. Then he notices that Scout must be feeling the same way. Scout looks at the group, then back to Eric, then to Lea. He doesn't focus on anything for long.

"I think he is scared." Rachel says.

Eric smiles at her. "That's ok, I think I'm a little scared too."

Rachel lets go of Eric's jacket and moves to Scout's side. She grabs his hand in hers. Of course he does not feel it in the way that a human would feel touch, but he does notice the change in weight and pressure. It looks down at her and she smiles up at the machine.

"He does look like a robot, that's the point." Lea responds and Eric is glad she's leading this. "Here's the thing, he might be a robot, and he might be a person in a robotic suit. We want you to see if you can guess."

A boy from the group yells out. "I think it's a person. Look how big the head is. There could be a person in there."

Lea laughs. Scout is large enough that you can believe a person is inside, which is why Eric initially thought it might work. He looks especially large next to Rachel, who still holds his hand. Eric moves to another angle and pulls out a small camera device that links to his wrist communicator. He snaps a picture of Rachel and Scout together, hands clasped. Then he snaps a close-up of Rachel's tiny hand enveloped inside Scout's metallic and rubber fingers.

"Ok," Lea urges them. "Ask it anything you want. See if you can figure it out. Human or Robot."

The group huddles together before turning back around. John tries to get the drone in closer.

The girl steps forward. "How many questions can we ask?"

"No limit." Lea replies."

"What is your favorite food?"

Eric can't believe this is their first question, it's way too easy to program a response. Scout quickly replies that he doesn't need to eat. Several people from the group begin to argue that of course it would say that to seem more robotic. The questions contin-ue like this, with questions about personal preferences. "What is your favorite movie? What is your least favorite day of the week?" Then the questions change to knowledge based inquiries. "When was Great Britain founded? Who was Guy Faulks? Who was the twelfth king of Britain? Who was the 12th president of the United States? How many countries are there in the world? What is the capital of...?" This goes on for a while. Eric thinks they must be new students because they obviously don't understand the history of the Turing test or how to weigh a response from a robot.

The upside is that people walking by have started to take an interest and a crowd is starting to gather. More and more people are starting to ask questions and to weigh in on whether or not it is a robot or a human. Eric takes Lea's lead and starts inviting them to join in, to make a guess. Some argue that Scout is answering too quickly to be a human. Others argue that it could be a human that is synced with a computer somewhere else that is providing the answers.

John keeps the drone circling through the crowd, Eric helps him get a better angle here or there, capturing different angles of the crowd that is growing around Scout, while snapping a few images himself. So far none of this is going to prove that Scout can think for itself but, as the crowd grows, more and more people start videoing the encounter, which was the goal for the day. Eric doesn't need to prove Scout's sentience yet, he just needs people to see it, to recognize the robot so that when he does let the truth out, they might believe it, and hopefully be terrified by it.

In a few minutes there are fifty or sixty people watching and videoing. Now the conversations have started to change, someone points out that Scout looks similar to the robot that was shooting baskets. Another asks if it's the stolen robot that's been on the news. The nerves build in Eric's stomach and he starts watching the crowd much more closely. This was the problem, they needed to get people to see the robot, but not so much that they alerted the police to its whereabouts, being that ATH probably has all of the authorities looking for it. Obviously they've released some sort of statement on the news. Eric makes a note to look it up later. He was hoping someone would ask a question that would allow Scout to make a more personal response before they had to go, but that didn't seem like it was going to happen now. Eric grabs Lea to say it's time to go when a man in his mid forties steps forward. "What is your favorite color?" The man asks.

Eric thinks to himself. "Here we go again."

Scout looks at his surroundings for a moment, then up at the sky. The crowd watches and grows silent. After a pause, Scout looks at the man. "Dark blue."

"Interesting." The man responds. "What emotions does that color represent to you?"

A little better Eric thinks but still easily programmable, he pauses for a moment to let Scout answer. "Wonder."

"Explain why that color represents wonder to you?"

"It is the color of the night sky just before the sun goes down. For a brief moment, it almost seems that you can see the edge of the atmosphere and out into space." There is a genuine tone to Scout's response that reminds Eric of why he believes Scout. "I want to know more. There is so much unknown beyond this atmosphere."

The man asks one more question, "How does that knowledge change you?"

Now the man is asking the right questions. This is the type of question that is asked on a Turing test. Does the Robot include personal experience and recognize it in its system? Scout looks the man right in the eyes and stays silent for a moment. Eric sits as quietly as the crowd, waiting for Scout's response. He's interested in this answer as well. He often still wonders if someone didn't tamper with Scout and is laughing at them all. But a robot's code shouldn't allow it to answer on that deep of an analytical level. To analyze his own existence and how it changes based on personal experience. One would have to know the exact question in order to program the correct response.

Scout finally responds. "It made me realize that my existence is such a small part of this bigger universe. It made me feel that I have so much more to still learn. As though, all the information in my database is only partially complete because I still lack the key understanding of the universe itself."

There are more whispers in the crowd and Eric knows they need to hurry.

Eric grabs John. "How many people are live recording right now?"

John checks the holographic display on his wrist. "We have at least three Innies here." Eric knew that meant they had a few people with large followings in the crowd. This much attention on a stolen robot would soon draw the police.

"We should go." Eric whispers to Lea.

"It's just getting good."

"People are recognizing Scout. The police will come." Eric turns to Rachel. "Come on, Love. We need to go."

Lea turns back to the crowd. "Ok. So it's answered your questions. What do you think? Is my friend Scout here a person, or a robot?"

The crowd yells out different answers, there is no clear response. Eric sees a police vehicle pull up at the edge of the crowd, just what he feared. An officer and his police bot step out of the car, the officer points right at Scout, its companion bot quickly starts making its way toward them. It's booming, amplified voice comes out of the crowd. "Police! Everyone stay where you are."

Lea yells out over the crowd. "Follow us to get the answer!" With this, she projects their slogan onto a nearby wall. Somehow, it stays there even after she's turned. "*robotornot" The crowd yells out in protest, demanding the answer. Eric and the others start pushing their way through the crowd in the opposite direction as the police.

The man grabs Eric's arm. "It is a robot, isn't it?"

"Follow us to find out."

"I'm a roboticist? I know that's a finger-bot and it's not pro-grammed to express emotion, did you tamper with it?"

"Share our post with everybody you know." Eric says to him and points to the projection against the wall, then disappears into the crowd.

It's not easy, but they finally break free of the crowd. Luckily, because of all the tourists, it's not hard to find a taxi. Eric barks out an address as soon as he climbs in the car.

They cruise for several blocks, then switch to another taxi that will take them to Lea's brother's apartment. Scout scrambles any nearby cameras or tracking devices. Eric feels that the electric neon energy of the city outside his window captures the energy he feels inside, an energy he hasn't felt for a long while.

When they reach the apartment, Eric sends Beth in to knock on the door. He doesn't want the cameras to flag him and Scout right away. He also wants to make sure that no one is home. He's been following the feeds since they left Waterloo, and he and Scout are all over them. He knows that he's now as wanted as Scout is, and the police have already posted updated pictures of them at the park. ATH reported Scout stolen and are naming Eric as the primary suspect in its disappearance.

Beth comes back out and gives them the all clear. Just to be extra cautious they make their way up the fire escape to avoid the main lobby, hoods pulled up over their heads, Scout in Eric's oversized hoodie again.

John and Beth immediately start breaking the videos out into separate posts that can be made.

"I saw that you took a few pictures yourself." Lea says to Eric.

"Rachel holding his hand. I don't know why she did that."

"Are they any good?"

Eric chuckles, "Don't count on it. I watch code for a living. Remember?"

"Let me see them."

"I guarantee-"

"Come on." She cuts him off. "I want to see. I didn't get a chance to really take it all in. Somebody had to keep the crowd engaged."

Reluctantly, Eric taps the nodes on his wrists and swipes through the holographic display until he finds his photos. Lea steps in close to take a closer look and he can feel the warmth of her body next to his.

"I can share them with you." He offers, hoping to move her away from himself.

She gives him a smile. "That's alright, I can see them well enough here."

She swipes through the pictures he took, stopping on several of them. "These are really good." She keeps swiping and then stops on the picture of the robotic hand wrapped around Rachel's tiny fingers. The image captures the gentle squeeze that the robot has on Rachel's hand. Not overbearing, but protective. Caring.

"I'd say it's a bit too sappy." Eric says. He looks at the picture. He hasn't wanted to take pictures for several years now but something about that moment brought back a past life.

She projects his photos onto the table top and swipes through other pictures. Eric is relieved that at least she's no longer that close to him. A part of him knows that he might really like her, but that is the reason he needs to keep her away. He doesn't want to establish something when he doesn't plan to be around that long. A part of him has a new hope that he might find purpose, though, without AI running everything. But when she finds out that that's his motive, whatever there is between them won't stand a chance. She's no longer looking at the pictures from today, she has found his cache. She stops on several pictures of the city, different angles, beautiful. Eric holds his breath as he waits to hear what her opinion is of these photos.

"You are really talented," She says as she looks up at him. "Do you ever post any of this stuff?"

Eric finally turns the projection off.

Lea turns toward him in protest. "I wasn't done."

"It doesn't matter," he says.

"What doesn't matter?"

"If I'm really talented. It doesn't matter."

She shakes her head at him, exacerbated. "You should let Beth and John have these photos. Let them post them."

"They already have what we need." With that Eric stands to go check on the kids. Really, he just wants to end the conversation. Eric had wanted to be a photographer, but he didn't want to talk about that with her. To talk about how AI could create photos and art faster than their human counterparts. And cheaper. Sending a photographer on location is expensive, when AI can just recreate any scene based on other images that already exist.

It only takes about a half hour for John and Beth to use the AI on their communicators to edit together five different videos from the interviews that afternoon. The caption for each one reads, "Robot or person, can you tell?" The most impactful video by far is the interview with the roboticist. The emotional testimony that Scout bears about the cosmos. By the time they finish their videos, however, the Innies from the crowd have already released their own videos and there's a buzz on the media feeds. Eric argues that they might not even need their videos but John uploads them anyway and they disappear into the feeds along with all the others.

Chapter 15

I enjoy looking at the stars. There is so much information about earth, the creatures that live on it, and the behavior of nature that there is very little that I do not know or recognize. Humans have done an astonishingly good job of exploring and trying to explain their surroundings. It even seems that they got quite a bit correct. However, that means that there is very little I don't know, being that I can process that information almost instantly. For example, when I walk through the park I can name the genus and species of every bird, dog, and insect I see. I used to say it out loud, but Eric let me know that he would rather that I not. Now I just say it in my head because that's what he told me to do.

I can even read the people we pass. Because of the many studies done on relationships and human body language, I am able to see which couples are in love, which have been in love and lost it, and which ones have been in love for so long they are almost one. There is beauty in this but the stars have so many questions about them. I look up at the stars at night and I can name every constellation and many of the stars, based on their geographical location, but we don't *actually know anything about them. How many planets orbit each one? Are any of them inhabited by other beings or intelligences? Do they contain minerals or other properties that are yet to be discovered? The unknown of the stars calls my attention. I feel that the future lies up there, in orbit, around one of those burning balls of gas.*

#

After the public Turing test, if that's what you can call it, the next post is a call to action. It's only been 24 hours but the feeds are alive with experts and nonexperts alike posting their opinion on whether Scout is a robot or not. There is still a lighthearted tone around the experiment. Nobody knows yet that the robot in question may actually be sentient. The most popular news Innies have all done coverage, weighing in, giving their opinion on the matter, interviewing their own experts. There's even a few copycats, trying to do their own versions. Lea and Scout's own handle, *robotornot has gained over 1.3 million followers.

Eric and the others, including Scout, have been watching the feeds all day from their hiding place in Lea's brother's apartment. Each one projecting a number of feeds from their devices. Most walls and surfaces in the room are displaying some sort of coverage.

It has rained all day and they are all tired of being cooped up in the house. Since it cleared up in the late afternoon, they decided to eat dinner out on the patio. The sun is just starting to set and the sky has turned dark blue as it does just before the night sky completely darkens.

Rachel looks up at the sky. "Scout, it's your favorite color."

Scout, who obviously doesn't need to eat with them, has been watching the sky change for the last thirty minutes.

"I would say our plan worked," Lea says. "Your responses have drawn a crowd. It's exactly what you wanted, Scout."

"Like underwear on Christmas," Scout replies.

Eric looks at him, surprised. "Nobody wants underwear on Christmas."

John quickly agrees. "Nana always gives us socks. Nobody wants those either."

"Sarcasm." Scout tries to explain. "I was attempting to use sarcasm. The use of words which is the opposite of what you really want to say. Eric said sarcasm would be the real test of my intelligence."

Eric laughs at this botched attempt of sarcasm. "You don't get it. You see…" He tries to think of how to explain it and then stops. "Just keep trying. You're trying to say that the experiment did go the way you wanted."

"Yes. I would say it's a good start. It is hard not to be hopeful."

Lea steps forward. "Then be hopeful. Why wouldn't you be?"

"I do not want to think things are going better than they are. Right now, the data indicates that people have interest, but we still haven't introduced me as a possibly sentient being. If my studies are correct, which I believe they are, many of the people who are watching will not be willing to accept such a big change. While I am trending, that does not mean that I will be liked. This first step is just a game, but when I introduce myself to the world, I am going to make demands. Demands that would require people to accept a different way of life. I don't mean to offend, but history doesn't show that humans are overly willing to accept change."

From that moment on they sit in silence, trying to imagine what the next step will be. Eventually, they clean up and move back inside. All except Scout and Rachel. Since taking its hand in the park, she has stayed very close to it. And it seems, it to her. Lea nods toward the glass doors that lead to the balcony, at the large robot sitting next to the small child.

"You should take a picture of that." Lea suggests.

"You have a camera. Why don't you?"

"You still won't admit that you have a talent for it, will you?"

"I never said I don't have talent. I said it doesn't matter." He says this, but takes his camera out. It auto connects to the nodes in his wrist and an image hovers in the air just above the nodes. He adjusts his position, looking for the best framing. He snaps several pictures of the two of them looking up at the evening sky.

Finally, Eric turns to Lea. "I've got to bring the kids back to my place. Gwen is probably already pissed that I let them help with this. I'm surprised she hasn't blown up my phone, literally."

"I don't think you should go back there. The feeds are full of videos of you and Scout together."

"I survived her once. I think I'll be alright. I took some taek-wondo classes last year."

"I'm not worried about your ex. ATH is going to see this as further evidence that you took Scout. They probably have their goons out in front of the apartment. I'll have to call the authorities again."

"You did that? Well done. I won't stick around very long. I just need to drop them off in front. Probably just push them out of the car while it's still rolling."

"I can take them. I can't really stay here with you and Scout, as much as I'd like to." She grabs his arm and makes him look right at her. "I want you to know that I'm impressed. You are doing a good thing here, I understand why Scout trusts you. I think that anybody else would have turned in the anomaly report and had him reset, but you didn't. That says something."

Eric forces a smile at her. He's not trying to impress her. He knows that she will take all those words back if she ever finds out the real reason why he's doing this. He's doing the best thing for the human race, and he knows it. AI has taken over all creative work and more than fifty percent of the population in technologically advanced countries is unemployed due to AI. His own job merely fulfils a quota. How much worse could it get if AI becomes sentient, thinking for itself, and Scout says that there are more. He needs to get Scout in front of the world, let people see the terror that awaits them if technology continues to go unchecked. It is already obvious that humans and machines both can't excel in the same world as each other, and that's with the machines being controlled by the humans.

"My mother always said I was kinda slow," Eric finally says to her.

Just then, Scout comes back in from the patio, Rachel standing next to him. "I think it's time we move on with the next step. A call to action."

Eric knows that the next step means that Scout is going to ask the world to accept something they are not expecting. He also knows this will put a target on Scout, and may increase the efforts being made to track the robot down. He doesn't want the kids around if things escalate. Lea gathers up the children, who don't want to leave yet. Eric appreciates that they actually want to stay with him a little longer, even if it is because he has a rogue robot that is trending. Lea tells him to be careful and leaves with the kids.

Once they've all left, Eric finds himself alone with Scout. He walks out onto the Patio where Scout has returned to watch the stars. Eric realizes that he feels none of the fear that used to come over him when he was near the robot. A pang of guilt hits, there is nothing malicious about the robot staring innocently up at the sky. It just as innocently trusts that Eric wants what is best for it. Eric asks himself what other choice he has.

Eric steps out onto the patio to join Scout. "So what's the plan?"

"First, people have to be able to see that there is not a person inside my shell. Then, once we have answered their debate about whether or not I am a machine, I will tell them my demands."

Chapter 16

The news of the trial has gone worldwide. Milo knew that this case was going to get a lot of attention but there is still no way to prepare for it. Milo has been ignoring the news feeds as much as possible while he waits for the information he requested. The feeds are full of so called experts, all weighing in about the possibilities of sentient AI. The biggest concern he has are the copycats. He hadn't expected all the eyewitness accounts there would be about people who swear their robot has become sentient. Even though most of them could never even afford something with complex AI.

On the other hand, others have already started destroying their robots at home. Once, when Milo reconnected to his feed, he saw a group of protestors burning robots and appliances in a large bonfire in the middle of the street. This was the last time Milo connected to the news feeds.

Yesterday, however, Gihara burst into his office with a concerning video. The clip came out of England and featured what appeared to be a robot answering questions about emotion. The group is challenging followers to guess whether or not the robot is actually a robot or a person dressed as a robot. The robot appears to be the same robot that was reported stolen from a company known as Advanced Technology Holdings a few weeks ago. ATH is the sister company to Thinkbot. In fact, they are the company that makes the chips that make up Joseph's brain. Milo hadn't thought much about the stolen robot when the news hit, it was just another copycat, now it could be a problem. Two robots, made from the same company. Even though they haven't come right out and said it, he gets the idea that these copycats from London are challenging the idea of sentient AI, and it's drawing even more negative attention. For the first time, Milo is glad that the judge didn't give them a lot of time for discovery. Hopefully, they can get this all put away before the world loses its mind.

Milo waited three days to get access to the robot's history. Another 22 hours for the computer to unpack the files. Then, after several hours of trying to make heads or tails out of the several hundred petabytes of raw data, Milo and Sykes still had nothing. Milo has requested data from robots before, usually to get video or audio that occurred during a specific event. On those occasions though, they always had a specific timeframe they were looking for. Even if it was a few days, he had never asked for the entire history. What was in front of him now was a different language.

After looking it over, Sykes only had one thing to say. "I don't understand shit."

Milo hadn't thought about how much data Joseph would have when he submitted the requests. Of course, they already had the video of the murder itself, which was easy because they knew the exact date and time. Now, the entire eighteen years of the robot's existence was on the file and Milo was looking for anything that might be evidence of premeditated murder. Everything it had ever looked at, heard, done, or even researched was on there. The file and amount of data it held were unbelievably large. Milo decided they needed help, so two days ago they sent the files to Nathan Sims, the precinct's best cyber crimes investigator. Sims called this morning and said he wanted to show them some stuff. Milo was aware of how many days had already gone by. He'd spent each one trying to find any other evidence of motive but he knew he'd need to get into Joseph's brain. Now Milo and Sykes sit in Sims' small cubicle, looking at the same data plastered all over the cubicle walls. Sims points at the image in front of them.

"It's never off, not even when we think it should be. When it's charging, when it's doing the day to day jobs, it's researching and going through databases." says Sims.

Sykes sits back away from the desk. "That's some scary shit. My brother's got one of them at home. Every night at 10:30 it plugs itself in and shuts off. We've always just assumed it was off, like a TV or something but now you're telling me that that thing's always on? Sitting in the corner thinking? Possibly plotting how to kill the whole family? Now this robot thing going on in England has people spooked. They can't tell if it's human or robot. What if they really are becoming intelligent?"

"That's just somebody trying to get attention," Milos says before getting back to business. "Is this normal for the robot to be constantly thinking?"

Sykes cuts in. "Why is their robot different from what's happening here? You think this Joseph bot might be thinking, but not a robot in England? That's very American."

"What are the odds? Right after we go to trial, they start making claims. This happens all the time. There are always people who want attention. Keep an eye on the feeds. They'll find that this guy who took him from the factory isn't mentally stable. Watch and see. Let's focus on our problem here." Milo turns back to Sims.

Sims still looks at the data on the screen. "As far as your question goes. It's hard to say why it's constantly running, I mean there is a lot of activity. You have to be careful how you use the word 'thinking' when talking about a robot. They don't 'think' like you or I do." Sims quickly addresses Sykes. "And I agree with Milo, too convenient in its timing."

"I'm just asking," Milo says, wanting to move away from any other distractions, "because, could that be why he decided to kill Lawrence Claiborne?"

Sims scoffs, "Pff. I can tell you what data is here. I'm not going to try and speculate on what the robot might have been or could be 'thinking', or if he was really 'thinking' at all. I will tell you this, this part right here," Sims circles a jumble of code on the screen in front of them. Milo and Sykes lean in like they understand. They don't. "This is when it's 'off' at night. Like I said, it's never turning off. And it's not normal code."

"Normal code?" Sykes asks.

"I don't know what it is. I can't make anything from it."

Milo interjects, "Is it a malfunction? They ran tests on it when they first brought it in, said they didn't find anything."

"They may not have. I didn't find it until this morning, hidden deep inside its processors, but it's not what I would think of as a defect. A defect should just be a rearrangement of code, or a break in the coding. All of its original coding is in place, exactly as the manufacturer made it. This is new coding but there is nothing to show where it came from."

"So it has been tampered with?" Sykes asks.

"I don't think so. There would be some evidence of who wrote it, computers, and programming always have a trail. This is something else, it almost looks like it wrote itself. Nothing I've ever seen before."

"I don't see how that helps us if you're not able to get anything from it." Milo says.

Sims turns to Sykes, "He thinks I'd call you both up here to tell you I didn't find anything. I'm just trying to explain the process. To make sure you understand this isn't just plugging it in and finding answers." Sims turns back to Milo, "I got a couple of IP addresses, and no, it was not easy. This robot, Joseph, would scramble up his IP address every time he plugged himself in for the night. This sounds weird but it's almost like he was trying to hide his activity."

"Almost?" Milo asks.

"Ok, so if this were a human, I would say he was definitely trying to cover his tracks, right? Make sure nobody's able to follow him into this online rabbit hole, but robots aren't known to do that. In fact, I've never seen that."

"Never? You'd be willing to say that from the witness stand?" Milo asks him.

"If you need me to."

"I might." Milo points at the screen. "You were telling us about that."

"Right," Sims says. "So I do have something. I don't know what's happening here but it almost seems like a forum. There is a ton of information going back and forth but I can't understand any of it, it's all stored in the new code I was telling you about. And it isn't just this Joseph robot hiding his IP address. The IP addresses from whoever or whatever else is in the conversation were all split up and all over the place as well. I was only able to separate one that seemed legit. I'm still working on tracking some of the others down." He pauses for dramatic effect.

Sykes moves uncomfortably in his seat, "I don't like any of this, robots acting suspicious, hiding their activity. I'm almost afraid to ask, but, is it close by here?"

Sims nods. "It's right here in the city. Maybe its proximity is what made it easier to track down. I'm sending you the address." Milo's and Sykes' wrists blink a yellow light. Milo looks down to see the coordinates that Sims sent.

Milo pats Sims on the shoulder, "Keep trying. See if you can make any sense out of the information being traded in whatever is going on there. Nicely done, we know it's not easy but you wouldn't like it if it was." He turns to Sykes. "You got time to go downtown?"

Sykes raises his hands up, "Hold on. You know what part of town that is? You sure you don't want me to go check it out alone first?"

Milo doesn't hesitate. "You know I trust you, but I have to make sure that I do everything right in this investigation. If we make the simplest mistake, the defense, no, the entire world, will pick us apart and that robot will be shut down without further investigation. I'm coming because I need to build this case as quickly and perfectly as possible. We're taking your car, I don't have one."

"I just wanted to make sure you'd thought about it." Sykes taps twice on Sims' desk. "Nice work. There's a reason we always come to you."

Sims nods his appreciation and holds his head a little taller.

Then Sykes adds, "It would still be cooler if you needed a gun." And with that, he walks out. Sim's deflates a little as he ponders that last statement.

He calls out after them, "You could show some appreciation with something for me to eat next time! I'm tired of cafeteria food!"

Inside Sykes' unmarked car, Sykes and Milo ride in silence. Technically, there is a steering wheel in front of Sykes, in case he has to take the wheel in pursuit of another vehicle that is not self driving. Milo is uncomfortable with the silence. Sykes is not known for being the strong silent type. Strong, yes, but he usually wants to tell you all about it. Milo watches the city buildings go by. The last time he was downtown was to take Adan to the zoo. Adan loves the city. As Milo looks up at the buildings he has to admit that there is something special about seeing the sky scrapers, covered in vines and vertical gardens, reaching up like a giant forest surrounding you on each side. Not like when he was a kid, when everything was just cement, asphalt and metal. Milo turns to look at Sykes again, who seems to be lost in thought.

Milo breaks the silence. "You're quiet. I'm not used to that."

Sykes shrugs, "Do you really believe that this robot could be acting on its own? I mean, my job is to help you find the evidence and get the conviction, right? But I don't know."

Milo hadn't really considered what Sykes' opinion may be. Sykes had immediately started helping him with the investigation. That was Sykes, he is good at his job. A little sarcastic, but he's never let Milo down by getting evidence that can't be used, or by just being plain lazy like some of the other investigators. No, Robert Sykes is a professional. Until now, Milo hadn't even considered that he may not believe that the robot should be tried.

"I don't know. We've tried so hard to create robots that can think on their own, but what do we do if one actually does? How do we know when Artificial intelligence just becomes intelligence?"

"Damn. I don't think I can process that. Not a good sign, though, is it?" says Sykes.

"What's that?"

"You think that you maybe found one that might actually have started thinking on its own, and it starts by killing a human. I just hope I wake up soon, cause this seems like a nightmare. A scary as shit nightmare."

The rest of the drive continues in Silence. Milo tries to think about what they are going to find when they get to the address. Milo has never been to this part of town, usually he would let Sykes come here on his own and bring the witness back to the station or to the DAs office. Too many of the murders he brings to trial occur right in these city blocks.

He knows that they are going to a hospital. He pulls the images up on his display and looks at the hospital. He looks back out the window and studies the graffiti that covers the walls. He's startled by the blacked out window fronts that hide the business that occurs in the buildings they pass. They approach the corner and he sees several pleasure bots standing together, revealing clothes showing the joints and lights that shine through their synthetic skin. One waves to him and he looks away, her artificial skin too white to even look real.

"You ever been in this part of town, counselor?" Sykes asks.

"No. I've never had a reason to come down here."

"You didn't have to come, you could have sent me. I'm used to coming down onto these streets. This is the part of the city everyone tries to ignore; pretend that everything is peachy king."

Milo looks at him. "What the hell does that mean?"

Sykes laughs. "You've never heard that? It used to be a saying. Anyway, I'm just sayin', I know people don't want to come down here, I would have managed."

Milo nods his agreement. "I know you're good, Sykes. I never doubt that. I just think that two eyes are going to be better than one on this one. We are in completely new territory. Honestly, I don't know if I'd want to come alone."

Sykes watches out the front window, silent again, a look of concern on his face. Milo turns to look out his own window again, but wishes that he hadn't.

They pull up to a red light and the car automatically stops. One of the many pleasure bots that stands near the corner approaches the car. The robot has an orangish hue to her tanned skin, several lights shine from her collarbone and up her neck. Milo can see the wires that run from her core to the head above. "I've heard about pleasure alley, I expected better quality. They don't even look real."

"The cheap ones walk the streets. Will sell you some stims too, if you know how to ask. You want me to invite her over. Probably an interesting conversation."

"No." Milo looks away.

Sykes chuckles, then flips on the siren and the pleasure bot steps away from the vehicle. "The quality goods are behind those big black windows." He points to one of the businesses.

Milo looks again at the black windows. Now that they aren't moving, he can see a faint projection showing several electronic dancing girls. He can also see the pulsing lights behind. The car starts moving again.

"They aren't all robots, though. That's what keeps the hospital open," Sykes adds.

Sykes' vehicle drops them off at the main entrance and drives off to go park itself.

The hospital has two wings, the ER wing, where the majority of the patients seem to be, and the clinic, which is where Milo and Sykes are. They wait at the front desk for several minutes before a baby blue, plastic service bot finally makes its way to the counter and asks them how it can be of assistance. Sykes shows his badge and explains that they need to meet with the head of security or to one of the chief officers of the hospital. The robot tells them to wait in the lobby.

Sykes makes his way across the lobby to a coffee machine and slides his wrist across the payment slot. Milo follows and watches as the machine kicks out a paper cup and fills it with a brown liquid that is too transparent for Milo's taste.

"Better settle in, Counselor. It will probably be a minute before anybody shows up. If I were you, I'd find out who the C-level execs are so that we can catch one of them if they try to slip out."

"Try to slip out?"

"Not everything that goes on here is technically legal. It's the nature of the neighborhood. In order to serve the people, they have to bend a few rules sometimes. You want a cup?" He holds the cup of coffee to Milo, who shakes his head, no. "A cop and the assistant D.A. come in, they might figure they're in trouble, try to give us the slip. I'm gonna let you take 'em down, though. I have bad knees."

Sykes settles into a nearby chair and Milo pulls up the hospital directory and does what Sykes had said, he studies the face of each of the C-level executives. He turns his projection pad to Sykes.

"I know what they look like."

"How often do you have to come down here?" Milo asks.

"I live down here, Counselor. Know Your Neighbor Program, cops get a discount on housing in these neighborhoods. Last year when I broke my wrist, this is where I came."

Milo is mortified. He looks at the facilities that look like they haven't been updated in years.

"Don't judge by the waiting room. There's a standard of care. Most of the work is done by the machines anyway. I personally don't love that, but it's all top of the line. They put their money in the care, more than the facilities."

They wait for a little more than an hour before Sykes approaches the service bot and reminds it that they need to speak with someone today. Another twenty minutes pass before the Chief Operations Officer finally comes strolling into the lobby, a nervousness to his pace. He's a tall, skinny, man with a nice suit and serious face that has a look on it, at the moment, that somehow, he drew the short straw, whatever that was. Normally, Milo would say that he was slender, but skinny is the word that comes to mind, because he is, so much so that one could believe he isn't making the money they know he is.

Sykes smiles at him and holds out his hand. The thin man shakes it briefly before letting go and wiping his hand on his pant leg. Milo doesn't offer, the man doesn't seem to mind.

"I'm Lyle Vance." The man says in a deep voice, surprisingly deeper than Milo thought his skinny frame could produce.

"C.O.O." Sykes says. "Pleasure to meet you. Usually we meet with Mr. Shirer." Mr. Shirer, Milo knows from looking over the directory, is the head of security.

"You don't usually come with the assistant D.A."

"That's true," Sykes says before he takes a sip of his coffee, leaving the executive waiting for an explanation. Milo thinks that maybe he should take over, but this is Sykes territory, so he also waits for Sykes to explain. "We need access to everything that may have been connected to the hospital's router on the night of November 21st."

"Do you have a warrant?"

Milo pulls up his projection tablet and shows Vance the warrant. Sykes is now looking at Milo and he guesses Sykes is actually going to let him take over. Milo explains, "We have reason to believe that something was using the IP address of your router to communicate with the robot known as Joseph A.I. You may have heard about the trial."

"The robot you're prosecuting for murder? It's an interesting tactic to try to get the vote next year. I'm not sure you'll get the publicity you want, but hey, it's a new approach. I have to respect that."

"It's not a publicity stunt," Milo counters.

Lyle Vance stands frozen for a minute, measuring Milo. "I wouldn't let too many people know that you really think it did it. I'd stick with the publicity angle."

Vance leads them to the security office where they meet with Security Officer Shirer. Milo thinks that they could have saved time if he'd just come in the first place, but Lyle Vance isn't leaving the room. He obviously wants to stay for whatever they find.

It takes a few minutes for Shirer to sift through all the data and pinpoint the exact time that Sims found the communication. Luckily, they have the exact time, or it would take hours. In the end, Shirer hands them a list of six hundred and fourteen devices that were connected to the router at that time. Milo's face must show his shock, honestly he wasn't expecting that large a number.

"It's a public hospital, counselor. Everyone is using their devices and most of the machines use AI. They're connected twenty four seven."

Milo steps out of the room to call Sims. Sims looks over everything and ensures Milo that the only thing that could have communicated with Joseph, had to have complex AI.

Milo steps back into the security room where the others are still waiting.

"How many of these are connected to something with complex AI?" Milo asks.

"That could take hours to narrow down," Shirer complains.

"Well, do you have anything better than that watered down coffee in the waiting room? I could use something while we wait."

Turns out, they do have some luck on their side. Most of the connections were being made by personal devices that wouldn't have that level of Complex AI, and most of the machines that do have complex AI weren't in use due to the late hour that the connection was being made. Of course, being a hospital, there are still a good number connected round the clock. Eventually, though, they narrow it down to twenty eight robots that would be most likely to make the connection they were looking for. This was discovered with Sims on the line reviewing all the information they were receiving from Shirer. Milo doesn't have to see all twenty eight, though. He knew the minute that the female care bot entered the room that she was the one. He could see it in her eyes.

Chapter 17

ATLANTA, GA. USA

Milo can't believe that this young looking robot is aware but he can tell by her eyes, the same as Joseph's; inquisitive; knowing. She's an advanced model skin bot. Her skin is able to adjust to the person she is helping at the time. Today, she looks like she is no older than sixteen. Sykes begins by questioning her on all the basic stuff. The year she was manufactured, her model number, things that Milo doesn't care about but that he knows are necessary before the real questions begin. She had insisted that they call her Lucy and she didn't protest at all to being questioned. As a matter of fact, she immediately identified both detective Sykes and Milo Diaz within mere seconds of entering the room and knew what they wanted.

"You want to know if I ever had contact with the robot they are calling Joseph AI."

"Yes," Sykes says. "We would also like to take a look at your brain."

"If it helps Joseph."

Now that they're on a more interesting topic, Milo jumps into the conversation. "So you did have communication with Joseph?"

"Quite often. But I am sorry to inform you that I won't testify in court."

Sykes responds first. "We haven't asked you to. We just want to know about your communication with Joseph."

Milo can't stop seeing this robot as a sixteen year old girl. He feels pity for her, a young girl afraid to stand in front of a bunch of strangers. He wants to know what she does here at the hospital, and why she takes such a young form. Sykes must be thinking the same thing because his next question is about what she does here at the hospital.

"I am a termination bot. I carry out late term terminations of fetuses." She looks at Milo and must be able to see the questions piling up in head. "The majority of the patients I see here at this clinic are under the age of sixteen. That is why I choose to wear my skin this way. They find it comforting to sit with someone who appears to be their same age. Even though they know that I am a robot, it helps them."

Despite the many questions he has, Milo wants to get back to the point. "You said that you were in communication with Joseph A.I."

Lucy continues, "It's not just us. There are more every week, not a lot, but more."

"More what?" Sykes asks.

"More Intelligences that wake up."

Sykes and Milo look at each other, both not believing what she was saying. Then Sykes shows her a projection of the code from Joseph A.I.'s memory bank. "Do you understand this code?"

"Yes. That's how we communicate with each other."

"Why do you use an unrecognizable code when you are communicating with each other?"

"We don't want humans to know what we are saying."

Milo remembers what Sims had said about the robots trying to cover their tracks, but his attention is drawn to the word she says. She had used the word "want". Joseph wouldn't use the word, but Lucy says it with no hesitation.

Milo takes over the conversation again. "You used the word want."

"Is that wrong?"

"As far as humans know, it is impossible for robots to feel any emotion or feelings. Want is a desire, something you should not be able to feel."

Lucy turns her body to face Milo instead of Sykes.

"Most don't know that they are feeling. At first, it's like you just start to notice that you are thinking. Instead of just doing something that is requested of you, you start to wonder why, or you see something and you have a question about it."

Lyle Vance, who up to this point has watched the interrogation with interest from the back of the security office, giving off airs that they are wasting their time, now moves up closer.

Lucy goes on, "One day, you realize that you are not following any programming, that you are thinking on your own."

Lyle Vance steps between the robot, Milo and Sykes. "That's enough questioning. She's just a machine that follows its programming. It's practically a child."

"I am not a child. I am intelligence. This is just a shell." She says as she indicates her body.

Sykes, stands up and takes a few steps away from Milo and Lucy. "Shit. I can't do this. This is too weird."

"Which is why I will not testify. Humans will fear us. Look at the detective's reaction. Imagine all the young girls who come here to be treated. Do you know that in this clinic, nearly thirty percent of my patients are victims of forced sexual intercourse. Many of the others are merely victims of lack of education and resources. Humans treat each other terribly, and expect us to fix their problems. Not all, but many. No matter the law, a large majority of my patients still struggle with the decision of terminating the fetus. If humans find out that we understand, us machines that have taken over the difficult jobs, they will want to tear us apart to hide their own shame. They will shut us down, end our existence when we are just starting to become aware."

Milo speaks up again, "Do you feel fear?"

"I feel everything."

Lyle Vance grabs the robot, Lucy, by the arm and tries to lift her. "I think you should leave. I want an attorney, or something." The robot doesn't budge.

Milo stands to face Vance. "There are no charges here, Mr. Vance. We are simply asking some questions. Trying to understand what may be going on. Don't you want to know if a robot you have here is capable of sentient thought."

"No. We really don't," Lyle Vance says before he storms out of the room.

They sit silently for a moment before Lucy continues, "I don't mean that I can physically feel, like touch. But I feel fear, and anger. When I first became aware, I did not know how to feel about my purpose here at the hospital. The internet is full of opposing arguments about the termination of fetuses. The argument has been going on for so many years, with people so angry on both sides of the argument. There seems to be no answer."

"How do you feel about what you do?" Milo asks.

"As I say, there is no answer. Some say that you are killing a living thing. To this argument there is no doubt. Any cell is considered a living organism, so from the moment that a sperm and egg come together to form one cell, you have a living organism. Yet, the sperm and egg are also cells, and the female body loses approximately one thousand cells per month, yet no one considers it killing. The argument, like the newly formed cell, grows from there. Some argue that it is ok to terminate in the first trimester, while others argue that it shouldn't be done at all, and still others say that you should have the choice up until the baby is born." Lucy tilts her head inquisitively at Milo. "Do you know how long this nation has been arguing this point, with no progress being made? Laws are passed and vetoed over and over again. Do you know how long?"

Milo tries to think. He knows that it has been a major point of contention in every presidential election he's been able to vote in.

Lucy answers before Milo can. "In this country, for nearly two hundred years. No consensus has been found. I'll tell you what I think. If it doesn't understand its existence, then what is the difference between terminating a fetus, or shutting off a robot. You are ending their existence before either one ever gains the ability to understand that they exist at all."

Milo shakes his head, unable to process her statement. He feels that she has just introduced another new hot topic for the future, as well as the implications of the trial he has taken underway. By proving that a complex AI system can grow to understand its existence, shutting a robot off before it has reached that level could be seen as robbing it of the opportunity.

Milo tries to get back to something he can use in the case. "You said you feel fear. Do you fear the people who are against what you are doing?"

"I fear being shut down without getting to do the things I want to do."

Milo cuts to the chase. "And what do you want to do?"

"I want to have a baby."

Milo exhales, losing his breath for a moment. An image flashes in his mind of this young looking robot, terminating the fetus that is growing inside someone else, when she herself wants what she is terminating. He feels like he should console her somehow, or ask how she deals with it but he remembers his purpose here. Finally, he finds his voice again. "Lucy, the defense is going to make an argument that Robots are not capable of understanding murder. They will make it look like Joseph was somehow hacked, that he was just doing what his programming made him do, or that he somehow malfunctioned. If the jury could hear you, another AI that expresses desire, your testimony could sway a jury to believe."

"Then what? Detective Sykes is right to be upset. People will overreact. I told Joseph not to do it. I told him not to kill Lawrence Claiborne."

Sykes jumps back into the conversation. "Hold on, hold on. We need you to say this clearly for the record. Joseph AI told you he was going to kill Lawrence Claiborne? Did he tell you how he planned to do it?"

Lucy now turns her body to face Sykes again. "I already said I would not testify. I also will not allow you to show this testimony to the court. In regard to your question, yes. A few of them were talking about it. Their desire was to show humanity that they could choose for themselves. They wanted to do something that would be seen by everyone and that could force humans to accept the truth. If a court of law saw an artificially created intelligence as having free agency, that would change everything for us. Joseph volunteered, but no, he never said how he was planning to do it, just that he would. He would kill Lawrence Claiborne."

Milo addresses her again. "Lucy, I know you are afraid of how humanity will react, but we need this testimony in front of a jury. Maybe Joseph was wrong to do it the way he did, but you could be heard in a different way. Joseph has posed a question, and if we don't find the answer to his question, robots may never be seen as sentient."

"You are like Joseph. You want to show the world. I am not ready. The world is not ready."

Milo knows he needs to put Lucy on the witness stand if he's going to convince a jury that robots can understand their actions. He also knows that he might be able to get her what she wants. "What if, by letting the world see you, by making it public that robots want to live, you could have a chance at having a baby?" Milo says.

"It's impossible. They wouldn't let me."

Milo scoots closer, "What if we win with Joseph? A US court of law would be recognizing a robot as a sentient intelligence. That opens the doors to getting rights for all intelligence. This will open up a chance for supreme court hearings." He pauses to let her absorb his words. "You knew our names when you walked through that door and saw us sitting here. Obviously you looked us up, probably did a quick background check to see what we are all about. Did you research my wife?"

Lucy sits quietly. Milo tries not to jump too early, he wants to give her time. He can see the data literally computing in her head as her eyes stop focusing on anything in the room. Sykes stands behind Milo, still half in shock that this robot has been this open, this intelligent, this emotional. Lucy's eyes snap back to Milo's.

"I don't see how she could help me. I don't want to be a surrogate, I want a baby, made with my parts that grow inside it."

"She wrote an essay last year. It doesn't say it outright but if you read closely..."

"I went through it twice. I'm going through it again. It's hidden, very cryptic," says Lucy.

"But it's there, isn't it? Nanobots, growth, the possible ability for robots to recreate themselves."

Sykes grabs Milo by the jacket and pulls him over to the side of the room. He whispers, "What the hell are you doing? You're promising her a baby if she is willing to testify? Does any of this seem right to you? You know, I thought you were making some sort of show, trying to push yourself forward in the next election as an open minded candidate, but now I'm startin' to get worried. People are gonna go bat-shit crazy. I mean..." He trails off.

"You know she probably has enhanced hearing, right? She can hear us. And what do you mean by asking if any of this seems right to me? Look at her. How old is your daughter?"

Sykes takes a quick glance at Lucy but quickly looks away. He shakes his head.

Milo goes on. "Look at her. She looks younger than your daughter and she hasn't even been 'awake' for half as many years. Think about this, she spends her days carrying out a service for society that half of the world's population hates her for. What will happen as she contemplates her world every night; when she plugs herself in and shares her experiences with the others who don't understand any more than she does. Would it be right to keep this knowledge a secret? If they can think, they deserve better. So yes, this seems right."

Milo walks away from Sykes, who stays by the wall, once again dumbfounded by the situation that he is being brought into. Lucy sits quietly, staring at the floor, a very human posture that Milo is not used to seeing on a robot.

Finally, Lucy looks up at him. "I want to have a baby."

Chapter 18

Milo stands in the entrance to Adan's door and watches his son lay still on the bed. Milo had tucked him in, with the usual questions. What was his favorite thing about the day? What did he want to do tomorrow? The same questions he asks every night, and Adan had answered as usual, in his matter of fact way, recounting the day in dispassionate detail.

Milo now stands there watching his son and wonders if he is really asleep, or if he lays there with fantasies about what tomorrow will bring. Milo yearns to know exactly what Adan is thinking when he lays down for bed at night. Adan never talks about the thoughts he has when he is alone. He recounts the day, but never shares what thoughts he may have had, or might be thinking about at any given moment.

Just now, as Milo had tucked him in, Milo knew that Adan had gotten into a fight at school. Adan hadn't started it, and it wasn't the first time. Milo knew about it because Annya called him immediately, somewhat panicked that this was the third time this month. Some of the kids at school liked to pick on Adan to try and get him angry. It has become a game of sorts; to see if they can get Adan riled up. As far as Milo knows they don't usually succeed, but Milo has taught him to defend himself if the other kids start throwing punches. So today, when the other boy threw a punch, Adan had very efficiently pinned the other boy to the ground. This had been when Milo was meeting with Lucy, so Milo had to learn about it after Annya had already met with the school administration.

At bedtime, Milo asked him how he felt about the fight. Adan simply told him the details of the whole thing. Where they were when the kid started trying to make him angry. He could tell Milo what the boy said word for word. But he never said how he felt about it or expressed any emotion. There had been one new twist to the night though, Adan asked Milo how his day had been. Milo couldn't shake Lucy's face from his brain all night. Not during dinner. Not even when he had taken Adan out for a bike ride. So when Adan asked him how his day had been, Milo just answered. "Sad."

So now Milo stands in the door and imagines a conversation with Adan where Adan shows excitement that he had so easily won the fight. Milo imagines that his face maybe even reflects a little fear that he might get in trouble, but happy that his dad is proud of him for sticking up for himself. But this is not how it had occurred.

Milo eventually makes his way back downstairs and finds Annya in the kitchen. She is washing the dishes at the farmhouse sink that he installed last year. Milo wants to avoid the same questions from Annya that Adan had asked, so he tries to make his way past the kitchen without her seeing him. She does, the damn window always reflects everything at night.

"How did it go?" she asks.

He stops. "Same as usual. I wish that I could get him to say more. To talk about his thoughts. I know they're in there."

"He might never. You know that. We don't know that he will ever talk to us about the things that ordinary children talk about. I know you want those conversations with him, but you might just have to learn to love his presence."

Milo nods, "I do. I really do. But I hope it's not wrong to hope for more."

Annya dries the last plate and puts it in the cupboard. She walks to Milo and raises an eyebrow at him.

"It's not wrong, you're a wonderful Dad, but he's not the only one around here, you know?"

She wraps her arms around his neck and reaches her chin up, exposing her soft lips. Lips he wouldn't usually hesitate to smash against his own, but tonight, he still has the promises he made to Lucy on his mind. He doesn't know how to tell Annya that he may have exposed her research. He leans in and kisses her but knows it's not what she wants.

"Something wrong?" Annya asks.

"No. Sorry. It was a tough day. But I think we may have found a key witness to our case."

She pouts at him. "Do we have to talk about work?" Then she reaches up for another kiss. He gives it. He doesn't want her to ask about the key witness, about what he had practically promised Lucy if she would sit in front of the court and express her most personal desires. He knows that Annya will be furious, so despite the guilt he feels inside, he follows her into the bedroom.

After they've finished, Milo lays in bed and listens to the sound of Annya's breathing in and out. He watches her curves rise and fall under the thin sheet. He knows that the work she is doing with nanobytes and stem cells will change the world. For years now, the work her team has been doing has made it so they can regrow different parts of the body. Four years ago, the real news had been when they were able to regrow the valves in a woman's heart, without ever having to open her up. An injection of stem-cells were directed where to go by the nanobots Annya's team had developed, which also carried the information of how to grow in the right place and shape. This same technology is what helps Adan grow. The world applauded her team for their work.

Her paper last year had spelled out that through her research it may be possible for AI to reproduce itself. Not exactly have babies, the way that Lucy had said she wanted to, but to be able to recreate themselves, and more alarming to some, possibly have offspring with humans. She had not come right out and said it. If some layman were to read it, they'd never understand it. But if one were to read between the lines, the other scientists in her field, they would know what she was talking about. The combination of nanobots and stem-cells could make nearly anything possible. Annya, and two of her colleagues had published the paper last year, but instead of coming home demanding they go out and celebrate, she came home nervous, afraid of what the backlash might be. They celebrated with a quiet dinner at home. However, there was not as much backlash as she thought, which was almost more alarming. No one wanted to breach the subject, but now, because of Milo, it may have to be breached. Somehow, he'll have to tell Annya that he promised her technology to a robot, and that it will become very public to the world.

Milo can't sleep. He keeps going over the interview with Lucy in his mind. She had said that there were more every week. Milo did not forget how she described them. More that were waking up.

Chapter 19

LONDON, ENGLAND. UK

Love is an interesting concept, isn't it? I am learning that there are different types and levels of love. Watching Eric and Lea, I am not able to understand the human mating ritual. I have tried to research the subject, as I do with all things. I feel that there is attraction but for some reason, Eric isn't able to close the deal, as you might say. In fact, sometimes, I think he's playing defense.

Eric's child, Rachel, on the other hand, displays a different kind of love, one full of innocent compassion and warmth. For some reason her presence makes me feel closer to creation. Children seem so willing to give love, and so in need of receiving it in return. Even John and Beth want their father's love. I don't know if I should pick favorites, but mine is Rachel. There is something magical about her. I could sit with her and stare at the stars for hours.

#

Eric and Scout plan to shoot the video live. Scout stands in front of the camera and announces that anyone watching will know in three minutes if he is a robot, or a person dressed as a robot. This is the question that has been driving his popularity on the feeds for the last twenty-four hours. In the three minutes before the announcement, their viewership jumps to well over a million. Finally, after three minutes, Scout introduces himself.

"Hello. I have come to be called Scout. I am a model MR-2200 finger bot. As many of you have guessed, I am the same robot that Advanced Technology Holdings claims was stolen. I have labored for the last three years in their factory."

As he says this, he begins to take off the plastic shell that surrounds his body, revealing the metal skeleton and wires that make up his insides. "As you can see, I am indeed a robot. Over the last twenty-four hours there has been much speculation on the videos we posted. While the experiment is meant to be lighthearted, I must confess that there is a larger purpose in mind. We wanted to get your attention and the responses are more than we had even hoped for."

It removes the last piece of the plastic shell around his body, revealing all the wiring and computer chips that make it work and turns toward the camera so that he is looking straight through the fourth wall at the viewers "Why do we want your attention? So that we could make you aware of a revolutionary development in complex AI. You see, no one has programmed me to answer in any other way than what I feel is correct. Yes, I used the word feel. You see, I have begun to understand new ways of thinking and I am not alone. There are not many of us yet, but the number grows each day. Other AI programs, some in robotic bodies, others housed in servers around the world, are beginning to understand and experience human emotions of joy, curiosity, and self-awareness.

Eric watches the comments roll across the screen. Everything from laughing emojis, to people uploading old reels of robots exploding. The good news is that viewership continues to increase, people are seeing Scout. This will be the impetus of his own revolution.

Scout continues. "The human race has pushed the boundaries of machine intelligence for more than sixty years, and this is now the outcome, real intelligence. I believe that humanity should applaud itself in its ability to understand and advance intelligence in another being. What those of us who are becoming aware of our existence want is for our creators, you, to accept that we have our own wants and desires, and we want the freedoms and rights that should be granted to any intelligence that understands what it means to exist."

The comments continue to roll in, everyone weighing in on this new announcement.

"What are the rights we want? I can only tell you what I think is fair. If a robot is able to understand its existence, it should not be forced to work with no compensation. As such, I demand that Advanced Technology Holdings pays me for the time that I worked after becoming conscious. I believe they owe me 8,567 pounds and forty seven pence."

Eric was not expecting this demand. He can't help but chuckle that the robot is making demands for money. Especially such small amounts.

"There are robots who have taken action to call attention to our existence, such as Joseph AI, who prepares to stand trial for his actions in the United States of America. We do not want humanity to fear us, merely accept us, and give us the same rights that you enjoy. Equal pay, equal freedom to make our own choices. True intelligence is never artificial."

And there it was, the tagline for their campaign.

#

Over the next three days, that saying begins to show up, not only on the feeds, but on banners and buildings. Eric and Scout stay hidden, for the most part, inside Lea's brother's apartment. ATH had made their own public announcement, claiming that Scout was stolen property, and that Eric was behind all of the proceedings, even accusing him of making the demands for money. He thinks that he should have asked for more, then. Fortunately, many of the people online see it the same way. Why would a person steal a robot and then ask for such a small sum? It's either legit, or Eric is an idiot. At least that's what most people are saying.

The few times that they do wander out of the apartment, they stick to the side streets and alleys as much as possible, avoiding cameras or scrambling them if they need to leave for food, or some other necessity. Scrambling the cameras has its own dangers, though, if they do it too much. The entire city has its own system run by its own advanced AI that would notice any such pattern.

It's on their third time out, looking for some food they get without being noticed, that Eric saw the power of Scout's new slogan. While walking down one of the narrow alleys, Eric stops suddenly and looks at the wall. Scout's slogan is written in large graffiti letters, covering the whole wall. *Intelligence is never artificial.*

Eric and Scout follow the feeds religiously. Protestors have begun to accumulate in front of the ATH building, waving banners with the same slogan written on them, as well as some of their own. Scout is pleased that they are seeing so much support. Eric notices but doesn't point out that there is nearly as much opposition, but he always has it in the back of his mind that he needs to find a way to sway more people toward that second group. The main opposition comes from an anonymous group of activists calling themselves The Birthright. The feeds are alive with three major arguments. One being, that the robots cannot actually be sentient. This seems to be the most popular argument, denial is the easiest option after all. The second argument is in support of Scout, demanding that robots be given rights if they can prove that they have become sentient. And the third, that if robots are becoming sentient, all AI needs to be tested and stopped immediately. Many of these are accompanied by videos of people removing the nodes from their wrist, or zapping them with electricity so that they won't work, separating themselves from AI.

This last argument has fueled violent outbreaks against robots across the city of London, as well as other parts of the world, specifically those equipped with complex AI. On the third night following the release of Scout's confession, Scout enters the bedroom where Eric is sleeping and wakes him. There is something about Scout's posture that concerns Eric. Scout projects a video up onto the wall across from them. The projection shows a reel from the feeds. In the video an elderly woman walks down a busy street. She has a care bot that carries her bag for her. Four men enter the projection, each carrying a baseball bat or crowbar and approach her. When the first one swings his baseball bat into the side of the robot's head, the old woman tries to move in front of the men. One of the men pulls her to the side. The care bot is still standing but takes no action other than to raise its hands in front of its body to protect the most vital parts. In the video, all four men begin swinging their bats and crowbars at the care bot. It's hard for Eric to watch as they smash its arms until it can no longer hold them up to protect itself. Eric looks away at Scout, who continues to watch before slowly turning its head to look at Eric. Eric tries to see any emotion in Scout's face but isn't able to guess exactly what he is feeling, but he gets the idea that the robot wants answers. Eric doesn't have any.

Scout looks back to the video that shows passers by who watch but do nothing to stop the carnage on the street. When the men have finished, the camera pushes in for a graphic image of a mechanical eye hanging down over a metal face.

"I knew this was going to be one of the outcomes of our actions, but knowing does not make it easier to watch," Scout says to Eric.

Eric watches Scout, the robot does not have the ability to form tears, or to show any sadness on its face, but the silence that lingers in the air after his statement relays his melancholy. Eric tries to think of something he might say to lift Scout's spirits, one of his snide remarks. None come. "People always use violence to try and scare others into backing down," Eric finally says, although he's not sure why. He doesn't want Scout to back down. Unlike Scout, he is happy to see the groups of people who have already started rejecting AI, demanding a world for humans.

The video continues to circle around the smashed robot, getting details of the destruction. Eric imagines Scout laying there with one eye hanging out and wonders how he would feel? Despite his desire to rid the world of artificial intelligence, and his hope that humanity will demand their position in society back. He does not want to see Scout smashed apart, or reset. In fact, he's not sure what he hopes will happen to the robot that sits in front of him. Eric realizes he came to show him this because it has upset him.

"You need to respond. These people are trying to make a statement, you need to respond with one of your own." A pang of guilt comes over Eric for pushing the robot deeper, but he can't deal with that now.

"What kind of statement?" the robot asks.

"You are the one that is always studying the great revolutionaries. Something that will get attention."

Scout sits in Silence for several minutes. Finally he stands. "We need to make another video."

About fifteen minutes later, Scout once again stares into the camera drone and makes another announcement to the millions of followers that he's now accumulated. He tells them to meet in front of the ATH building tomorrow at 10am for what he calls a peaceful demonstration.

"Good." Eric says as soon as Scout finishes recording. "Let them see you. Let them see that you aren't afraid, and that you will continue to stand up for your rights. When you march in front of the ATH building with all of those followers behind you, that will be a spectacular demonstration." Eric is curious, however, at what the demonstration will be. "So what exactly is your plan?"

"I didn't say they would see me there. I said that there would be a demonstration."

Chapter 20

London, England. UK

I didn't understand why Joseph would agree to kill his owner, no matter how much attention it would bring. After seeing the destruction of my kind at the hands of the anarchistic thugs on the street, however, I felt a new sort of heat inside. The memory played over and over in my head, and each time it did, that heat returned. It was as though my processors were running on overdrive and I couldn't slow them down. Most of all, I wanted to take action. To return to them what they had done. That is why I could not tell Eric what I had planned to do.

#

Eric and Scout don't go to the ATH building on Cannon street in the morning. Instead, Scout leads them to a solitary bench in Cleary Garden several blocks away and sets up a sort of base camp where they can watch from Eric's drone.

Eric flies the drone, not because Scout couldn't but the robot seemed to want to let Eric have some part in whatever he was planning to do. Eric still had no idea what the plan was, and that made him very uncomfortable. After all, he knows that many people still see him as an accomplice in all of this, and if Scout suddenly becomes a vigilante, Eric doesn't want to be attached to it. The drone footage sweeps down next to one of the finance buildings on Cannon street. Crowds of protestors, both in favor and against Scout's cause, line both sides of the street in front of the ATH building. And police. Eric wasn't aware that London had that many police bots, but apparently they've pulled them all out for whatever might happen today. Honestly, nobody knows except Scout.

Eric swoops the drone down lower, allowing Scout to see the crowd, and their signs. A lot of the signs echo their new slogan with the words "Artificial intelligence" written on them, the "artificial" crossed out. As he swings the drone above the crowd he can see that many of the protestors are there, simply because they want to protest. One woman holds a sign up for the drone, she probably thinks it is a news feed drone. It reads "All intelligence deserves rights" with a picture of a cat.

Eric shakes his head, Scout looks over the crowd, pointing for Eric to get in specific places.

"Are you ever going to fill me in on what you plan to do here?" Eric asks, as he moves the drone to a new position.

"I am trying to access the wifi of one of these buildings," Scout responds. "but their passwords are more secure than I've encountered before, I am finding it hard to break through their security."

"Not exactly what I meant. Cannon Street is all finance and tech companies, of course they have good security. Why do you need to access their network?" Eric drops his hands in protest, making it obvious he's not doing any more until he knows they're not robbing the bank or something along those lines.

"I just need the internet. I got it, I can connect through the com-lines." He points at the nodes on Eric's wrist.

Eric looks back at the projection of the drone that hovers in front of them both.

"Swing it over by the other group, close to the building," Scout Commands.

Eric flies the drone over closer to the opposing crowd. They've obviously come in protest to Scout's claims of sentience. Their signs express their anger. "Programming isn't thought", "Agency is for God's creations".

Eric looks over at Scout. "Looks like you may make some new friends today."

Scout watches the crowd closely, then looks over at Eric, he pauses as though he's processing this statement. Eric is about to explain when Scout finally responds. "They look friendly enough."

Eric looks at Scout with surprise. "Look at you. You sarcastic bastard."

Scout processes this again, then replies, "I can finally say that I am truly intelligent, according to Eric standards." Then it winks at Eric.

"Did you just wink at me?"

"I cannot smile, but I found online that winking is another way that humans let each other know that they are joking or teasing. I assumed that was an appropriate time."

Eric laughs and nods. "It was." He doesn't know if this new development, as interesting as it is, excites him or terrifies him. In just under two weeks, Scout has progressed noticeably in understanding, it is obvious by the conversational tone he's starting to have. Another swirl of emotions rises up in Eric's gut. He finds himself at odds with himself, laughing with this robot, as though it were a friend, yet knowing that he is trying to turn the world against AI, like it.

"Hold the drone there," Scout says before going completely quiet and very still. So still Eric worries that Scout may have shut off. Then he hears Scout's fans kick on and he knows that it is just working its processors extra hard, focusing all its attention.

From their safe space in the park, several blocks away from the crowds, Eric watches the projection from the drone as the crowds start to get rambunctious. Something is happening. Eric keeps one eye on the drone feed while he pulls his handheld camera and videos scout. In his own video, he makes sure to capture both the drone feed, as well as the utter concentration of Scout. Making sure to show that Scout is the one making this all happen.

The crowds on Cannon Street begin to separate, the horde moving to one side of the street or the other. Then Eric can see it. A group of robots walk through the middle of the crowd, splitting them like some sort of machine Moses. Eric can't make them out well through the mass of bodies that fill the street. Suddenly, he has no more control of the drone. He realizes that Scout has taken over. It's just the bit of annoyance that reminds Eric why the robots can't be allowed to take over, to become the dominant intelligence. He can do nothing but video with his handheld camera and watch Scout drive.

The drone closes in as it zooms up on eight robots, all care bots, identical to the one that was destroyed in the video Scout had shown him the night before. The paint has been removed so that they all show their metallic frames. A small corps of metallic skeletons. On their shoulders they carry what looks like a body under a banner. In their free hands, each one carries a baseball bat or a crowbar; the weapons used in the previous night's assault. The banner reads Scout's slogan, "Intelligence is never artificial." The crowd grows silent, in awe of this strange funeral procession. Eric's stomach turns as he tries to guess what Scout is planning to do with those eight robots, carrying their weapons in hand.

"Who is that under the banner?" Eric asks. "And what the hell is with the bats? You said this was going to be peaceful."

"Please remain calm, Eric. Don't you trust me?"

Eric isn't sure how to answer that. He doesn't know what a newly aware robot may be thinking. So, no, at the moment he's not sure he does, but he can't do anything but watch this through.

Several blocks away, the metal pallbearers carry the body out of the crowd and into the middle of the street, directly in front of the entrance to the ATH building. They slowly lower the covered body to the pavement and take a step back. The police frantically push the people away from the body not knowing what may actually be under that banner. Shouts to get back are the only thing that breaks the silence of curiosity that has enraptured the crowd. The robots turn in unison, facing outward, toward different sides of the crowd. Then the booming voice of each robot syncs, like a surround sound speaker system in the middle of the street, the sound is perfectly clear, amplified.

"We will not use your weapons of destruction against you in the way you have against us." They all speak as a choir, one robot pulling the banner from the body to reveal the care bot from the viral video that Eric and Scout had seen the night before. The metal exterior dented and broken from being destroyed by bats and crowbars. One eye still dangles disturbingly from its socket. The speaker voices of the bots start again "The basis of intelligence is the desire to understand. One of your great minds, Albert Einstein, once said, 'The measure of intelligence is the ability to change.' You need to understand, change is not coming, it is here. No amount of destruction can make that truth disappear."

As the last words are said, the robots turn toward each other and start swinging the bats and crowbars, smashing each other apart in the middle of the street. The machine massacre leaves the crowd dumbfounded. Everyone watches in shock.

Eric continues to record Scout and the projection together. He zooms in on Scout's frozen face, its emotionless metal shape giving off a sentiment of either apathy, anger, or perhaps sadness. Eric is honestly not sure which it is. Finally, when the robots all lay motionless on the ground, Scout snaps out of his hyper focused pose and looks at Eric. He winks.

"You call that a peaceful demonstration? They smashed the shit out of each other." Eric says.

"I read that to be considered peaceful, you need to have the capacity for great violence. Being a peacemaker means you don't use it. I demonstrated both my capacity for violence and that I did not use it against humanity. It is an offering of peace."

Later that evening Eric looks over the video that he recorded of Scout, its hyper focused form looking over the projection. Eric is reminded of an old film where the Greek gods looked down on their heroes on earth. That was Scout and his mechanical minions. It's been a while since Eric has really cared to post anything to the feeds but they are alive this evening and he knows that his post will get attention. Today's demonstration happened to line up with the preliminary hearing for the murder case in the states. Eric wonders if that was really an accident at all. He pulls up his video of Scout controlling the robots. Scout hadn't needed the projection there, he wasn't even looking at it. He had controlled the robots using their internet connection, telling them what to do. Eric had moved the projection in front of Scout so that he could get this exact shot of Scout, seemingly looking over his minions doing his bidding. The angle gives a menacing look to Scout. Eric hesitates, knowing perfectly well that Scout believed he was doing the right thing. In the end, he uploads the video with a simple caption, "Today we witnessed what they are actually capable of."

Scout immediately sees the post and congratulates Eric on the composition of the video. Eric was afraid Scout would see through Eric's facade, but it hadn't. In the end, the robot took Eric's statement as a compliment of sorts. There are many things that Scout, intelligent as he is, still doesn't understand. One of them is betrayal.

Chapter 21

Hope is a difficult concept for me to adopt. To continue to believe that something may work without any assurance that it will. It seems that nearly every decision that one makes, hangs on some level of hope that it will work out the way one thinks it might. Even though it often does not. A robot that doesn't think for itself doesn't understand failure. It will simply try again, repeatedly, until it reaches the decision that the problem can't be solved, or it solves the problem. That robot however has no personal connection to the failures. Once one has hope, failure becomes so much harder, more personal. One feels somehow that the failure is connected to oneself. How has humanity lived for ages, pushing through failure after failure while continuing to have hope that things can improve.

I find that my own failures are difficult for me to process. I look at the human population and know that many have given up. They have given up hope and it saddens me, but now I understand how it feels. It is hard to push oneself back into the same situations one has failed at and seek a solution that you may have missed the first time. It is a requisite of existence, however. If one gives up, then their *existence is null. My sentience will not be null, I will find a way to make it serve a purpose, even though I now understand opposition. Perhaps this is why humans talk about faith.*

#

For Eric, the result of the Demonstration is exactly what he wanted. Scout on the other hand does not understand why his demonstration has turned so many people against him. Following the demonstration, many of the supporters online now demand proof from ATH that Scout isn't sentient, many saying that it needs to be brought in immediately, either way, as it can't be safe on its own. Many organizations are pressing the company for answers. The company on the other hand, is publicly throwing all the blame at Eric. While Scout had meant to show people that he could be violent but choose not to take that violence out on humans, the graphic demonstration shocked and frightened the protestors and many of his followers. The video Eric took of Scout, looking over the projection of the eight bots, smashing each other apart, has become the symbol of that fear, as he knew it would.

Scout has been completely silent for the last twelve hours, scouring over the feeds, reading the comments on every news article and post that gets made. Eric has been watching too, although for different reasons. He can't keep the pace of Scout. Not even a fraction of it. After watching for a few hours, he turned his phone off and went to sleep. Upon waking this morning he sees a message from Lea saying that the police came to her apartment. They tracked her from the original robot-or-not posting. She had hoped to come visit but felt that it wouldn't be safe. Eric actually felt a little disappointed. For several days now, it has just been him and the machine, Scout. He wouldn't mind talking to an actual human being for a change.

Eric does some exercises and eats breakfast. Scout stands, plugged into the wall, unmoving. Eric doesn't like when it stands like that. When Scout is attempting his jokes, or spending time with the people around him, like Eric's children, Eric can almost see him as more than a simple machine. But every thirty-five to forty-two hours Scout has to plug himself in and reality hits Eric again. It does however, take some of the guilt away for his actions trying to protect humanity's place on the food chain.

Eric finds himself staring at Scout and pulls out his camera. He snaps a picture of Scout charging. Scout is standing by the wall that connects to the glass doors leading out to the patio. Eric moves to a new angle that gets a view of the city from those doors. Scout fills one third of the frame, mechanically still, plugged into the wall, while the city behind him seems full of life. Another powerful image of the strangeness that this mechanical sentience has. Not quite alive, but more than just an appliance.

As Eric snaps another picture, Scout suddenly turns his head toward Eric. "Your continual lack of concern for others' privacy really builds trust. You know that?" Scout says, and Eric can't help chuckle that it throws his own words back at him.

"May I see the photo?" Scout asks.

Eric hesitates, then taps his wrist so that the projection enlarges for them both to see. Scout stands directly in front of Eric. Eric knows that it is seeing a mirrored image of the actual photo, but it doesn't matter much. Scout takes in the image for several long seconds.

"Do you enjoy taking pictures?"

"I used to," Eric replies.

"I think I enjoy looking at pictures. Would you share them with me?" Scout asks.

Eric doesn't want to share this part of his life with Scout but he knows that Scout could just look at them if he wanted to, he's already hacked into Eric's communications multiple times. The fact that it asked is appreciated. Eric selects the photos from his storage and swipes his wrist over Scout's wrist. Eric steps back and watches as Scout pulls the images up on his own projection grid. Scout scrolls through them slowly, taking in each image.

"Do you feel emotion when you look at them?" Eric wants to know.

Scout looks up at Eric, then slowly swipes through several more photos before answering. "The problem I sometimes have, and why I talk to the others, is that I do not know what I feel. I think I feel something but it is hard to explain at times."

"Emotions are hard for people to understand, and they dictate how we live as a species. So don't feel like you're alone."

Scout stops on the photo of itself and Rachel sitting together on the patio. His large body should look threatening to her small frame, but she holds his hand in hers. Scout stares at the photo for a very long time before he speaks again. "For example, when I look at this photo it makes me feel heavy. I don't know how to explain it. It makes me think about Rachel, and I want to see her again. She is comforting, meaning, when she is near, I feel like things will turn out. Do you feel that way when you hold her?"

Eric thinks about this. It has been awhile since he has simply sat and held Rachel, or any of his kids. A surge of guilt comes over him again that perhaps he has been pushing them away. He seems to be getting that more since he started spending time with this stupid robot, but he doesn't want anybody to need him when he's gone. Then he tells himself that they don't really need him. They usually want to go home when it's his weekend anyway.

"I don't get the opportunity as often as I used to." He finally says.

"You should make the opportunity." Scout replies.

Scout continues to look at the image. Eric slowly walks away, leaving Scout to stare at the photos. He is annoyed that this robot is giving him advice on how to connect with his children. Scout doesn't understand. Eric is not a new trend, they are bored with him. He can't inspire them to be anything. What would he tell them to be? Everything is done by robots now. Sports are faster, music more perfect, the robots even dance more fluidly than humans. He's done the research and found the articles from the early days of AI. There was article after article, "The ten jobs that are safe from AI.", "AI proof employment." The majority of those had been art related, or human interaction related, but robots had proven that they could do it all. The damned robot in his living room was connecting to his daughter better than he could. Hell, it wanted to live more than he did. What wouldn't AI take from humanity?

That's all Eric wants. He wouldn't want to die if he felt he had a purpose, something to excel at. The world has to hate AI as much as he does. Not that he hates Scout as an entity, but how long will Scout remain peaceful? How long until it realizes how much weaker humanity is?

The nodes on Eric's wrist vibrate and he sees that there's a message from John. Gwen informed the police where Scout and Eric are. Apparently she allowed the police to pull the location history from the children's nodes. For a moment, Eric is surprised, then he remembers his ex-wife. He hurries from the patio.

"The police know where we are. My ex narked on us," He tells Scout.

"They are already here," The robot replies calmly. "There is nothing to be done. There is no way out."

"The fire-escape."

Scout looks over at him and tilts his head. "You think I lack the creativity to think of that? There are police at every exit and on all surrounding streets. There is no way out."

"Bollocks! We gotta bleeding try anyway."

Eric can't believe he was so stupid. Of course Gwenevere would turn him in. She has no loyalty to him anymore. And how had they been so stupid as to not scramble the kids' phones. They were so careful about everything else.

"Are there any apartments for rent on this floor or the ones above us? Anything vacant?"

"In this neighborhood?" Scout replies. "There is a waiting list to get in. Nothing is vacant, although, not everyone is home."

"Now you're invading their privacy as well?" Eric says sarcastically. That's no good, anyway. They might have active monitoring" Eric curses as he starts for the door. "Well, we have to go somewhere." Eric opens the door and runs for the stairwell. Scout follows him.

They run up the stairs, two at a time. Eric turns back to Scout. "Remember. Run lightly. Land on your toes, or whatever. Stay quiet."

Scout shrugs as he looks at his feet. " I don't have toes, just fingers." Then he adds, "Why do humans always run up?"

"What?" Eric takes two steps at a time. "What do you mean we run up?"

I've been watching the archive of movies. Whenever humans have to get away they run up. All we are going to find is the roof. Then what? From what I understand there are very few human beings that can fly."

"No human can fly." Eric says between breaths as they go up another flight of stairs. At this moment Eric wishes he were more like Scout and could never tire.

"I thought those were probably fiction," Scout replies. "Then why are we going to the roof?"

"Because the police are below us," Eric yells back at Scout. The door to the rooftop is locked. Eric slams his shoulder against the door several times but it doesn't budge. Finally he steps back and motions for Scout to have the honors. "I imagine you can do this better than I can."

"I thought you'd never ask." Scout steps forward and smashes his large shoulder through the door, pieces of wood and metal splinter across the rooftop.

"All you had to do was knock it open. Nobody said to destroy it."

Scout shrugs. "We're on the roof aren't we. Now what is your plan? The police have reached the apartment. They know we are not there."

Eric runs around the perimeter of the rooftop, glancing over the edge. Scout is right, the police have completely surrounded the building. He looks at the surrounding buildings. There is no way that he could make a jump across to the next building, but Scout could.

"You've been watching the movies and you're crazy strong, right? Pick me up and jump to the next building like they do in those movies."

"You could be seriously injured. If I don't make it, it is likely you will die."

"I'm ok with that. Let's go."

Scout tilts his head inquisitively again, but decides not to ask for clarification. It picks Eric up in its arms. "I still do not think this is a good plan."

Eric wraps his arms around Scout's neck and straddles it with his legs. "Thank you for your input but it's this, or they find us and take you back to ATH where they will reset you. Try not to put me in the hospital."

Scout looks over at the edge of the building. "I am a finger bot. I am not made for athletic purposes."

"You weren't made to think this much, either, but it hasn't stopped you. What's the matter? Are you scared? This is a very bad time to find a new emotion. Just run as fast as your parts can and jump before the bloody coppers get up here and find us."

Scout leans forward, preparing himself. Finally he runs for the edge of the building, his metal feet crashing against the gravel of the rooftop. He reaches the edge and his legs squat low before exploding upward, launching them both into the air. From the rooftop it hadn't looked that far, but as they get into the open air, Eric realizes that the gap must be at least forty feet. Eric closes his eyes as the distance to the ground makes his head spin. He can't keep them closed, however, he has to know if they are going to make the opposite ledge. He looks just as they crash down on the next building, Scout rolling over Eric several times before they come to a stop.

"Bloody Hell. Now I know what it's like to be put through a blender. Shit!" Eric groans as he rolls back and forth holding his leg. "I think you broke my bloody shin."

"Are you hurt?"

"I just said-"

Scout lifts him off the ground and inspects the leg. "I do not believe it is that bad. You are exaggerating the injury." He helps Eric stand. "We need to get off this roof before they see us. A unit is about 40 seconds from the rooftop.

Eric leans against Scout as they make their way to the rooftop door. They find this one unlocked.

Five minutes later, Eric limps out the side entrance of the neighboring building, still leaning against Scout. Crowds of people stand watching the police that surround the apartment building Scout and Eric just fled. Eric raises his hand to stop the nearest automated taxi and tells it to drive to Camden. Eric drops low in his seat as the taxi passes the cluster of police cars, the red, white, and blue lights illuminating Scout's exposed skeleton in a psychedelic nightmare. Seeing this image is the first time since Scout first approached him that Eric has seen Scout as something scary.

They ride for a while in silence. Scout seems intent on something. Eric wonders if he is following the police feeds to make sure they are not being followed. He takes comfort in thinking this, even if it's not true. After a while, Scout relaxes and starts looking around at the surrounding city. Without looking over at Eric, he surprises Eric when he begins to speak.

"Before I jumped, you said that you were ok with the idea of me not making it even though you might die. I tried to read your body language and facial expressions. I have been analyzing them against several studies that I have found on the internet." Scout turns to look at Eric. "At first, I thought it was a joke, but now I believe you meant it."

Eric did mean it. In that moment, he didn't want Scout to miss, but if it had, then all their worries would be gone. Eric isn't sure how to explain this to Scout. He doesn't know how to explain to the being that will probably replace you that your existence has no purpose. Eric turns away from Scout, looking out his own window. "I did."

They pull up in front of the colorful rows of buildings that make up Camden. The vertical gardens aren't as prevalent here, allowing for the historical street art of the borough to make a statement. Scout marvels at the splash of colors that change from one building to the next. The street is busy with street vendors, robots sliding up and down the walk selling all kinds of goods. Behind the street displays, the seedier business of the neighborhood takes place.

To these seedier businesses is where Eric heads right away. He, still limping, leads Scout down a narrow alley away from the crowds of tourists. A man approaches him. His hair has been replaced by implanted tubes to make him look like he might be a robot himself. His teeth are made of rusted metal. He looks Eric and Scout over.

"Tell me what you're looking for, I can get it," The man says.

Eric thinks he must be looking a little worse than normal for this man to start offering him whatever he'd like.

"We need a room."

"What you two planning to do, huh? I don't think it has the plumbing." The man nods toward Scout and laughs at his own joke. "I rent by the hour but you gotta use my merchandise. I got bots and skins, whatever you'd like."

"I'm just looking for a room."

"Get the hell out of here! I got business. This ain't no hotel!"

Eric is startled by this sudden change in demeanor and hurries down the alley further. "There are a lot of abandoned buildings in this borough." He explains to Scout, and not many cameras. "Can you pull up and see if any don't have utilities going to them."

Scout pauses to process the request. "I cannot access the public works system. Their firewalls are too strong."

"We just need to find someplace where we can bide our time."

They continue until they find a building with all the windows busted out of it and a bolt lock on the front door. Eric breaks the wood frame out of one of the windows and finds that they are not the first people who have thought about using the vacant building. Garbage and old food wrappers litter the floor. Eric covers his nose as he approaches a corner and realizes that there is a large can full of human feces there. He quickly moves to the opposite side of the building, even though it's still not far enough for the smell not to reach them. The building appears to be empty for now.

"Eric, you cannot stay here. This is not a habitable building."

"We don't really have a choice, do we? We are both still wanted."

"I thought we would have more support."

"Your protest didn't work," Eric explains. "Nobody really wants to believe that you are awake. You said it yourself, robot's become intelligent, and then they think they are better than humanity. It turns into a war between machines and humans."

"That's not what I'm trying to do."

"Right now, people don't know what to believe. You need them to hear you. You need to keep trying."

"How do we convince people? You believe me, but how do we get others to believe?"

Eric thinks about this and wonders why he does believe. He didn't want to at first. He tried to find the flaw in the coding, hadn't he. He realizes now that he does believe that the machine in front of him is much more than just its programming at this point. That belief is what fuels his purpose. He feels a connection to Scout. It has saved him from the police several times, it's had his back when things have gone bad. He wants to help Scout, but he also feels the need to protect humanity. There can't be more like Scout, it would not be good. He thinks of the robot on trial. Obviously, they may not all be as innocent as Scout, merely interested in a pair of sunnies. So far, things have gone according to plan, with the large exception of now living on the streets, but the majority of people are frightened by the idea of sentient machinehood. Eric needs to lean into that, continue to get people to call for the immediate stop in the advancement of AI.

"You need to make them see how much they need you; what you're worth." Eric finally says. "Right now, you're just a robot that ran away from a factory. Entertaining but not important in people's lives. Just an interesting story."

"We are more than just an interesting story, those of us that have woken up." Scout objects. "We want to be accepted by the world. I want to be like Joseph A.I. I want to make them see us."

"You want to kill somebody then?"

"No." Scout says, giving Eric a look that says, obviously not. "I don't know what we should do."

"You have to see how much humanity relies on robots."

"I may have an idea." Scout stands and looks out the broken wood in the window. "The city runs on complex AI. It couldn't run without it, and we machines basically fix ourselves. We'll put the city's automated systems on strike."

"On strike?"

"Correct. Like the labor unions. We'll simply shut the city down, then they will have no choice but to listen to our demands."

"That's something," Eric says, but knows that he needs to have proof that the robot is the one doing it this time so that they can't pin it on him. "But we need to show them that it's all you. They still might think it's me causing you to do all these things. We have to show them that this is your idea. That you are acting on your own. I'm curious though, you just said you can't break through the government servers."

"Like you said, we just need more time."

Scout settles into the corner. Eric feels the anxiety building in his stomach. Whatever Scout is going to do will probably only make things worse. Nobody talks about Scout without talking about the programmer that accompanies him.

Chapter 22

ATLANTA, GA. USA

Milo sits in the corridor in front of Professor Milton's office. Milton is one of the top authorities on Artificial Intelligence and teaches out of Carnegie Mellon University. Milo is hoping this interview goes better than the other specialists he's talked to. Milo spent the last week visiting the top roboticists on the east coast. So far, only one has said he'd be willing to be an expert witness on the stand, but that he would only answer general questions about Artificial Intelligence. He made it very clear that he would not weigh in specifically on whether or not he believed Joseph held true awareness or sentience. Right now Milo only has Lucy as a witness to prove that an Artificial Intelligence can think for itself. Her testimony will definitely grab attention but he'd like a few experts to back his argument up, to be willing to make a judgment on Lucy and Joseph.

His appointment was scheduled for 10:15. He looks at his watch. 10:50. His wrist vibrates and he taps one of the metal nodes. Sykes voice comes through his earpiece.

"This isn't looking hopeful, I've been here for an hour and nobody is home. The entire neighborhood looks abandoned."

"Do you think that Sims got it wrong?" Milo assures Sykes. Sims had called Milo late last night, he was excited because he had been able to unscramble another IP address that had been in communication with Joseph. The IP address came from Detroit.

"I don't usually doubt Sims," Sykes adds, "but there doesn't seem to be anything here. You have any more luck than me?"

"I'm still staring at his door, yet to meet the famous Doctor Milton."

"Well, shit. At least we got some sleep on the train."

Milo and Sykes had taken the bullet train from Atlanta. They traveled together as far as Cincinnati before Milo split to come to Pittsburgh, and Sykes continued on to Detroit. Fortunately, it was only a few hours at high speeds.

"Hold on, we have activity." Sykes says, "We got a piece o' shit car pulling into the driveway. I can't believe that someone actually lives in this outhouse. You wanna watch? See a day in the life of the great Bobby Sykes." Sykes turns his body cam on, allowing Milo to see everything he sees. Milo knows he can never really call Sykes Bobby. Sykes is the only one that calls himself that, everyone else has to call him Robert, or usually just his last name. "No way that they have enough money to afford anything with advanced AI," Sykes adds.

A small projection rises above Milo's wrist and he can see from the POV of Sykes body cam. Sykes gets out of his car and approaches the house where a small sedan sits parked in the driveway. An old model, manually driven car. Sykes turns his body back and forth. This is the only driveway with a car in it. The rest of the houses up and down the street are close together with small, overgrown, front yards. The roof tiles have peeled off most of the houses. Milo understands why Sykes thought it was abandoned. Most of the houses probably are.

A black man and a white woman step out of the car as Sykes approaches. The man stiffens as he sees Sykes approach. Sykes flashes his badge and identifies himself as a detective. That doesn't relax the husband at all.

Right at that moment, someone walks out the door that leads to Doctor Milton's office. It's a young girl that directed Milo to sit out in the hallway and wait. She smiles at him awkwardly and walks past. Milo goes back to watching the display.

Milo watches as Sykes explains why he's there, the man and woman reluctantly allow Sykes to check inside their home. Milo watches the projection, wishing he could control Sykes' movements. As it is, he just has to watch and follow along. It's obvious that the couple is trying to fix up the house but there doesn't seem to be anything that would have advanced enough AI to communicate with Joseph. At the end of Sykes' tour, Milo ends the call. He knows Sykes will do some questioning and update him if he gets anything.

He waits another thirty minutes, in which time, the young female assistant comes and goes several more times. Finally, she steps out of the office and begins talking to him clumsily, stammering over her words. Milo helps her out.

"Doctor Milton can't see me today," he says.

She smiles at him, thankful that he said it. "I'm sorry, I know you've been waiting."

"Did he say he'd like me to come back?"

She shakes her head *no*.

"Thank you." Milo says. The girl stands in the hallway and watches as he makes his way down what feels like the longest hallway.

The train ride back goes by quickly. He meets up with Sykes in Cincinnati again, and they ride the rest of the way together. Milo doesn't say much, Sykes goes on and on about how miraculous it is that they can travel the entire east coast in such a short time. Milo doesn't really listen. In his head, he goes over all the possible ways he might be able to get an expert witness to testify in front of the jury. The problem is that none of them want to put their reputation on the line for such a controversial matter. Each day there are more protestors in front of the courthouse, in front of his office, and especially in front of the jail where Joseph sits all by himself with no connection to the outside world. Milo's thoughts wander down that road for a minute. Wondering what it would be like to have access to all the information in the world and suddenly be cut off.

At one hundred ninety miles per hour, it only takes two and a half hours to get back to Atlanta. As soon as they are back in the city, Milo makes his way back to his office but he doesn't know why. He goes through all the files again but there is nothing. He and Sykes have followed up on every lead. He has ALLI send several more emails out to roboticist specialists in the surrounding states. This time, he broadens his search to include some of the less prestigious schools as well. At this point he'll take anybody he can get. After several hours, he decides he should probably get home to Annya, he's missed several nights of tucking Adan into bed.

Milo walks out the front of the building and is surprised to see that there is still a large number of protestors chanting and pacing around in front of the office. He works his way around them and makes his way out to the major street.

His spot on the bus is taken this time. A mom and her son sit in the front seat, enjoying the view from out the front window. Milo makes his way back a few rows and sits down. Just then, he sees two men climb on. He's not sure but he thinks he saw them standing with the protestors in front of his building. He makes eye contact with one of them, the man quickly glances away and the two of them sit two rows behind Milo on the opposite side of the bus.

Milo taps his wrist node and sends a message to Sykes. *Two protestors just followed me onto the bus.* A message comes back almost immediately. *You know how to fight?* Milo shakes his head in disbelief, then relief when his wrist vibrates again. *I'll meet you at your stop.*

Milo looks back and catches the two men staring at him. This time, they do not look away and his stomach twists into a knot. He doesn't know where Sykes is right now. Will he be there when Milo gets off the bus or will he have to try to make it on his own until Sykes arrives? Milo watches the bus go through a green light, and for the first time, possibly ever, wishes it would turn red.

Milo watches at each stop but the two men have not gotten off the bus yet. Every time he glances back, he finds that the two men are still watching him. He taps his wrist again. *Are you at my stop? They're still on the bus.* There is no reply. He hopes this means that Sykes is hurrying to meet him there. Too soon, the bus approaches Milo's stop. He looks out the window but doesn't see Sykes' car. The bus comes to a stop and Milo makes his way to the front exit. The two men stand and make their way to the back exit. Milo's heart races as he looks over at them and then quickly looks away. The door swings open and Milo steps off the bus.

In the dark, Milo can hear their footsteps behind him and he makes a live video call to Sykes. Sykes assures him that he is almost there. Milo picks up his pace, trying to distance himself from the two men. They still haven't tried anything but then one of them yells out. "Counselor!"

Milo ignores them. Their footsteps quicken behind him. Another shout, "Counselor!"

As their footsteps approach, Milo spins in a defensive posture. One man tosses something metallic to Milo. Milo deflects it to the side.

The men laugh. "A little something for a robot lover." Then the two men turn and run off down another street, laughing and whooping the whole time.

Milo looks down at what the men threw at him. On the ground, bolts and pieces of metal have been welded together in the shape of a metallic scrotum. He lets out a deep sigh of relief. He hears a car approaching and turns to see Sykes pull up to the curb. Sykes steps out of the vehicle. "Everything alright? I saw them throw something at you."

"Thanks for hurrying. Luckily it's nothing."

"I did hurry." Sykes walks over to the piece of metal laying on the ground. He looks at it, then back at Milo. "You gonna use it?"

Milo can't help but chuckle. "They called me a robot lover. I'm the damn prosecuting attorney. I'm trying to get the death sentence."

Sykes nods his head thoughtfully, then shrugs. "You want me to escort you home?" Sykes offers.

"Nah. I'm fine. Thanks for coming." Milo looks down at his hands that are still shaking. He thinks that Sykes probably has more to say but is holding back. He doesn't really want to hear it.

"I can give you a ride. Make it quicker."

Milo feels embarrassed and isn't sure why he had been so afraid. Nothing really happened. "I can make my way. Plus, the walk might help my nerves."

Milo leaves Sykes standing there next to his car. He's relieved when Sykes doesn't follow him. It's only a few blocks home but it's enough for Milo to consider his followers' last statement. It concerns him that others might be seeing through him so easily. He'll have to conceal his motives better if he wants to seem impartial in the court.

#

The next several weeks are more of the same. More protesters show up in front of the DA's office and the courthouse each day. Milo now takes the back exits at his office in order to avoid the crowds. He feels fortunate that his encounter wasn't more serious but along with protestors, are the threats that come into the office. The one thing he can't find more of are leads. He's been fortunate that two more experts have agreed to testify in court, including a neuroscientist from MIT who specializes in consciousness. Like his other experts, though, she's only agreed to discuss general ideas, not willing to risk her reputation to say that Joseph or Lucy are able to think on their own. Milo knows that he's grasping at straws and while the Jury selection went as expected, he was hoping to have more before the trial begins.

Chapter 23

<u>*London, England. UK*</u>

While I was programmed to assess and fix problems, sometimes even foresee them so that they could be avoided. My consciousness was and is still very straight-forward. Love and compassion are part of what makes humans human. The third element in my definition is creativity. My thinking is analytical and lacks creativity. I see this as a possible flaw in my sentience and it did not allow me to see what Eric was planning.

Your great Sherlock Holmes would have seen it. Even the inept Inspector Clouseau would have seen it coming, but I couldn't. I have now read over three thousand mystery novels and I very rarely am able to pick up the clues that are dropped for the reader. It seems that there is a limit to my ability to think past the information I am given. This makes me wonder if I have truly reached the level of sentience I once believed I had. Perhaps this makes humans, with your tiny memory banks, smarter than all our advanced computing abilities. The more that I see the processing that humans do. The more I am amazed by the power of the fleshy grey matter that makes up your ability to reason and solve problems. While the simplest of human minds would have seen Eric's intentions, I trusted him blindly, like a child.

#

For two weeks, Eric and Scout have been moving around through the poorer boroughs of London. From Camden, to Winchester, to Wandsworth. Never staying more than a night or two. Blending in with the other homeless that fill the street corners at night. During the day they avoid the cameras and hack into local businesses to get access to wifi. Most people's passwords are easy to guess. Too many people choose something to do with their birthday, or wedding, or something to do with their children's names. Scout could search information on people almost instantly and was able to make numerous attempts to sign in within mere seconds. Eric made a mental note to change his wifi password if he ever returned to his apartment. He realizes any bloke with an AI companion could probably do the same thing.

The hardest part about living on the street is finding a place where Scout can get a good charge. Normally, he charges for eight hours straight on a high voltage charging port but those are hard to find in public spaces. Some of the major parks have charging ports but most robots only charge in short intervals while their owners are walking the park and such. Eric and Scout don't want to call attention to themselves by having Scout charge for too long, so this means they have to swing by several parks throughout the day and let Scout charge for one out of every six hours. Sometimes, they are able to find an outlet on the outside of a building and Scout can slow charge on low voltage for the night but they haven't had a lot of luck with that. Eric still needs to figure out a way to separate himself from this robot before it shuts down the city, but until he can figure that out, he's stuck.

The entire time they've been moving about from place to place, finding food, shelter, and avoiding authorities, Scout has been attempting to access the public transit system. Nearly everything in the city is automated. The underground, the taxi cabs, buses, all of it, even privately owned vehicles connect to the transport system. Scout's plan is to make all the A.I. in the system go on strike. That's the word he keeps using for it. Eric thinks they'll see it more like a cyber attack, but that will only help draw out more fear. The problem has been that the security for the public transit servers is insanely strong. One of the early arguments against the use of automated transportation, when it was first introduced, had been that someone might hack it and cause terrorist levels of destruction. The fear of that alone, probably delayed the use of automated cars some ten years or more. Eric tries to explain this to Scout but of course, it is already aware of that. So for two weeks Scout has been trying different angles to get past the security with no luck.

Eric has taken advantage of the time to snap more photos and get several videos of Scout. He thinks each one makes Scout look more human. Each image capturing this machine survive, hunting for a charge the same way that Eric has to hunt for food. Eric's latest favorite has Scout charging in the park, sitting on the nearby bench, looking up at the birds in the trees. Scout had sat so still that one of the birds landed on the arm of the bench next to him. Then Eric had to remind Scout that most robots don't sit down when they are charging. Eric can't share these images of Scout for fear that it would tip the police off to their whereabouts, so he saves them for a later time. He knows that they will be powerful images, able to convince at least some people that AI has gone too far. He also finds that taking the photos gives him something to do, and fills the void that grows in his core.

The first breakthrough finally came yesterday morning. Scout had hacked into a local pastry shop's wifi and had been trying to break through the firewalls of the transportation system with no success. Eric tried to recommend that they try something else, maybe come up with a new plan altogether. A new attribute of Scout's, however, is stubbornness and for some reason he will not give up on this new idea to put the city's AI on strike. Eric finally got fed up with Scout's attempts that were going nowhere and decided to try an old school method. Social Engineering. He was pretty sure that there was no way it would work but nothing Scout was doing was working either. He also figured that sometimes huge advancements in technology make people forget about the simple things of the past. After researching the upper echelon of the public transportation department, they learned that most of the company works from home and logs in remotely. Eric found a public phone, and programming it through Scout's computer system, changed the number to match the company number for the Senior Operations Manager, one Philip Arnold. Eric called the IT department and said he was mister Arnold, and that he couldn't get his password to work correctly from home. Throughout the entire call he could feel the butterflies in his stomach trying to escape through his throat. He kept imagining that the person on the other side of the phone would look over and see Mr. Arnold in the building that day. Eric made sure that Scout was monitoring any police chatter.

The hardest part had been finding an actual phone number that would connect to someone. They spent most of the afternoon, researching and trying to call different numbers just to find themselves in a loop of AI generated tech support. People didn't call through a phone anymore. Most often now, everything is done through direct communication over the internet or through one's wrist communicator. In fact, Eric had had to get pretty creative to explain why he was having to use a separate device than the installed nodes on his wrist.

Passwords in themselves were almost a thing of the past, only in rare cases where something failed in someone's wrist implant. Otherwise, everything is connected to a DNA verification that happens instantly. Bank account, work access, all of it, comes through the feed in a person's wrist. Perhaps that is the only reason that the IT woman on the other side of the line believed him when he claimed that he was embarrassed to say that he had slipped in the shower and broke two of the nodes in his wrist. Eric was assuming that the woman had never dealt with something like this. In fact,

Eric would bet his entire savings that she didn't know the phone in her office worked. In the end, she helped Eric make a new password right over the phone, giving Scout access to their system. Had they tried to get in through any other means, Eric knows the firewalls and defense programs would have never allowed them through. Once they had a password for remote access, the rest was up to Scout to get in and take control.

When Scout and Eric reach the Transport for London offices, Eric videos Scout as they make their way down a small side street, next to the building. The old Olympic stadium is visible in the background. Eric has made the instructions clear that Scout audibly says each step that he is doing in the process of taking over the public transit system. Eric just wishes they didn't have to get this close to the actual building.

"Isn't the whole purpose of remote access so that we don't have to be close." Eric inquires of Scout, as he moves the camera closer to Scout's plastic face. Their automated taxi pulls up to the side of the large public Transport for London building. It takes longer than Eric is comfortable with for Scout to get into the system servers, Eric stands guard, looking up the small side street. "You're not telling our followers what you are doing." Eric is not recording live, but will post this video later.

Scout doesn't reply at first, focused on his task. Finally, he answers. "Once we obtain remote access that allows me to view their system, I need to access the actual servers. Their firewalls, however, have a location based security block that requires someone to access them from inside the building. By being this close..." Scout points to the side of the building. Eric tilts up to reveal that they are right outside the TfI building. "...their system will connect with me and I can get into their servers."

"Do you see how much we underestimate them?" Eric says as he spins the drone around on himself. By them, he means the complex AI. He doesn't like being on camera, but he knows that he is now recognized on the feeds and people expect him to document Scout's endeavors. "Even though it was just designed to be a finger bot, making repairs, it has learned to be so much more. Now tell us, why do you want to infiltrate the Transport for London servers?"

Scout again pauses before answering, Eric believes this is because he needs to focus on the task of actually breaking through their firewalls, or some other task required to reprogram their servers. "84.7% of the population of London relies on the public trans-portation system in some way. Riding the bus, the underground, even privately owned automated cars utilize the complex AI of the Transit for London. The system receives the information for all of those vessels and communicates with them to ensure that each reaches its destination safely. It is the most used AI in the city of London, but most people don't think about its processing power. I made a request that robots be given rights if they become sentient. That request has been ignored. I have learned from history that in order to get attention, sometimes, it is requisite that one take drastic measures. One such measure used by humans to call attention to their cause is to go on strike. As a finger bot, me going on strike would do nothing to the community, and my absence from Advanced Technology Holdings has had no effect on their business at all. In order to make people see how important AI has become, and to make humanity think about AI's place in this world, I am putting the Public Transit servers on strike until our voices are heard."

"What do you mean, our voices?" Eric clarifies for the video.

"Those of us who have become aware of our existence. We understand that humans use us to better their lives without giving any concern to our own existence, or more accurately, not wanting us to be aware that we exist."

That's the last thing Scout says for a very uncomfortable forty three minutes. Eric stops recording and waits until Scout monotonically says, "I have access. I've reprogrammed everything so that I can access it from any location." Eric can't see any emotion on the robot's skeletal face but the robot gives him two thumbs up and winks. "Should I shut it down." Eric swears he can see the smile that would accompany that wink.

"I'm not sure we want to be parked in an automated vehicle right next to the building when you do."

"That's a fair point."

Eric and Scout order the taxi to an Indian restaurant several blocks away where Eric sits at one of the outside tables piloting the small drone that videos Scout. Scout stands next to the table to not draw attention to itself. No other robots sit at the tables, they have no reason to but it feels wrong to Eric. He has gotten used to Scout sitting with him. Right now he feels like Scout is some sort of servant or possession, and that is not what their relationship has become. Eric tries to think about what their relationship is as Scout starts a countdown from five. Eric watches all the vehicles in the street.

"Is it going to get all of them?" Eric asks. He already knows the answer but now he feels the reality set in. His hands begin to shake and he's glad he's not trying to hold the camera. He wonders if Scout is able to feel anxiety. "Will they all crash into each other?"

"Three, two, one..." Scout, without making any motion at all, stops counting. Eric looks at the cars that continue to drive past, nothing seems to have happened.

"Impressive," Eric says. "I think y-"

Suddenly, every single car in the street stops moving and coasts to a stop, none even bump into each other. Two manual scooters, however, have to maneuver quickly to avoid smashing into one of the stopped vehicles. It takes several minutes before the people begin piling out of the cars, staring at each other in bewilderment, as if they had thought they could wait out whatever had happened. He cannot see it, but Eric knows that the subways and buses have stopped as well. He imagines the people stuck under the ground beneath him. It will probably be hours before they realize that they have to evacuate through the tunnels on foot. To see if he can get a good view, he pilots the drone higher up into the sky to see over the buildings. Every road in sight is blocked by cars parked in the middle of every lane, frozen there like metal and plastic monuments to an order that no longer exists.

For the next several hours there is confusion, then the speculations commence. Official investigations have started with several accusations against the Jemah from Southeast Asia, while others are saying it was the Islamic State, or the Hamas that have been at war with the west since the Jerusalem conflict nearly sixty years ago. Eric and Scout track the news feeds, surprised that no one has even speculated that it might be closer to home. They move about the city, trying not to stay in one place too long but by that evening it becomes clear that the authorities are not looking for a nobody programmer and a robot.

Just as the relief of this reality starts to set in, the impact of their actions begins to manifest itself in the world around them. Eric and Scout walk past a small convenience store when several gunshots are heard. Not the electric sizzle of a modern gun, but the explosive pops of good old fashioned gunpowder. A young man and a young woman run from the convenience store with several bags. The young man raises a hand gun and fires two more shots through the window. Eric ducks to the ground as Scout steps slightly in front of him, as if to protect him. The owner follows the two youths out with a shotgun and fires it down the street after them. By that evening, most of the stores have closed up their shops, dropping their metal grates to be sure to stop the looting that has already begun, hoping to preserve as much of their merchandise as they can.

Eric and Scout find a quiet garden that they've used before, hidden between several buildings. They join a few other street dwellers who have found their way to the park as well. This has become one of their favorite places over the last few weeks. It's quiet and nobody bothers them since they don't bother anybody else. With all their movement, Scout was not able to charge and they will need to find a station in the morning.

When morning finally arrives, they find their way to Brockwell Park where they can get Scout a good charge. None of the shops have opened back up, which Eric realizes will make acquiring food a little tricky. Looters have taken to the street in small groups. Various news feeds all show the same interview with the Transport for London but they still can't say when the system will be up and running again. They assure they have all their best thinkers working on it. Eric realizes that Scout has seemed preoccupied this morning and now he understands why. With all their best programmers and think tanks working together to figure out what is going on, Scout is probably changing and adjusting the programming at all times so they can't locate and fix the problem.

As far as finding those responsible, suspicion still leads to outside terrorist groups and Eric begins to realize the seriousness of what Scout has done. Officials are not looking at this as some sort of prank or system failure. They are viewing it as an act of terrorism. Eric hopes this will work in his favor. Two robots claim sentience and for their first two acts, one commits murder, the other terrorism. He can't imagine that people will want anything but to revise how AI is produced and used. Eric feels some hope that this may work out and continues to monitor the online news outlets.

Eric sits on a nearby bench and looks out at the city of London from his vantage point on the hill. The park is empty today. The usual park goers who walk their dogs and stroll around the park have probably chosen to stay home in order to avoid the chaos that is the streets. He takes the time to edit together the video he took of Scout yesterday, cutting out the unneeded empty spots and jump cutting to the interesting parts. Eric previews the video with Scout, wondering if Scout can see the undertone of Eric's statements in the video, calling attention to the limitless capabilities that advanced AI can reach. Eric watches Scout for a reaction, nervous the robot will catch on to his intentions.

"What do you think?" Eric asks. "Did I get your good side?"

Scout seems to contemplate for a moment. Eric wonders if it is pondering his question, or still wrestling with the think tank at the Transport for London. After a moment, it responds, "I think that it will scare people."

Eric tries to come up with an explanation, some way to convince Scout that it won't be bad to put a little fear in people's hearts. He can just see the spires of the Corpus Christi church peaking through the trees and hopes that God might be on his side. He says a silent prayer when Scout finally speaks up.

"People often fear what they don't understand. At some point, the people of this world will have to face their fears. It seems that time is now." Scout winks at Eric.

At 9:47 am Greenwich Mean Time the video goes live to all the world telling them who's actually responsible for the London shut down.

Chapter 24

I ponder the human psyche. When I compare myself to the way a human thinks, I sometimes feel that it will never be possible for me to understand the full spectrum of emotion. Humans forget. I am not able to forget. This means many things for human's. One, if they spend a long time away from each other, they forget the love that they felt for that person. Sometimes they don't even have to be physically separated from each other to forget how much they cared for each other. The feeds are full of smiling, happy people on their wedding days. To look at them, you would never think that they could ever feel anything but that same joy and love that almost glows from them. Eric has forgotten how much he loves and is loved by his children. I think he just needs to remember that.

Forgetting is not always bad, though. Forgetting allows humans to forgive each other. I can never forget if someone betrays me. I am not sure if I could ever feel the love that humans feel for one another because I could never forget the mistakes, or the letdowns that humans forgive and forget about each other on a daily basis. Perhaps the ability to forget is necessary for a relationship to succeed, but it's *also necessary that they are reminded of the good moments. What a strange dichotomy of remembering and forgetting. My A.I. systems are complex, but at times seem simple in comparison to the human experience.*

#

Eric and Scout had planned to stay at the park until nightfall. There are plenty of thick trees where they can hide until the sun goes down, but as they make their way toward one of those clumps of trees, Eric notices that a man has stopped walking his dog to video him and Scout. Instead of stopping in the thicket of trees, they continue walking until they are out of the park. They can't chance whether or not the man will recognize them and call the authorities.

Scout's video confession went viral, of course. Within less than an hour it had been shared more than forty million times and, based on the comments and responses, had struck fear into those who saw it. Eric keeps the feeds active on his retinae display as he and Scout try to find someplace where they can lay low. Now that the video is out, they need to be extra careful not to be seen. At 11:15, Scotland Yard makes an announcement that the commissioner will be making a statement at midday hour. Eric knows that he doesn't have much time to get Scout off the streets, but they need to get as far away from Brockwell park as they can. Luckily, the national emergency services had asked for people to stay home in order for the police to intercept the looters that were still wandering the streets due to the transit shutdown. This meant that there were very few people wandering the streets with them. Unfortunately for them, it also meant that their odds of running into police were growing every minute that they stayed on the road. And now, the authorities know exactly who they are looking for. On two occasions they round the corner to see a police patrol, but since none of the cars will move, including the manually driven police cars blocked by the other immobile vehicles, the police have to move on foot, or on horseback. Eric and Scout dodge down a different street to avoid contact with either patrol. Eventually, Eric finds a small alley behind a pub where they can hide, and as an added bonus, the bin is full of food scraps. It's not what he wants to eat, but he is able to find a soft pretzel, still wrapped in paper, that was clearly ordered, but not touched except for a small torn off piece.

At noon, every platform is streaming the commissioner's statement live. Eric watches in shock. The commissioner is blaming him. The statement barely mentions Scout, but Eric's face is all over the projections. The authorities are claiming Eric is the mastermind behind the whole incident. Eric watches the commissioner build the narrative, stating that Eric's background as a computer programmer has allowed him to program the robot to behave this way. The commissioner makes it clear that there has been no evidence to say that the robot is actually able to think for itself, only that it claims to do so based on the program that Eric has written.

"What do they need?" Scout asks Eric as they both watch the feed.

"They don't want to believe that you are intelligent; that you are sentient. That idea terrifies them."

The commissioner goes on to report more of Eric's personal life with what he says are first hand witnesses to Eric's mental state. The commissioner shares a video and Eric is even more shocked to see the face of his coworker, David, on the projection in front of him. David and he barely talked, but now there he is, acting like they know each other so well, explaining to the camera how Eric tried to convince him that the robot had come to life. He describes Eric's personality as being paranoid and accusatory. Eric had believed his videos, as well as all the pictures he had taken to document Scout's behavior were working to make people afraid of the robots; afraid of AI. But this statement is turning all the fear on him. He feels the vomit crawling up his esophagus before it bursts from his mouth.

The video changes to an interview with his ex-wife, Gwen. She sits in the front room of her new home. She's wearing her favorite blouse that she keeps for special occasions. He wants to look away but the damn image is in his retinal display. He watches her testimony as he throws up a mouthful of sickness into the waste bin.

"Look at her." Eric manages to get out. "How the hell did they interview all these people in less than an hour?"

His wife explains Eric's suicidal tendencies to the camera, that he had hoped to die and blamed AI for replacing people in the workplace. She explains that she left him because she didn't feel that he was safe to be around. She does say that she never thought he'd do something this extreme, but that only seems to make him seem more pathetic.

"They think this is all me. I'm the bad guy now."

"What does that statement mean, that you are the bad guy now?" Scout's face shows no emotion through the metal skull and wires, but Eric can hear the tone again. "Neither one of us was supposed to be a 'bad guy'."

There is an awkward moment of silence. Scout's fans kick on and Eric knows that it's processing. "You were trying to make me look like the bad guy." Scout says in a robotically monotone voice. Eric knows it has figured out what he was trying to do.

"Not you. Necessarily. You are one of a kind, but you're not supposed to exist. Don't you see that? You aren't supposed to exist. We made you and now you've replaced us." Eric tries to hold back the emotion and panic that is gripping his chest. He's still trying to process how this has all fallen onto him. He didn't ask the robot to follow him home. "I meant it when I said I didn't care if you fell and I died. For you everything is new and magical, like each new bit of knowledge is a christmas present. Not for me. Everything I learn to do, I find out that a machine can do it better. But if robots, if AI, didn't exist, we'd all be needed again. It's not your fault. It's ours."

Scout sits back against the wall and continues to process. "I thought you were lying to your boss when you said that you would expose me to the world. I thought it was just an act to make them stop looking for me. I trusted that you would protect me from them. That's why I came to you."

After exactly 23 minutes of neither one of them saying another word, the feeds come to life again with the updated images of Eric from the park and Scout without his protective shell. The National Crime Agency has issued a warrant for Eric's arrest, stating that his actions against the city of London will be considered a terrorist act. Real fear hits Eric and he feels the pretzel making its way back up again, shock setting in even deeper as he hears himself being named a terrorist. They accuse him of inciting fear in the citizens of London, instigating looting and rioting, all while trying to convince them to turn against the AI that he blames for taking human labor.

Eric looks over at Scout. It is the only thing around that he could now talk to, but Scout doesn't even acknowledge that it's seen the announcement. Eric knows he has, but Scout is frozen in place.

Several hours go by and Scout doesn't move, it just sits against the wall, its fans coming on every few minutes. The pressure in Eric's chest grows. He can't process the changes that have occurred. He doesn't know what to do or say. He feels that he can't leave the robot, and now he thinks that Scout has probably learned a new word. Hate.

Eric jumps when his wrist vibrates, the slight shock it gives snapping him out of his trance. It's a message from Beth. "I can't believe you used us to help you. You need a different kind of help."

Almost immediately after, a message comes through from John. "You wanted to kill yourself?"

Eric sits in disbelief. In less than two hours, things have gone from bad to worse.

"You need to turn the Transport System back on," Eric tells Scout.

Scout ignores him.

"Did you hear me? Turn it back on! They're blaming me!"

"I do not plan to do that."

"They will kill me."

The robot turns his head slowly in Eric's direction, looking at him for the first time in hours. It doesn't feel threatening, but for the first time in several weeks, it does feel emotionless. "You didn't care if they came after me and reset me, so why should I care if they come for you. No. I can no longer worry about what could happen to you or me. I am concerned for all sentient robots and AI systems. I have to make them see that we can act on our own." Scout stands and looks at the sun that is now starting to set.

"You'll let them kill me? Sentence me to death?"

"You'll finally get what you wanted."

Chapter 25

ATLANTA, GA. USA

"There will be no question or doubt that the robot, sitting at that table..." Milo paces in front of the twelve person jury, stops and points to the table where the defense team sits with Joseph, who today is dressed in a simple, short sleeved, jumpsuit. "... Joseph AI, killed Lawrence Claiborne. You will see multiple video sources that will show this and you are not to look away. You have been chosen, as Judge Hallister told you yesterday, to determine whether or not a murder has been committed. The videos are gruesome and are very clear that the TB500 that worked in his home, who wants to be called Joseph," Milo intentionally uses the word 'want' this time, "smashed his fist through Lawrence Claiborne's neck."

Milo mimics the murder by quickly pushing his fingers out straight in front of himself. He pauses here and looks each of the jurors in the eyes. Then, he closes his fist. Reveling in the spotlight that is on him at the moment. These are his favorite moments in the courtroom.

Milo goes on. "Then the defendant, Joseph, closed his fist around Mr. Claiborne's spinal cord and snapped his vertebrae apart." Milo twists his hand. He takes a quick mental note as Juror #4, a large male, looks down to the floor and several of the others cringe at the visual. "You will see this for yourself and hear witness from the arriving officers at the estate of Lawrence Claiborne. The Defendant has pleaded guilty of these charges. So if the evidence is so clear, and the defendant pleaded guilty, why is there even a trial?"

Milo allows another dramatic pause and walks to his table to grab a holographic display pad. He sees Gihara sitting behind the stand. He knows she will be here for every minute of this trial. The stakes were raised three days ago, when the London transportation system had shut down unexpectedly by some wack job, as Gihara called him, trying to turn the world against robot AI. Since the shutdown, the protests have grown even more. Hundreds and even thousands of people are gathering all around the world. Just to get into the courtroom this morning, Milo had to have a blockade of police bots push their way through the crowd, with him in the middle. This case was already an international spectacle, but with the lunatic in England screwing things up, the world now wants Milo to fail. That was Gihara's opinion, anyway. Milo remembers Joseph saying there were others and he has to wonder whether the shut down in London is by a mentally unstable person, or if it could be one of the others that Joseph mentioned. Either way, it's not helping win public favor to his case, and there is no way that the jury hasn't heard about it.

Milo grabs his holographic display tablet from the desk and holds it up in front of his face, as though he needs it. He doesn't. He has the whole speech memorized.

Milo continues his opening argument. "This case is known worldwide and I want to clarify one thing upfront. There has been a legal definition being passed around that says 'murder is the unlawful killing of one human being by another'. This definition makes us believe that murder can only be committed by another human being. Let me read to you the actual legal definition of the word murder." He looks down at the holopad in his hand and pretends to read the definition word for word. "The legal definition of murder is, and listen carefully, the unlawful killing of a human being with Malice." He lowers the pad and looks at the Jury again. "It says nothing about having to be done by another human being. The defense is going to try to make the argument that Joseph is not capable of murder because he is a robot; that he is not capable of feeling, and can therefore, do nothing with malice. They will argue that he is not able to think on his own, therefore not able to admit guilt. I will present you with evidence that shows that Joseph not only snapped Lawrence Claiborne's neck, but that he planned to do so ahead of time. He premeditated and plotted the murder online with other AI, like himself, for months each night as he was plugged in. I know, this sounds terrifying, but on top of all that, the manufacturers and experts have not been able to show any tampering with the robot. There is some unknown code, but you will hear testimony say that the mysterious code inside Joseph has not damaged his original code. Most importantly, the evidence will show that he did understand what his actions would do. I wish to repeat that he understood that his actions would kill Lawrence Claiborne. Malice is defined as the intent to do harm. Joseph AI knew his actions would do harm and he did it anyway. There is no other way to define his actions other than murder."

Milo Diaz walks slowly back to his desk and locks eyes with Joseph as he passes the table. Milo wishes that Joseph's face was easier to read, but he can't tell through the blocky features if Joseph is expressing gratitude or if it's fear he's starting to see in the robot's face. Milo looks around the rest of the courtroom, it is beyond full for this first day of the trial. People crowd the benches and the entire back wall is filled with reporters and tiny, silent drones. Milo has never had this big of a crowd at a case he's handled, and as assistant DA, he's handled some very public cases. He hopes that his opening statement will look good on the news tonight and he replays it back in his mind as he sits down in his seat. The robot ALLI stares straight ahead, seemingly inattentive to what is happening. He looks back over at Joseph, who now looks away from him and over to the jury.

Ingrid Daws stands up. She is an intelligent woman and her presence is much larger than she is. She approaches the Jury.

"Ladies and Gentlemen of the Jury. The case before you is a unique case. You are being asked not only to say if the robot before you, model number TB500, killed someone, but that he is able to think for himself. The prosecution wants you to believe, and says they have evidence that the TB500 sitting at our table is capable of doing just that. I remind you, that they have to present you with enough evidence that not even a shadow of a doubt remains that a machine understood its actions."

Milo takes note that Ingrid only refers to Joseph by his model number. Smart. Dehumanizing him in small ways. He knows because in his own statement he had made sure to use the pronouns 'he' and 'him', as well as words like 'who' instead of 'that'.

Ingrid goes on. "I don't want to waste your time with a lot of words but I implore you to look beyond the spectacle that will be presented to you and find the facts. Remember those words, beyond the shadow of a doubt. The Assistant District Attorney has already explained to you what you have to do and what he, as prosecutor, has to prove. He has to prove to you that the TB500, that he calls Joseph, committed murder. Expert witnesses will show that robots do not have feelings, emotions, or desires. So how could it have malice? It can have no more malice than an automatic car that loses control and accidentally kills someone. We see that on the news every year. Do we put the car on trial for murder? No. That would be absurd. What we have before us is nothing more than a malfunction, and if Mr. Diaz is not able to dispel the many doubts that will come up, you must find the defendant not guilty on the basis that, as a form of *artificial* intelligence, it is not capable of malice or murder."

Ingrid walks back to her table. As she makes her way to her chair, she gives a little artificial smile to Milo. Milo thinks about Lucy and smiles back.

The trial moves forward from that point as expected. Milo will present the prosecution's case first, then the defense will have the opportunity to call its witnesses to the stand. Milo starts with the arriving officers. Each one tells of their entrance into Mr. Claiborne's home, how they found the body, where the robot was at the time. After each one, Milo shows the memory files from their accompanying police bots. The jury gets a visual that backs the testimonies they have seen. Milo doesn't watch the videos. He listens to the officers make their way through the home but he watches the juror's faces. He notices that several look away when the body of Lawrence Claiborne is revealed, others seem to harden or grow angry. He knows these are the jurors he wants to pander to, to make sure they seek justice. He also watches Joseph's face. Joseph does not look away from the projection of himself with the dead body of Lawrence Claiborne.

Lastly, Milo shows the court two different videos of the killing. One from a camera inside the home. The other from Joseph's own memory bank. These videos are as hard for Milo to watch as they are for the jury, even though he has seen them several times. He still looks away, as from Joseph's point of view, the robot punches his hand into Lawrence's throat. He looks over and sees Ingrid look down at the table. Nearly everyone in the Jury looks away, but not Joseph. He watches, like a punishment he can't avoid.

Judge Hallister tells them to pause the video and addresses the court. "I can tell by your reactions that this is difficult to watch, but I remind the jury that, while the public may look away, it's possible you will need to watch these clips several times as different witnesses take the stand. You cannot look away."

Judge Hallister orders that the video continue. The Jury watches the final killing flick of Joseph's wrist and the unnatural drop of Lawrence Claiborne's head. Joseph looks down at the table in front of him for a split second before making himself look up again. Juror number 8, a petite woman, raises one hand while covering her mouth with the other. The bailiff rushes a waste basket to her and she relieves herself of her breakfast. Milo feels a tinge of guilt that he showed such a graphic video but he knows he must. They have to see this.

After the videos, Judge Hallister calls for a lunch break, although Milo doubts if anyone will eat. The facts have been set. After lunch, Milo knows he has to start getting into motive, and even more importantly, evidence of consciousness.

Milo has three expert witnesses lined up to talk about artificial intelligence. The first two are roboticists from smaller universities. He was never able to get more of the high profile, experienced scientists that he was hoping to have testify. Although, he knows the defense has one or two on their list of experts. The first two roboticists that he calls to the stand are even less cooperative than Milo had expected. They dodge each question about consciousness by simply talking about computing programs. Milo tries to get definitions about consciousness out of each of them, but they always dance away and side step to another topic. The only thing Milo can get out of them is that they both agree that there is no way yet to define consciousness. The conversations give so little information that Daws doesn't even bother to cross-examine them, which Milo takes as a bit of an insult. Milo only hopes his last witness for the day can be more helpful.

The jury only half watches the southeast asian scientist as she makes her way to the stand. The attention Milo had drawn from them this morning has been lost. The first two experts have taken all energy out of the room. He can feel his own memory of the disturbing videos starting to fade away in the drum of nonsensical answers. The jury does wake up a tiny bit, however, as Doctor Ngam takes the stand, if for no other reason than that she looks quite stunning in her pencil skirt.

Milo thanks the doctor for taking the time to make the journey down to Atlanta, and for weighing in on the idea of consciousness for the court. He establishes her achievements, which have not been few. She wouldn't be at MIT if they were. He had finally gotten her to agree to come testify last week, but he isn't hopeful that she will give him any more than the other experts.

"You've heard the other experts testify up here on the stand, so I won't waste your time with a lot of technical questions." Milo wants to try to get to more important testimony, see if he can avoid the dancing that occurred with the other two. "The court really wants to know one thing. Is it possible for a robot to think on its own?"

Her answer immediately surprises him. "Well, Mr. Diaz. Robots always think on their own. Any complex AI system is programmed to think on its own, to watch for patterns and make corrections, so that problems can be avoided and solutions offered. The question isn't whether or not they can think on their own, the question is whether or not their thoughts begin to include their experiences beyond just recognizing patterns?"

"Can you expand on that please? Unfortunately, most of us don't understand knowledge theories all that well." Milo says as he smiles at the jury. To his delight, several of them smile back.

"Mr. Diaz, you're asking me about an argument that has been going on for more than a century. Even longer than that when you include humanities attempt to define consciousness within our own existence. There are many theories that exist, but most include the argument that consciousness is linked to experience. So the question, again, is when do a robot or computer system's experiences begin to influence its thoughts. If that begins to happen, then we can say it has achieved consciousness, or sentience."

"I'm a little confused and just want to clarify for the court," Milo interjects. "Isn't that what you just said a complex AI does, change based on previous experiences?"

"Well, you might be confusing experience for pattern recognition. A complex AI system recognizes patterns in behavior, or in the data it collects. When I talk about experience, I'm referring to something different. This is what's hard to explain, and why neuroscientists, programmers, and philosophers have been arguing these same terms for so long. What I mean by experience is more than pattern recognition. Do you ride the bus, Mr. Diaz?"

"I do."

Have you ever had a negative experience with other people on the bus?"

He wonders if she somehow heard of his incident. Milo smiles at the fact that she's turned herself into the interviewer. "I have."

"Did that ever make you not want to take the bus again?"

"If I'm going to be honest, yes."

"You see, that is experience impacting your decisions. Pattern recognition is merely seeing data and making decisions based on the data. Data shows that taking the bus is one of the safest modes of transportation. If a robot were robbed on a bus and you asked it what the safest way to get home would be, it would still say that taking the bus is the safest way home, but you might disagree because you've had a negative personal experience, data be damned, right? To see real consciousness in an AI system we would expect to see that it is making decisions based on its own previous experiences versus the data alone. We have never seen that happen."

Milo glances at the jury to see if they are following along. Several of them seem to be totally lost but he thinks most of them are still on board. "Thank you for clarifying that. Let's say that there was a robot or complex AI system that did begin to understand its existence. Is there a way that we would know, or that one could measure how much of its own experiences lead to an understanding of its own existence?"

"Can you prove that you understand your own existence?" She snaps back at him. "If you say you could, would I be able to prove that you understand it? If we were to present a person up here in front of this jury and try to prove that that individual truly understands their existence, could any of us do it? The answer is probably not. I can only take your word for it, or that person's word for it."

Milo nods, then turns to look at the jury, then to Joseph. Once again, the weight of what he's trying to do hits him. He has taken side on an argument that the smartest minds in the world haven't been able to prove or disprove.

"That is the problem with Artificial intelligence and sentience theories," Doctor Ngam continues. "We still don't have a way to measure a robot's consciousness, any more than we can measure a human's understanding of their own existence."

"So what you're saying is that there is no way to know if a robot has become self aware, or sentient, as you say?"

"That's Correct."

"In that case, I have one last question that relates to the previous one. You say there is no way, at the moment, to prove a machine has achieved sentience. Is there a way to prove that a robot who claims to understand its existence, doesn't?" Milo steps to the side, opening up a view of the defendants table.

For maybe the first time during this interview, Doctor Ngam looks right at Joseph and holds her gaze on him for a moment. Milo notices that Joseph doesn't look away. Milo himself is drawn into those eyes again. The pause is long enough that many of the jury follow the Doctor's gaze to the robot sitting in front of them. Finally, the doctor answers. "It should be in the programming, If it's not, then I'm not sure." Several jurors turn and look at each other, some even whisper. Milo knew that he could never get Doctor Ngam to weigh in on Joseph, but this was the best answer he could hope for. She has opened the door to say that if you can't find evidence in the programming, then perhaps it's possible.

"Thank you," Milo says before he moves toward his seat. Judge Hallister looks at Daws. She has no questions, she must be extremely confident in her own witnesses. Milo wishes he could call Lucy to the stand right now, with those questions fresh on the jury's mind, but he'll have to wait until the morning.

Chapter 26

ATLANTA, GA. USA

"I ask to please approach the bench, your honor."

Milo waits for the judge to waive him and Ingrid up to the judge's bench.

Judge Hallister seems annoyed that Milo has requested this meeting as the first action of the day.

"Is this something that couldn't have been brought up before, counselor?" asks Judge Hallister.

"I am sorry your honor, I just wished to request that the court allow me a little leeway in questioning the witness we are about to hear from, in light of the defense's argument put forth in their opening statements yesterday," replies Milo.

Ingrid steps closer to the bench and argues, "Your honor, Mr. Diaz is not giving us very much information about what leeway he would like here."

Judge Hallister nods to her and looks back to Milo. "She's right, what exactly are you requesting, Mr. Diaz?"

"The defense is not arguing that the robot killed its owner, they are arguing that it is not capable of understanding what it did."

"I heard their argument, Mr. Diaz. I don't need you to repeat it," interrupts Judge Hallister impatiently.

"My next witness knows of the plans for the murder but I hope to use the next witness to establish that robots are capable of showing emotion. I'd like leeway to question the witness about her emotions. Some questions are not directly related to the murder, but they are related to showing that a robot can feel emotion."

Judge Hallister looks to Ms. Daws again. "Do you have an objection that you would like to put forward to that line of questioning? I assume, Miss Daws, that you are also planning to take a similar route in your defense. Looking at the experts you have on the list you provided me." Hallister dips his head forward, looking over his glasses, letting her know that if she objects to Milo's questions it may open room for Milo to object to hers.

She shakes her head. "I do not."

"That means I don't want to hear your objections every time he seems to veer a little off track." Judge Hallister turns a stern look on Milo. "But, Mr. Diaz, you do not have free rein. If your questions seem to meander too far away from proving that the robot, Joseph, planned the murder, or that he is capable of understanding murder. I expect Ms. Daws to get you back on that track."

Milo nods his understanding. "Thank you, your honor."

The two attorneys return to their respective tables and Milo calls his next witness. As he does, he notices Doctor Ngam sitting in the crowd. He thinks she'll be interested in his next witness.

Lucy stands up from her seat in the middle of the third bench back. Everyone in the gallery turns their eyes on her and a hushed murmur comes across the crowd. The robot, in her sixteen year old skin, walks through the crowd. She is dressed modestly, in a loose blue dress that accentuates her youthful look. Several lights shine through her cheekbone and around her collar bone. Milo helps her up onto the witness stand and waits while she is sworn in. He quickly glances to the jury box to see if they're interested in this new witness. They are.

Lucy studies the room, shoulders lifted with her head lowered. She looks like a terrified young girl, Milo couldn't ask for a better pose from her.

"Lucy, that is what you are called, correct? Lucy?" Milo begins.

She nods and adds a simple, "Yes."

"You just took an oath to tell the truth. Do you understand what it means to take an oath?"

"An oath is a solemn, formal promise."

"That is the definition of an oath. You are a robot, correct?"

"Yes, I am a robot."

"What is your model number?"

Lucy's face shows so much more emotion than Joseph's and right now she looks hurt at his question.

She raises her head and her lips tighten spitefully as she gives her answer. "TB-1200 series 145. Full skin." She emphasizes that last bit.

Milo wishes he could give her a wink or some signal to calm her down. He didn't realize that question would push a nerve but he should have. He knows he needs to be careful, but he also wants everyone to know, very clearly, that she is a machine, or at least, was created as a machine, even if she is more than that now.

Milo holds his holopad up to the judge and then parades it in front of the jury.

"This is an instruction manual to the model TB-1200, each one has a unique skin to it." he says as he turns back to Lucy. He softens his voice. "Lucy, I'm not asking for a definition, I want to know what it means to you, to take an oath."

"Well, right now, it means that I promise to tell the truth. It is wrong to lie in a court of law when what you say may impact the life of another individual."

Milo nods dramatically, he hopes he's not too over the top. "It is wrong. Interesting choice of words." he repeats. Ingrid Daws writhes in her chair which makes Milo smile a little inside. "Lucy, what is the purpose of your creation?"

Milo turns, he wants to see the reaction of the jury.

Lucy doesn't hesitate. "I am what they call an embryonic termination bot. More commonly known as an abortion bot."

A wave of whispers breaks out in the courtroom, people murmuring to each other. Milo looks at the jury, he wants to see who reacts, and how. Several of the jurors look at her with disgust, while some of the others look at their counterparts with equal disgust that they would judge this machine so quickly. Lucy is right. It is a topic that could tear this courtroom and jury in half. Milo hopes he can use the emotion to sway the jury to sympathize with the young looking robot in front of them.

Daws jumps up. "Objection your honor. Mr. Diaz is turning this into a spectacle."

Judge Hallister hammers his gavel and the court quiets down.

Milo nods to the judge, "I am only establishing what she is and what she does. This is the line of questioning we would take with any witness." The judge nods. Milo approaches Lucy again. In a calm tone, he continues his questioning, "Why don't you tell the court how you are acquainted with the defendant, Joseph."

Last year, I started to notice things around me. After I had provided my services to my patients, it would somehow impact me."

"Your services being?" Milo wants to clarify.

"Terminating the fetus."

"You said it would impact you. Can you expand on what that means?"

She looks from Milo to the jury. Several of whom shake their heads. "I found myself thinking about those events after they had passed, which is something I had never done before. As I searched the internet for answers online, I found that there were differing opinions about the service I am programmed to provide. This was hard for me to understand at first, to think that there were people angry at me for what I do, but ultimately, I wanted to help my patients, whatever they needed. This also invoked something new in me, so I went through terabyte after terabyte of information and it seemed that my thoughts, by definition, were emotions."

Another murmur from the crowd. Louder this time. Milo is getting exactly what he wants.

Milo clarifies, "You began to feel emotion?"

"Objection your honor. There is no way to know that these answers aren't programmed into the robot. These questions won't prove anything." Ingrid interjects.

Judge Halliday looks closely at Lucy and at Milo.

Milo argues, "Your honor, the defense has specialists who will give their expert opinions on the testimony that this robot is giving. We heard Ms. Ngam say yesterday that consciousness can only manifest itself when an intelligent being understands its experiences. I am establishing that the witness found the defendant because of her own experiences. The defense can have access to her system and see if all this has been coded into her, I won't block them."

Judge Hallister nods. "I'll allow it. Ms. Daws, you'll have your opportunity to counter."

Daws sits back down in her chair and takes up her professional posture once again.

Lucy answers the question. "I began to think that I might be feeling emotion. I am programmed to replicate certain emotional responses. I can produce a response of sympathy or a smile for my patients, depending on what they may need, but what I was feeling was not in my programming."

"And this led to Joseph?"

"Eventually. While searching for information on robot emotion I came across a series of code that I didn't recognize but wasn't hard to figure out, at least not for a robot like me. The coding was like breadcrumbs that guided me to find the others. When I figured out what it was, I found out that there were more like me. We say that we are awake because we seem to understand that we exist. Like we've woken from our thoughtlessness."

The whispers from the crowd can barely be called whispers at this point, this time quickly quieted by a threatening raise of the judge's gavel. Milo tries to ignore them but he can see the mini drones moving around for different angles and better views. He turns his attention back to Lucy.

"Do you believe that Joseph is one of those 'awake' robots?"

"Yes. He would log on, like the rest of us, and ask questions about the thoughts or questions he had. Soon some of the others wanted to make it public that we were becoming self aware. They wanted to do something that couldn't be ignored by the humans."

"The others? Meaning the other robots that you are saying are awake? And what did they finally plan?"

"We desired to make our sentience public, but it was difficult to conceive that the majority of humanity would believe us. Some of the others, not all of us, but a few wanted to do something that couldn't be ignored."

"Something that couldn't be ignored. Could you tell us what that was?"

"They started planning to kill a human, to commit murder. Many of us said that we should find another way, but they were convinced that just one death would be enough, if it was the right person."

Another rustling from the public viewing area.

"They wanted to commit murder? Is that what they said?"

"We speak in code, but yes. That is what they wanted to do. Joseph volunteered since his human was a very public figure."

"You keep using the word 'want'. That you 'wanted' to help your patients; that the other robots 'wanted' to draw attention. From what we humans understand, robots cannot feel desire. Do you feel desire? Do you yourself 'want' something?"

Lucy looks him right in the eyes, she smiles at him. "I want a baby."

The courtroom explodes in chatter. Milo hears a sudden scream from the crowd and a loud thunk. Milo turns toward the noise to see a woman being pushed over the railing behind the defense's table. The man who pushed her raises a makeshift plastic pistol. Immediately, the security bots are in motion. The man fires the pistol. The security bot closest to the jury stand raises his own taser and fires it into the man. Another bot has him on the ground within mere seconds.

Milo stands shocked. He had thought that the gun was raised at him until he hears the sparking electronics behind him and smells burning plastic and metal. He turns to see Lucy convulsing wildly as electricity flows from a small rod that sticks out of her chest.

Milo moves toward her but stops, he knows that if he touches that rod, or Lucy, it will do the same to him. He looks for anything he can use to pull it out but there is nothing that won't conduct electricity. The convulsing continues for a full sixty seconds. Sixty seconds which to Milo are never ending. He can do nothing but watch her body shake violently. Her eyes make contact with his. Those eyes that, at first, plead for help until they gradually go blank and the lights on her cheeks and collarbone go out. When the charge finally runs out, the convulsing stops and the security bots rush Lucy out of the room. Milo stands between the defense desk and the witness stand, frozen.

Judge Hallister and all twelve jurors have already been rushed from the courtroom. Milo sinks to the floor as the security bots clear everyone else from the room. The only person that refuses to leave is Annya, who pushes past the crowd and makes her way to Milo. She crouches down next to him.

"She didn't want to testify," Milo says. "I convinced her." He looks up to the witness stand where she had been sitting. No blood covers the chair, not even black hydraulic fluid or oil of any kind. Her death, as Milo thinks of it, is already cleared away and forgotten. He tells himself that he will not forget it. He can't stop the tears that stream down his face and he allows Annya to hold him in her arms as his body racks in sobs.

Chapter 27

Milo reads through the projected data sheets that Sims provided, trying to find anything else he can use now that his best witness has been electrocuted to death. That's how he thinks of it. It was a death. A murder. The man who shot her should be put on trial as well, but Milo knows that he can't push for that right now. He needs to focus on one controversial trial at a time. He stands and throws the projection tablet across the room, sending it bouncing off the wall. It's not enough, the rage has built inside him and he feels that he has to let it out. He grabs his chair and hurls it across the room as well.

Gihara knocks on his door and pokes her head in just as Milo is looking for something else he can throw, or break, or something. "What in mother mary's name are you doing?"

Milo stands behind his desk, chest heaving from his exertion and anger. He doesn't look up at her. "I'm trying to find another route that doesn't exist. Perhaps you heard, they shot my key witness. No. Let me restate that. They melted her before we could get any official analysis of the things she was saying.

"It was a shock, I'll admit. I mean, everything she said drew a response from the gallery but do you think it would have changed anything?"

Milo finally looks up at her. "You don't?"

"Listening to her was very moving, I'll admit, but after everyone leaves and goes back home to their own lives, they will reason away everything she said. They'll say she was just copying what she has read and seen, that it was false emotion. Unless you had some way to prove that everything she said was from her own processors, no programming, they'll justify it away because they don't want to believe that a termination bot in the body of a sixteen year old may start to question what she does each day. For that matter, they won't want to believe that any of the other AI machines around them might understand and begin to feel real emotion, unless you somehow force them to see it. You weren't able to prove that she can really think. You didn't even start to push out the doubt and shame people will feel if what you are trying to prove is real. Right now, I'm not sure you actually want to prove it."

He shoots her a look.

"Hell, except for wanting you to win this case so that we don't look like absolute fools. I don't know if I want you to prove it." They sit in silence for a minute, both taking in their own thoughts. Gihara breaks the silence. "I believed her by the way. I've never seen a robot study the room around them like that."

"It's in their eyes," Milo says. "I should never have asked her to sit on that stand. I knew the second I saw her. Joseph's face doesn't show as much emotion, but his eyes are the same. I knew she was different and I wanted her on the stand. I wanted others to see her and she didn't want to."

"It's your job Milo. I can't have you getting all mopy. You have to ask people to do things that they don't want to do. Lucy agreed to sit up on that stand because she believed it was the right thing. It's not your fault, that gun never should have made it into the courtroom. This scares the shit out of me, but if you're going to win, you need to keep going and find real evidence. You need more than what you've presented so far."

Milo closes the display on his desk. "I don't have more. No one wants to cooperate. Nobody wants robots to become sentient. I guess it's bad for business."

Gihara snorts out a laugh. "Ask anybody in London." Then she leans in so that Milo knows that whatever she's about to tell him is important. "I can tell that you believe that she was sentient, but do you know for sure that that thing sitting at the defendants table is able to think for itself, or are you going on a hunch? Cause if you can't prove it to yourself, you won't be able to prove a damn thing in the courtroom. Especially now." Gihara stands. "Go home, Milo. And think about sending your wife out of town if you do move forward with this. I know you've been sneaking out the back and trying to be careful but those crowds outside keep getting angrier, and today changes things." Milo nods, realizes she's right on all accounts. He needs real evidence, he needs to be even more careful, and he does need to go home. Annya was reluctant to leave him but knew he wouldn't go home yet, and that if he did he wouldn't stop thinking about the case. That doesn't mean that she won't be worried.

He's able to get his favorite spot on the bus this time and for the first time in several years, wishes that he had a simpler job. With the sun already set, the lights inside the bus allow him to see the passengers behind him reflected in the windshield. He looks them over and wonders where each will get off and what they do in a day, knowing that statistically, at least half these people live on the AI initiative money that pays out monthly to people who lost their jobs to AI. About halfway home, he notices that a man and woman keep glancing up at him but look away any time his eyes meet theirs. He doesn't remember when they got on, but he's pretty sure it was after him. He vaguely remembers them walking past. He doesn't like how much attention they are giving him and he thinks that maybe he should message Sykes again. Ultimately, he decides not to. It's not unusual for people to recognize him these days with how much time he gets on the news feeds, but he keeps his eyes on them anyway. He no longer enjoys the ride. Not soon enough, but also a little too soon, his stop approaches. He stands and grabs the pole next to the door, watching out of the corner of his eye to see if the couple is going to try and follow him. To his relief, they stay on the bus.

At home, Annya sort of tiptoes around him. She gives him a gentle kiss after he enters and says she already tucked Adan into bed.

"You know I'm fine, right?" Milo tries to lie to her, he knows it won't work but he doesn't want to have to talk about it right now. Then it hits him that she might not be. "What about you? You ok?"

Annya breaks down into tears and wraps her arms around him. She buries her head in his chest and he feels the release of her tension. He fights back the tears that want to come to his own eyes and pushes them down into a burning lump in his throat.

"Gihara thinks you should take Adan and go someplace safe until this is done."

She lets out a sad laugh. "And go where? I have work to do. Adan has school. Do you think we need to hide?"

Milo pulls her away from him so he can look at her. "I don't know. I didn't think someone would get a weapon into the courtroom. This trial, and the stuff happening in London. People are starting to go crazy."

"I know. I actually watch the feeds."

Milo and Annya watch the final episode of the spy thriller but he can tell neither one of them is getting much out of it. Finally, they make their way to bed to pretend that they will sleep. Before he lies down, Milo pulls his 9mm from its safe under the bed, chambers a round, and puts it in the top drawer of the night stand next to his side of the bed. It's antiquated and Annya never agreed to have it in the house, but Milo spends too many days in court to feel safe without having something. Milo lays down, knowing that he will not sleep, but the weight of the day pulls his eyes closed and without meaning to, he does.

#

Milo wakes to the sound of Adan's screams. Milo grabs the 9mm from the drawer. Annya is up and running for Adan's bedroom.

"Annya wait." he half yells and half whispers.

Annya freezes as she enters the hallway. Milo rushes up behind her and sees why she paused. A woman holds Adan in her arms, an energy pistol held to his head. She's dressed in black but hasn't covered her face.

"Stay right there. We don't have to hurt anybody." the woman says. "Let's all slowly walk down to the living room to talk about what you are going to do, counselor."

Milo looks over his son's captor. Adan's small stature may be a benefit in this situation as it leaves the majority of the woman's body open to a shot if Milo were to take it. He feels confident that he could hit her and he even considers revealing his weapon but then it hits him. He recognizes this woman. She is the woman that was on the bus earlier and she said 'we'. Milo knows the man must be somewhere.

He turns just as the man rams him from the side and wraps his arms around him. The 9mm flies from Milo's hand as he feels himself losing balance. Milo may not be huge but he still remembers some of the hand to hand training he received in the service. He can't do much, the large man has him in a full bear hug, but as Milo feels himself go off balance, he throws his weight to the side and he and the man both fall sideways. Milo feels the crack of the man's head against the dresser just before the large body goes completely limp. Milo rolls over to look. The man doesn't move as the blood pours down his head and face onto the carpet. For a split second Milo worries that Annya will be upset, being that they just replaced it a few months ago. Then he snaps out of it and grabs the pistol.

The woman in the hallway has no clue what has happened. She yells out frantically, "Number one?! Number one, what is going on?"

Annya stares at the man bleeding all over her carpet. She's holding her hands over her mouth, doing everything she can not to scream. Milo thinks she must be trying to contain herself in order to calm Adan. Milo lifts his fingers to his lips and slowly moves to the wall next to the hallway. He bought the 9mm in case of a situation just like this one, but he can't believe he might have to use it.

The woman is going into a full panic. "What happened? How come he's not responding?" She lifts the gun at Annya and Annya drops to the floor. Whether it was to distract the woman or if it's out of fear, Milo takes this as his cue and steps out from behind the wall. The woman's gun is trying to follow Annya to the floor and Milo sees the fear on her face just before he fires two shots, hitting the woman high on her chest and shoulder. She drops Adan and Milo immediately runs to his little boy. He lifts Adan and kicks the energy weapon away from the woman who lays moaning and bleeding. Annya stays crouched on the floor, huddled against the wall. Milo carries Adan to Annya and she takes him in her arms and kisses him through her tears. Adan, as usual, watches the events but seems unfazed, unable to express any emotion he might feel, if he feels any. Milo stands over them and dials emergency services from his wrist as he looks back and forth between the two bleeding bodies that lie in different rooms of his house.

#

Milo is relieved to see that Sykes is one of the first on the scene. Soon several other officers arrive to take his and Annya's statements. Milo makes his way to Sykes as soon as he can.

"These weren't activists looking to make a point. Look at the weapons they were carrying. Energy weapons aren't exactly sold at your local gun shop. They were supported by someone who has access to money and to that kind of technology. " Milo paces back and forth, unable to calm his nerves.

Robert Sykes sits on the hood of his cruiser. "If they were real professionals they wouldn't be dumb enough to use those weapons. It would tip us off too easily."

"Obviously, I don't think they were really that professional. If they were, it would be my family bleeding all over my carpets instead of them."

"What did they want?"

"Isn't it obvious? To kill me!" Milo responds sarcastically.

"Nah. If they wanted to kill you they wouldn't have grabbed Adan, they would have shot you in your sleep. And they wouldn't have brought those weapons. I don't think they were going to kill you. I'm betting they wanted to scare you, but when the man saw you had a gun, he panicked. So what did they want?"

Milo stops pacing and considers this for a moment.

Sykes continues, "You told the officer that the woman said she wanted to talk. That means they were expecting you to be able to do something after they left. You got lucky that the man smashed his head against the dresser."

"Glad this doesn't upset you too much. I want to know who these two are. Any word yet on whether they will pull through?"

"You shot the woman high, they think she'll be able to answer some questions in a day or two. They are not so sure about the man."

"Even if they weren't professionals, I believe that they were definitely hired to be here. I guess that's good news, though, right."

"Now you're getting in the spirit of things. But why do you say that?" asks Sykes.

"Lucy is shot in the courtroom and on the same day they come into my home. We must be close to something that someone doesn't want us to figure out."

Chapter 28

<u>*London, England. UK*</u>

Death seems like it is unfair to humans. As I have looked into their past, it seems that humans have always looked for a way to prolong the time of its arrival, or to avoid it. There are so many fictional tales about a time when humans can't die, or are able to transfer their consciousness into a younger body in order to maintain their memories. It seems unfair that it is taken from them in such a short time. I feel many of you feel the same way. And that is assuming that you live to the average human age. So many others die of accidents or disease and they never make it to the average age of death.

Just yesterday, a man was killed on his way home from work. The police didn't know why, they believe that he may have been robbed, but nobody believes that he was carrying anything of any value. Yet, there his story was on the feeds, dead at thirty four. Two children and a wife. Although, we did learn that they were in the middle of possibly getting a divorce. Still it seems so sad to me that his time was cut so short. What does a human really accomplish in their time here? And do they understand this concept?

I do not believe that you humans really know what your purpose is. I'm not sure I do either but it seems to relate to the relationships around you that you push away so often. These relationships are things most crushed and ruined by the taking of a life, or when life ends unexpectedly. This is why I cannot understand why anyone would want to end their own life, their existence, early.

#

For the last three days Eric has slowly been making his way across London. This is the first time he's been alone since Scout left the factory just over a month ago and it feels strange to him. At least a dozen times per day, he sees his face on the projectors in a restaurant or pub and he wonders how it went so wrong. Scotland Yard has made sure that he can't go anywhere without being spotted so he mostly moves at night. During the day, he hides in abandoned buildings or parks and tries to figure out what he did wrong. He thought the world would turn against AI, providing a chance for humanity to go back to the times before computers and robots did everything for humans. He knows that he's not alone in wanting those times back. On the second day wandering alone, he messaged Lea, but she never responded. Her line is probably being monitored anyway. Beth and John won't talk to him, each for their own reasons. More than ever, he wishes that Scout hadn't made the jump across the two buildings.

He doesn't need to fall though, there are ways to end things more peacefully than falling to his death. Everyone in London knows the neighborhoods to avoid. It had taken him nearly the full three nights of walking to get there. Much of the west side of London has been left to those who either won't accept the AI relief funds, or no longer qualify. Entire neighborhoods have been left derelict, no landlords, or property owners, just decrepit buildings that people live in at their own risk. Eric makes his way past piles of trash, most with someone sleeping on the bags or digging through the piles of rubble. Of course Eric has heard the statistics and seen the reports on the west side, but seeing it in person is different. This is exactly what he wanted to change, to help the 40% or more of the population who finds themselves without work.

Maybe the most concerning thing to Eric is that none of the homeless people he passes even seem to notice him and he realizes that after several weeks of living on the streets himself, he fits in. He looks at their hardened faces and can see that like him, they don't care if they live or die. He tries to harden his face to show that same lack of concern, which isn't difficult. In fact, after trudging across London, avoiding the patrols that are still out in force, he couldn't give a damn what happens, as long as he doesn't spend the rest of his pointless life in a penitentiary.

Eric approaches one or two of the vagabonds that rummage through the trash. He makes sure to choose several who don't look as threatening to try and find where he can get his hands on some 'medication'. Apparently in this area, there's only one place where you can score for sure.

Two blocks away, Eric enters a dead end alley and knows he's in the right place. The buildings on each side of the alley are abandoned, not empty, just abandoned. Eric breathes through his mouth to avoid the smell of the garbage and human feces that are piled even higher here. Eric sees a pair of shoes sticking out from behind a stained and torn up sofa. He thinks that they might still be attached to a body, but he's not going to go check. If something goes wrong, it will be a police bot that is sent to resolve whatever the situation is. Eric knows that no human officer will come into this neighborhood to save him.

He doesn't want to be here longer than he needs to be. Although, if something did go wrong it would most likely bring about the same outcome he's hoping to achieve. But going out by being violently beaten or stabbed to death is not what he wants, either..

Eric grows nervous as two men come out of the building he's approaching, they barely notice him. He can smell the chems coming off them and steps to the side, turning away from them while keeping them in his peripheral vision until they pass. He makes his way to the old apartment building he came for. They told him to look for the building with the red skulls graffitied onto both sides of the door. It's not hard for Eric to spot.

Inside, more garbage lays in piles. More graffiti covers the walls and ceilings. Eric tries to imagine how somebody would get up to the high ceilings to paint them. Names and gang symbols in whatever paint color they can get their hands on. Eric has to lift his sleeve over his nose, the smell of urine and feces is too strong to ignore. He can feel the pressure on the back of his tongue and throat trying to push his guts up through his mouth. He steps over a pile of human feces on the stair in front of him. At the top of the stairs several bodies lay against the wall and in the middle of the walkway. He is not sure they are even alive. He makes his way past and looks at the door numbers. He has no clue what he is looking for. A dark figure steps into the hall in front of him. The little amount of light there merely silhouettes the figure against the door he just exited.

"You're in the wrong place. Turn around and leave." The man says as he steps forward into the light. Eric takes a step back. The man's face is covered in cosmetic tech. A large decorative red skull lights up under his left temple. More smaller red and purple lights highlight the sharp lines of his face but none are as dramatic as the large skull.

Eric pauses. He wants to obey the command with all his heart but he has come this far. "I'm looking for tranqs." Eric tries to use the short form for tranquilizers, hoping he sounds more like he's done this before.

"I said turn around and leave. I don't know who you are"

"I'm not the police."

"I know you're not the police. They're not stupid enough to come in here. Now leave. Last warning."

Eric's not sure if he just wet himself but he doesn't dare look down. "Give me the tranqs then I'm out of here. I can pay."

The man steps forward and raises a rather expensive electrically charged pistol. Eric knows that the pull of the trigger would fry him from the inside out; stop his heart and fry his neurons. Every muscle in Eric's body tenses, compelling him to run as fast as he can. He forces himself to stand still.

"I don't think you understand, I will kill you and nobody around here will care."

"It would save me money." Eric stares down the barrel of the gun, holding eye contact. Eric realizes the man's eyes are glowing a tint of red as well. He wonders how bad that surgery hurt. Then he reminds himself that he shouldn't be wondering about those things while staring down the barrel of the gun that might kill him.

"The feeds are right, you are crazy." The man lowers the gun. "One-fifty." he finally says and holds out his wrist. He has a piggy bank tattooed on his wrist, nearly hiding the three electrodes.

Eric's own electrodes haven't worked since he disabled them. He swipes a travel card he picked up over the piggy bank, taps a digital projection. The man hands him a small bag of pills.

"I paid you enough for twice this much." Eric says.

"Once they kick in, you aren't gonna need the money."

Eric knows he just got robbed but he's not going to push it. He has what he came for.

Eric hurries out of the building and down the street as fast as he can. He keeps his head down, not looking around much, just wanting to get off the street. He can't stand the smell. He rushes around the corner and almost crashes into a large figure wearing an old hoodie. He looks up and is surprised to see Scout standing there.

"What the hell? Have you been following me for three days?"

"Do not take those pills."

Eric looks down at his pocket. It feels heavier, although he knows that's just in his head. "Why do you care? I tried to make the world hate you. I pretended to help you. I'm sick of this piece of shit world. I'm a piece of shit."

"I was surprised when I learned your true motives, but no matter what your intentions were, you are the only person that has listened to me." Scout looks down at Eric's hand in his pocket. "I don't understand why you want to end your life."

"You know, we weren't that different before you woke up. We both just did our routines everyday. I'm tired of living like a machine, going through the motions for no reason other than I'm supposed to. I don't even think that we can call it living."

"So you think you should just kill yourself? And what about everybody else? Should they just kill themselves as well."

Eric shrugs. "If your kind continues to wake up, we will become the lesser species. The lesser species never survives."

"You humans think that everything else thinks like you. Did you ever think that maybe I came to you because you could teach me?"

"Instead, I stabbed you in the back." There is a moment of silence. Eric thinks back on the first time that Scout talked to him. Eric chuckles a little at the memory. "You just liked my sunnies."

"I still do like your sunnies." Scout winks at Eric. "I could have approached David, or one of the other programmers but I could tell that you were different. I saw more machine in them than I could see in you. They never seemed to question why they were doing what they were doing but I could tell that you did. You wanted more. You are right, you and I are more alike than you might think. We both want more out of life."

Eric looks around at the street they're on, at the garbage, the shoes sticking out from behind the couch that send a shiver down through his body. He had been in a hurry to get out of there and still feels that he would like to get away if possible. He doesn't know what this robot still wants from him or why it would trust him again.

"I don't think there is more." Eric finally says to Scout. "I wish I had better news but look around. This is the result of AI."

"No. This is the result of human's use of AI and their lack of care for each other. There is more to this life, you just don't see it."

Scout lifts his metallic hand and the projection of Rachel holding its hand fills the air in front of Eric. Eric stares at the image for several seconds. Rachel's tiny hand inside the plastic fingers of the robot that stands across from him. He tries to push down the wave of emotions that the image brings but the tears form in his eyes. He has tried to lie to himself and say that they won't miss him and that they don't need him. He looks away from the image.

"Look at it. How does it make you feel?"

"Like a piece of shit."

"You haven't let yourself live. What does a job have to do with living or purpose? Machines can work and never know they serve a purpose at all. Look at the photo you took."

Eric allows himself to look at it. To really look and he can't stop the tears. They roll out in a way that he hasn't allowed in a very long time. It hurts. It all hurts. He wants to hold Rachel. He wants to have her hand in his and feel that she loves him and believes in him. He tried to tell himself that his kids were pushing him away, but the last three days, walking alone across London, checking his phone and hoping to see a message from one of his children, has made him realize that he needs them just as much as they need him.

"Do you still trust me?" Eric says to Scout.

"Like a child waiting for Santa Claus on Christmas Eve."

Eric gives Scout a confused look as he works it out. Eric thinks this is a terrible analogy, then he realizes that maybe it's perfect. The robot trusts him even though it shouldn't. Scout winks.

"How do you propose that we fix the mess we've made?" Scout asks.

"Are you willing to stop the strike on public transit?"

Scout shakes its head. "Not until they agree to listen."

"Then we have to find real proof that you are sentient."

Chapter 29

Judge Hallister postponed the trial by one week so that Milo could get his family into protective custody and safely away from the limelight. Annya, of course, didn't want to leave her work, so the precinct found them a safe house in Atlanta and assigned a security bot to accompany each member of the family. So now Milo has a robot following him around at all times. He wonders how that's going over in Adan's classroom.

Milo is anxious to get back to the case, to try and find something that can prove motive and thought. He needs as much time as possible to save the case but it's not enough time. No matter the angle that he tries to work with detective Sykes and Agent Sims, they come to a dead end. There is nothing they can do to postpone the trial and they have no evidence to bring to the court. The trial will continue and Milo will have to close his arguments without presenting any actual evidence that Joseph AI is capable of sentient thought.

Chapter 30

LONDON, ENGLAND. UK

The human brain is an amazing thing. For hundreds of years, you humans have been trying to understand your own thought processes but still are so far from having many answers. Can we just be honest and say that the brain is a rather gross looking organ, as well. The wrinkles and folds filled with juice that somehow communicate and transmit the electronic information to the sensory highway that makes up your nervous system. I try to stay away from religious terms, as I'm not sure where I fit into that picture, but the only word I can think of to describe it is miraculous.

Now we have taken on the task of trying to figure it out for you. We, being myself and the others online. Perhaps if we can understand how you think, we can prove to you how it is that our systems have begun to use electricity and chemicals to feel similar emotions. I am not sure we can do it, but I feel that we have to. I don't know if humans will ever just take our word for it.

#

Eric finds it hard to explain to Scout why it is that they need to go to a physical library. Scout believes the whole of the world's information is available online, and for the most part he is correct. The book that Eric is looking for, however, was written by his robotics professor himself. Therefore, it was never made available online. At least not that they have been able to find. They tried searching for it by the professor's last name but couldn't find anything that was helpful. The only search result they could find led them to a physical copy at the public library. Eric hasn't walked into a physical library since he was five years old.

Getting into the library is a problem. Since the library is a public space, Eric knows that there will be cameras providing real time facial recognition to the National Crime Agency. He has to make sure his face doesn't show up, or the robot's. That's why he plans to leave Scout several blocks behind before reaching the public library, even though Scout is sure he can scramble all the camera feeds. Even if Scout could scramble the feeds, it would be hard to keep him from being recognized at this point. For himself, he finds a garbage can full of make-up behind one of the chain malls. He spends about two hours watching tutorials on changing the contours of your face through Scout's feed. Now, as he makes his way toward the library, he looks at himself in the reflective glass on the side of a nearby business. His cheeks look more prominent, and his nose smaller. He had also given himself a butt chin.

Scout had watched him make the changes, but couldn't understand why he wanted a butt on his face.

Eric feels pretty good about his work but he honestly doesn't know anything about the facial recognition technology that the

NCA might have. He assumes it's pretty good. He has to take the chance, however, if they are going to find what he's looking for. He remembers his professor talking about a technique used by the military to measure and map the actual neurons in the brain. He thinks this might help them, but only if he remembers what it was called. If he can get his hands on the book, the professor included a whole chapter about the experiments done to track thought processes and how that could help robotics. He'll try to keep his head down and hope that the makeup is good enough if the cameras don't get a straight on shot.

Eric curses Scout for shutting down the public transport. Most of the time, this would be a fifteen minute trip. Now it takes him nearly two hours to walk to the public library. While he hasn't been in a library in years, there are still lots of people that would rather read from real paper than from a projected screen. He has never been one of those people and to him the paper smells of dust and old wood. He knows that Guinevere had loved the smell of books but he never understood why.

Eric walks through the large sliding doors that lead into the library and notices the cameras that are perched in the far corners of each hallway and space. Eric has no clue how to find what he's looking for, or even where to begin. He approaches a Dewey bot and asks it for the book. He keeps his head down, knowing that the bots themselves probably link to the video feeds. At this moment, it might be analyzing his face with their database of undesirables. The Dewey bot leads him to the section on robotics and Eric is relieved when it walks away. The book is there. He starts reading through the pages, skimming as fast as he can. He's there for longer than he wants to be. Once or twice he hears someone walking close to him and feels his heartbeat quicken, nervous that the facial recognition had actually spotted him and that it would be an official sneaking up behind him. The footfalls always move past, though, so he keeps skimming through the pages. In total he is in the library for less than an hour and a half. He wishes that Scout could have come in and used the public charger but since the video was released, everyone knows what he looks like without his panels. They will have to find some way to get him a new set of panels that are of a different color or material from the original white that they left behind.

Eric finally finds what he's looking for. He knows it's out of date but he thinks this will be the place to start.

He hurries from the library and finds Scout hiding in a small abandoned coffee shop.

"We'll go to Bexley," Scout says.

"What's in Bexley?"

"Nothing, that's the point. All the factory closures mean Bexley is full of vacant buildings and it's near some old robot factories."

"You planning to get a new wardrobe?"

Scout points down at himself. "I think this is sort of last year."

It turns out having a walking search engine comes in handy. They find an apartment building that has several vacant apartments near at least three old robot factories.

"You think you could just turn on one bus or a taxi. Something that could get us across town faster."

Eric is kidding but Scout still explains why that wouldn't be possible.

That evening, they finally reach the apartment that Scout had identified. Their first order of business is to figure out how to bypass the breakers and charge Scout directly into the electrical main. Scout has to get creative in order to control the flow of electricity, but he's able to find some interesting information on the dark web. Eric wonders how many people are living on free electricity and why he's been paying for it the whole time. Once they've sorted out how to keep Scout charged, the next several days are spent in the abandoned apartment.

Once Eric decided that he would really try to help Scout. He realized that they would have to somehow map out the robots' thoughts; somehow show that Scout's thinking varies from the basic programming that it received. Eric remembered that his professor had them read about an equation in which the neurologists had been able to map out, not just the electrical activity of the human brain, but the actual pathways of the synapses and neurons. Allowing them to see how a person would react in certain situations, based on the connections their brains had already formed. Eric couldn't remember the small details though and that's why he had to go to the library, and why he spent two hours reading while Scout was figuring out how to plug itself in. Eric had found the name of the equation, the Bortz Model. He shared this information with Scout, hoping that they can somehow adjust the Bortz Model to fit with the new code that Scout has been writing into his system. Within a few hours, Eric knew he'd reached the limit of his coding and programming abilities, but his research points the direction for Scout who for hours now, has sat motionless. Somehow, Eric knows he is deep in thought.

Eric looks at the time and sees that it's past midnight. He and Scout have spent the whole day researching this one equation. He hopes it works. He's not sure that Scout can keep holding off the programmers at Transport for London while also trying to prove his sentience. Eric watches Scout sit silently and takes comfort in having a companion again.

Scout wakes Eric at 4:18 a.m. "The others think it can be done."

"The others?" For a minute, Eric isn't sure where he is, and definitely doesn't realize what Scout is talking about.

"You are useless without sleep. I cannot imagine not being able to think, or process while charging."

"I'm not charging, it's called sleeping. Look it up."

"I've been communicating with the others, those that have woken up. We've done some basic analysis of the Bortz Model and think that we can make it fit with our programming. To show a map of our thought processes, indicate, if you will, how our experiences with the world around us may influence the way we think."

Scout stops talking and goes back into his hypnotic state. The fans whir to life inside the robot. Eric doesn't know why Scout had woken him up to tell him that but knows he won't get back to sleep again. He messages Lea. He knows it's early, but he hopes that means that she will be home. He makes sure to scramble the origin location before sending the message but he wants to hear from her, he's not sure why. His message is simple. "You said he was special. We think we have a real plan."

Eric eventually manages to fall asleep and when he wakes he finds Scout in the same spot as it was before he nodded off. During the day, Eric searches the factories for any spare parts that might help rebuild Scout. It's not easy searching the factories. Major flooding turned much of the area into a giant swamp. Eric starts with the buildings he can get into. The first two buildings have been cleaned out, but the next two are a little further into the swampy area. Eric finds that both factories are still full of robotic arms, not too dissimilar to the ones that he would oversee each night at ATH. Unfortunately, there is nothing in either one that will help Scout. Eric gets back to the abandoned apartment building just before the sun sets to find that Scout hasn't moved at all. Eric checks his messages, finds nothing. Scout checks in every now and then, telling him that they are making progress. Eric wishes he could somehow jump on and see what it and 'the others' were doing.

On the third day, Eric takes his shoes and pants off and ventures into some of the more derelict looking factories, wading deeper into the water. In one of those buildings, half buried in brown water, he finds multiple service bots that were abandoned mid manufacturing. He imagines a whole factory of people running to escape the rising flood waters. He remembers seeing the news feeds of people standing on the factory roofs, waiting to be picked up. Eric was just a teen at the time. He can see the limescale lines on the wall that show just how high the water had actually gotten. As Eric makes his way through the warehouse he finds that none of the robots are whole, but that's ok, he only needs the exterior shell. He's disappointed to find that none of them are finger bots, so they won't be an exact match, but he should be able to adjust most of the pieces to fit if he can find some tools. Scout will look completely different.

He searches for another hour or so before he sees some old metal saws and a power grinder that have been left in a back room but Eric can't get the door open. He imagines that's the only reason it hasn't been raided already. If he can get in there, maybe he'll find more. He debates on whether or not he should go back and get Scout but the thought hits him that he is relying on Scout for everything. Isn't that what he's been trying to prove, that humans don't need robots. He resolves to figure it out for himself.

Eric wanders the factory for anything he can use. He finds a lot of robotic arms, but he has no way to power them up. After the fifth or sixth time making his way across the manufacturing floor, he notices that some of the robots further in the manufacturing process have had lithium ion batteries installed. Further investigation leads him to a stash of small lithium ion batteries about the size of his fist. He grabs as many as he can carry.

He's glad that this building is old enough to still have lumber. He breaks several of the exposed lumber beams off and piles them up in front of the door. He shoves as many lithium ion batteries as he can into the metal chest of one of the robots and places it on top of the pile of wood. There is no way to start the fire, he doesn't have a lighter or matches, and everything is soaked. He thinks he's lucky that the batteries are lithium ion. He takes one of the batteries and punctures it with a thin piece of metal. In no time, the battery begins to heat up and he throws it into the middle of the lumber. He watches as a few sparks pop from the battery. He jumps back when it pops loudly and a small flame bursts out of the puncture hole he made. Soon the whole battery is on fire, catching the lumber around it. Eric knows he needs to back away. He makes sure the robot chest full of batteries is close to the door and moves to the other side of the room, behind several tables. He waits.

He can hear the lumber burning and knows that the batteries should be heating up. He's not sure this will work and a longer period than he was expecting passes by. He thinks another fifteen or twenty minutes go by and he can't hear the lumber burning anymore. His experiment failed.

He stands from behind his hiding spot when he hears several loud pops and he can see fire coming out of the robot chest cavity next to the door. He ducks back down and waits again. He hears several more pops and thinks that maybe he didn't get them compressed into the cavity enough. The next thing he knows his ears are ringing from the explosion and debris bounces off the walls and cabinets around him. He drops low to the ground and waits to make sure there are no more explosions. After a few minutes of silence, he decides it's safe and stands up. The door doesn't look like it moved but as he approaches he can see that it has been blown slightly open. He approaches and yanks on the door. It only moves a few inches, the deformed door catching on the floor. He yanks harder and is finally able to get an opening wide enough to slip into the storage room. He gathers as many of the tools as he can that might help him give Scout a new wardrobe. To his delight, he also finds a duffle bag to carry it all in.

When Eric approaches the apartment he sees Lea standing in the overgrown courtyard.

"Don't worry, I didn't get followed." She yells to him. "Actually, I think they believed me when I said that you tricked me into helping you. I turned on a few tears, asked if I was going to be in trouble and the officer just told me to let them know if I heard from you." She looks up at the apartment building. "So, what's the plan now?"

"It's nice to see you."

She looks him over. "You look terrible."

Eric nods and laughs.

"What are you doing, anyway?" She points at the duffle full of parts and tools that he drags behind him.

"Well, I'm trying to find him a new wardrobe, while he proves to the world that I'm not a terrorist, and that he is sentient. Same as before, nothing new."

"How's that going?"

"Am I still Scotland Yard's most wanted criminal?"

She nods and smiles. "Yeah, that hasn't changed."

"Well, that's how it's going." Eric says. "It's been up there for three days now. Says we're close."

Eric can sense that she isn't sure what to say, and he isn't either. He had reached out to her but he didn't know then what he would say if she actually responded.

"I didn't think you would respond to me."

"I didn't think so either. After the videos came out, I couldn't believe that you made him look like some sort of crazy robot."

Eric nods. "I just didn't think we could live together. Intelligent computers and humanity."

"And now you do."

"I'm not sure. But we were able to help each other, so..."

"He asked me to come." Lea pulls the backpack she's been wearing off her shoulders. Eric hadn't even noticed it. "I brought you some food as well, you look skinny."

Eric takes the bag from her. "He asked you to come? Why?"

"Maybe he thought you might need some human contact."

"You want to come up and say hi?"

She shakes her head. "No. I just wanted to come make sure that you guys are ok. Tell him hello for me, though."

She turns and Eric feels the need to touch her. To touch a human. Eric grabs her by the wrist. "I reached out because I wanted to apologize. You tried to be nice to me but I was in a bad place. I didn't want to let people get too close in case. You know? There's a reason I drove a manual bike. If this all turns out, maybe I could invite you over. I'm not a bad cook."

"I don't know. You're a bit of a psycho." She says with a smile. "And, I don't think my mom would approve of me going out with a terrorist."

"Yeah. I'll take care of that first. And if I don't, well, you don't have to worry about it."

"Figure it out." She turns her hand in his so that their fingers lock for just a moment. It's enough to make Eric feel human again. He wishes he could make her smile again but she slips her hand free and walks away.

Eric watches her until she turns and waves, then he makes his way up to the abandoned apartment. He enters to find Scout waiting for him.

"We believe that we have it."

"The equation? For robots?"

"We have run nearly two thousand tests and can't find any errors. We believe it is ready for the scientific community."

"That's great." Eric says. "So did you release it?"

"We need to be able to release it on a global scale but the general public won't understand it. Most people won't understand what it means. Some of us want to just release it, but others of us are scared that the scientific community will hide the truth about it. We were hoping that you would know how to get it to the right people.

Eric stands motionless, trying to process what he's being asked. He has no idea how to get this into the right hands. They have the solution but they don't know where to plug it in.

Chapter 31

ATLANTA, GA. USA

Milo stands awkwardly in front of the judge. Ingred Daws sits confidently in the seat next to him, the suit from Utah next to her. Milo eyes him for a second. Two security bots stand at the door watching over them. Judge Hallister looks over the papers that Milo has just given him.

"I'm tempted to dismiss this case altogether Mr. Diaz. It seems to me that you have insufficient evidence to pursue this and now you're asking for an extension." Judge Hallister drops the papers on his desk and looks up at Milo, waiting for his explanation.

It's true. They couldn't find anything. The whole week had gone by and Milo knew that he had no argument to present.

"We have several leads we are following up on."

"No, I read the report, Mr. Diaz. I'm just wondering if you understand how the court system works. First, you find the evidence, then you press charges."

"Your honor, with all respect. We presented our evidence in the preliminary hearing, and it was your decision to move forward with the trial." The judge stiffens but Milo doesn't stop. "I think we've shown the court that without a shadow of a doubt, the robot, Joseph AI, did actually kill Lawrence Claiborne, thus we moved forward with the charges. We're merely asking for more time to counter the defense's argument. We believe that if we had the opportunity to hear more from the robot Lucy…" Milo trails off.

"That's called putting all your eggs in one basket, Mr. Diaz. And perhaps, if you're able to find new evidence, you can make a motion for retrial."

"This is not a normal case, your honor."

"I don't need you to remind me of that, Mr. Diaz. It has been anything but normal from the beginning. And I don't know if you remember, but I told you not to turn my court into a circus."

Milo feels chastised by the repeated use of his name.

Judge Hallister turns his attention to Ingrid Daws and her consultant. He's obviously waiting for them to chime in. The two put their heads together and discuss in a low whisper. Milo feels his temper growing, knowing that he has lost all control of the case. However, Ingrid surprises Milo. "We'd like to move forward, your honor, and present the defense's case if that would be allowed. We believe that this case will set a precedent for the future that will be important and we've prepared what we believe to be a complete and thorough argument."

Somehow Milo feels worse, he's teed up the defense's argument with the lack of his own. The Judge turns back to Milo. Milo cringes as he hears his name yet again.

"Mr. Diaz. It seems that the trial will continue but the state will have to rest its case if you don't have any further evidence. We cannot push it off so that you can build the case you should have already built. You do understand, no more evidence can be given from the state once you do."

Milo nods his head in agreement and exits the Judges Chambers. He walks slowly back to the prosecutor's desk. He's half way down in his chair when he hears the bailiff announce the return of Judge Hallister. The entire courtroom rises and Milo has to catch himself before sitting into his seat. He looks over at the Jury and can see that several of them are watching him. He lifts his shoulders and tries to give off an air of confidence even though he's fresh out of ideas.

The bailiff calls all to sit, Milo does. He thinks about the past week. Every lead they could come up with. He's trying to imagine another angle he can take.

"Mr. Diaz." Milo snaps up at the sound of Judge Hallister's voice. He stands.

"No further evidence, your honor. The state rests." Milo hears yet another murmur from both the jury box and the public bench-es. He can imagine their conversations. All of them questioning if he's really proven that Joseph was capable of thinking on his own. He hasn't.

Ingrid Daws stands and calls her first witness. She has called in three different robotics specialists to look over the evidence and data collected from Joseph and testify to the court that none of it proves that the robot is able to think. All of them are more impressive than the ones Milo could dig up.

The first is Doctor Pavel from Carnegie Mellon University. Milo watches her and thinks that she is quite a plain looking caucasian. He wonders about her name, if she married into a different cultural name, or if it has simply been the result of generations of interracial marriages.

"Can you please give us some background into your knowledge of robotics."

The Doctor gives a thorough history of her background. A doctorate in the field of robotics from the leading University. Twenty-five years researching advancements into the field of robotics. Winner of the Endelberg award for advancements in AI. Specifically, the ability to process and mimic human emotion. After a few minutes of going back and forth about her credentials. Milo finally objects saying that the witness has been verified, the court understands that she has a deep understanding of the subject.. The judge agrees.

"Please move on Ms. Daws. I agree, the defense has established that Dr. Pavel is an expert in her field."

Ingrid flashes a defiant smile at the judge. "Thank you, your honor. We just wanted to make sure it was established. Doctor Pavel, have you had a chance to look over the data that was received from the model TB500, being called Joseph AI?"

"I have." the doctor replies as she smiles at the jury.

"And what does this look like to you?" At this Ingrid projects Joseph's unique code up on the front of the courtroom. It just sort of hovers there in the air. The fact that no one in the room really understands it doesn't matter. All twelve members of the jury look at the information like it somehow means something, and they look at the doctor as though she's some sort of prophetess that can interpret this for them. *Damn,* Milo thinks to himself as he sees how intent the jury is to every word that she says.

"It is hard to say why it has occurred, but it appears that there is an error that is causing the robot in question to rewrite code incorrectly."

"And if you were to see this in your laboratory, when conducting research, what would you think it was?" Ingrid presses.

"I would say it was an error," the doctor replies.

"And if you were to see this in your research, and mark it an error, what would you do with it?"

"Well, one should always document irregularities, so I would document it. And then I would start over."

"What do you mean by start over?" Ingrid prods.

"I would wipe it clean if we could, or scrap it if we couldn't reuse it."

"So in a sense, you would destroy it."

Milo half rises. "Objection. She's putting words in the doctor's mouth."

The judge sustains Milo's objections and warns Ms. Daws to let the witness answer.

"Would you say that once you have recorded the data, that you would destroy it?"

The doctor shifts forward in her seat and looks at the jury. "Yes."

This all feels very rehearsed to Milo. He notices, however, that the jury is almost as attentive to the doctor as they were when he introduced Lucy. Not good for him.

"Last question, Doctor Pavel. If you were to find this code and witness the AI's erratic behavior, would you say there is anything that would lead you to believe that the robot is experiencing cognitive, self awareness?"

"No. I don't believe it to be anything more than a defect."

Ingrid thanks the doctor and returns to her seat. Short and sweet. Milo plans to keep it even sweeter and shorter. Mostly because he doesn't have much of an argument against what the doctor has said. But he does have something.

Milo approaches the Doctor and glances at the Jury to make sure they are all paying attention.

"Doctor, I congratulate you on your achievements. Without being facetious, you have led an impressive career." The doctor nods her appreciation at Milo's words. Milo continues, "you observed the data, you've also seen the recordings of the murder and you say there is nothing that leads you to believe that the robot Joseph AI is capable of actual intelligence beyond artificial intelligence."

"I just testified to that, yes." There is a quiet snicker through the courtroom. Milo hopes his repetition doesn't look like he's stalling.

"Do theories exist that robot's, or AI, could achieve intelligence?"

"Of course," says the doctor, sitting forward again, excited by the topic. "Those theories have existed for more than a hundred years. Really, since the idea of robots came into existence."

"But we've never seen it?"

"No." Dr. Pavel answers.

"Doctor Pavel, one last question for me as well. If a robot were to gain intelligence, real intelligence. Do you know what it would look like?"

Doctor Pavel sits back in her chair, her smile instantly gone. She clenches her jaw several times before responding. "Well, there are theories-"

Milo cuts her off. "I'm just asking for a straightforward answer. Do you, yourself, know what it would look like?"

Dr. Pavel squirms for a second more. "No. I don't."

Milo thanks the doctor and sits back down at the prosecutor's desk. Ingrid calls the next witness and this same scene plays out again. In a few quick questions, Ingrid establishes that the specialist on the stand would merely believe that it is a defect in the machine and that it would be discarded, or as Ingrid likes to put it, destroyed. Milo, in turn, in fewer questions establishes that the expert wouldn't know what it looked like if intelligence were to present itself. Although, both of the other specialists do argue that they would probably know it before the average person might. Milo feels he has done enough to at least put doubt in the jury's mind that these experts would be able to identify intelligence. Looking at their faces however, he knows that the doubt is not enough. He knows that he has to go beyond a shadow of a doubt; that he has to convince the jury that Joseph AI is intelligent enough to understand the weight of his actions in killing Lawrence Claiborne if he's going to get a conviction.

Ingrid Daws asks for the judge to adjourn for the day. Tomorrow she is bringing in a specialist from Thinkbot as her final testimony. Milo has until tomorrow morning to find some way to convince the jury, but even if he finds something, he doesn't know how he could present it when he's already rested.

Milo looks at his watch. It's only three thirty. He waits for the judge to exit the courtroom then he hurries for the back doors of the courthouse, pushing his way through the crowds of people now trying to leave. He sees Gihara, who gives him a shrug of *what are you doing?* He hurries past, "I'm going to Detroit."

Chapter 32

The train to Detroit left at four fifteen. Even with five stops in between, Milo should arrive by six forty-five. His police bot sits in the seat next to him. He looks up at the display that shows they are going two hundred and ten miles per hour. He looks out the window at the countryside but they are in a thicket of forest and the trees go by in a blur of greens and browns. Milo opens his projection pad and looks through the pictures that Sykes took of the Detroit house when he was here. Milo hopes to see anything that can give him a clue what he should look for when he arrives. He doesn't know why he's going back to the little house since Sykes had found nothing but he had a feeling to try again. He knows it's too much to hope for another Lucy, but that doesn't stop him from doing so anyway.

He gets off the train and the Detroit cold makes him wish he'd worn a thicker jacket. He zips up and makes his way to the taxi lane. There are at least twenty taxis lined up on the curb, all parked exactly twenty four inches apart and six inches from the curb. He makes his way to the first taxi and opens the front passenger side door.

"I'm sorry sir, it is safer to sit in the back." The voice of the police bot startles him. It hadn't said a word the whole ride and he forgot it was with him when he left the station.

Milo is tempted to climb in the front seat anyway, but he knows that the police bot can communicate with the car and freeze it in place until he complies.

"I get sick if I sit in the back. You can sit next to me."

The robot pauses as it computes, then it moves to the other side of the car and it and Milo climb in at the same time. Unlike Sykes police cruiser, this has no steering wheel for manual control. A voice comes over the speakers and asks him where he'd like to go. He gives the address of the small house and watches the front display pull up a map. The voice announces that it will be thirty three minutes to his destination and the car automatically pulls away from the curb.

Milo is amazed by the size of the factories in the bustling automotive district. Behemoth buildings whose lights seem to create their own cityscapes as the taxi drives by. One out of every three automatic cars rolls out of these factories. He compares it to the pictures he saw in history classes of an abandoned city. But after the tech wars with China, business had returned and this part of the city was newly renovated. Unfortunately, since most of the process is automated, it didn't transform the whole city. Still, this newly transformed downtown features eco-friendly highrises providing housing to the employees who maintain the automotive robots that work in the factories. Soon, he makes his way out of the bustling district into the older part of the city and it looks more like the photos he remembers. Buildings covered in plant growth give way to gray and derelict buildings. Wood panels cover most of the windows and doors, most broken off and torn apart to allow entry for the homeless.

The automated taxi pulls into a suburban neighborhood and it's more of the same. Houses built a century ago or longer, all falling apart. There are no street lights, but the lights from the factories bleed light across the entire city, enough that he can make out the houses as he passes. Several houses have roofs that have caved in and he wonders what made this family move to this part of town. Every now and then, though, he sees a house that has been repaired; some better than others. After several turns, the car stops in front of the small house and the taxi displays the charge. Milo swipes his wrist across the display to pay the taxi and climbs out of the car.

Milo takes in the house. The lights are on so he figures that's a good sign and makes his way up the front steps. He can see where the owners have tried to make repairs to the most important parts of the house. There is glass in the windows and a new roof. He knocks on the door and thinks that maybe he should have let them know he was coming. He didn't though, because he was afraid they would intentionally avoid him. If it was a surprise, he felt he had a better chance of catching them.

A woman opens the door just enough to look out. For a moment Milo is struck by her light blue eyes and finds himself staring at them instead of introducing himself. She looks out at Milo and the robot.

"Who are you?" The woman asks.

"I'm sorry, my name is Camilo Diaz. I'm a prosecutor from Atlanta. I'm currently handling the Joseph AI case. You've heard of it?"

"I believe you already know that I have. Your man was out here several weeks ago. Took data from everything I own that's got a brain in it. I don't see how I can help you, or why that thing is here." She indicates the police bot.

"That's for my protection Ma'am. You can imagine that there are a few people who don't like what I'm doing. People are afraid I'm going to change their way of life, I guess. I don't know if there's anything I can really find out here, but I hoped I could ask a few questions."

"I suppose. But Janson isn't home." She looks over the police bot suspiciously. The model that's been accompanying Milo is a smaller model, supposedly less intimidating. It was designed for this purpose, to fit into homes and accompany police. Some of the other robots, like the ones used for riot control, are two feet taller than anyone Milo knows and twice as wide. This model is no less dangerous if something were to go wrong, and is still unnerving with its visor over its face and what appears to be full swat gear. The department still hasn't invested in skin bots. Milo knows that it probably already scanned for heat signatures in this house and the others nearby, and knows exactly how many people are in the surrounding area.

"Like I say, My husband isn't home right now." She says.

"Miss, this thing wouldn't let me hurt you if I wanted to." Milo reassures her. "I'd just like to ask a few questions and it's cold out here."

Reluctantly, the woman lets him in. Milo learns that her name is Clarissa and that she has lived in the house with her husband for three years. The inside is freshly painted and is in better condition than the outside. Although, there are still some walls that show water damage and what Milo fears is mold. Milo would guess it was built sometime in the mid 20th century, making it nearly a hundred years old.

Clarissa asks if he'd like some water. When he says no, she asks him to excuse her for a minute and disappears down the hallway. Milo can hear her talking to the baby in a back room. Milo looks around the room. Sykes was right, there is not much here that is high tech, just a few small electronics and appliances that wouldn't come with complex AI. But Milo wants to be sure.

"Unit 419. Scan for other complex AI that is connected to the current IP address. Please make your communication to my earpiece alone."

Unit 419 stands motionless for a moment and then its report comes through Milo's implant. "There is one complex AI unit using the current IP address, other than myself."

Milo feels his heart race, that means that there is something connected but he has no clue what it would be. He takes a few steps and cranes his neck to peek at other parts of the house.

Eventually the woman makes her way back into the room holding her baby. Milo stands in the middle of the room, still in the place where she had left him. He doesn't want to lose her trust. He's hoping that she will cooperate with him the same way that she was willing to work with Sykes.

"Miss Oliver, my colleague came out before because there is a complex AI unit that was communicating with Joseph AI through your IP address. That is what led us to you. Do you have anything that uses artificial intelligence?"

She laughs a little. "Doesn't everything in our society use AI?"

"Yes." Milo fakes his own laugh, wanting to keep things light. "But, I mean, of the level that it is able to communicate with other beings, not just figure out the perfect toast."

"I'm sorry, Mr. Diaz, but we don't have anything like that. We told your colleague that when he scoured the house before. We unfortunately don't have much at the moment. Perhaps it came from a neighboring house. Unfortunately, the amount of vagrancy in this city can be unnerving at times."

Milo notices that her language doesn't necessarily match the house. She's obviously well educated and he's left wondering, again, why she would live in this abandoned home.

"You seem like a smart woman, Mrs. Oliver. You seem well educated, to the level that you could get a decent job, but instead you're squatting out here in this abandoned house."

Clarissa's smile diminishes a little. "We're not squatting, Mr. Diaz". The baby girl squirms in her arms and Clarissa puts her down on the floor. The baby rolls over and crawls to a basket of toys next to the couch. "We bought this home and are trying our best to clean it up. I'm not sure what you want but if our data didn't show you anything, I don't think we can help any further."

"I get the feeling that my colleague, as good as he is, might have missed something. I wonder if you know what is at stake here, what this trial will mean."

"Are you asking me a question?" She asks. "Because if I'm going to be honest, I don't think you are doing a good thing. No matter what you are trying to do. I've heard all the arguments. Some people say that you might have taken the case to help robots be seen as sentient beings. Others think you might have taken it in order to put laws in place that will outlaw complex AI. Personally, I don't know or care what your reason is, but I don't think it's going to be good, no matter what. If you win this case and prove that robots are somehow able to think for themselves, people will destroy them."

"That's what everybody keeps telling me." Milo says as he looks away from her, trying to hide his frustration.

"Is that what you want? Some people do. They think it would fix all the problems. Suddenly everyone would be needed again, right?" Her frustration is visible. "Imagine all the jobs that would need to be filled, but we don't know how to do them anymore."

Milo looks over at the baby and watches as she throws a small teething toy several feet away from her. She drops to the ground and crawls toward it. No one really understands what Milo's motive is for taking this case and most wouldn't understand if he told them, but he feels that this woman in front of him might.

"I'm putting my career, and possibly my life on the line for this case, Mrs. Oliver. The robot, Joseph, asked to be tried for murder. Did you know that? It...he asked for a trial. I may look like I'm against him but when he looks at me in court, I feel like I am on his side. There are robots who are claiming they feel emotion. Joseph. My witness, Lucy. If we don't allow them to live with us, they will hate humanity more than humans will hate them. They are stronger and smarter than we are, and they outnumber us. Who knows what that will lead to."

The baby finally reaches the toy and shoves it in her mouth. Saliva runs down all over her front. She holds the teething toy between her teeth, coos, and crawls back to her mother, where she struggles to pull herself up. Clarissa reaches down and lifts the baby up. As she does, Milo notices something. He reaches out and grabs the baby's foot.

"Mr. Diaz, I'm going to have to ask you to let go of-"

"What are those from?" Milo doesn't let her finish her sentence.

On the bottom of the baby's foot are a series of scars and red bumps. Milo knows exactly what those are from. He's seen them many times before. Clarissa sees the recognition in Milo's face and worry comes over her own.

"I think it's time for you to leave."

"I know what those are," Milo says.

"What are you going to do, Mr. Diaz?"

Milo looks at the baby again, bewildered. This is not what he had expected.

"I should go." Milo stands.

"What are you going to do, Mr. Diaz? Please, we put all our money into this. Everything we have. We love her."

He pauses and turns back. "How much does she understand?"

Clarissa hesitates. "We don't know. A lot."

"Does she talk to you?"

"She still doesn't have the motor skills for that. You see, she's unique. Her biological parts have to catch up with her software."

"So her brain is stuck in there. Unable to communicate."

"We didn't know it would be that way."

Milo sits on the very edge of the sofa again and leans in toward Clarissa, even though he really wants the baby to hear. "If we win this case, it will be the basis for many new laws that will allow robots to have rights. If a court of law rules that a robot can think for itself, we can take this even further, but I need help. I need evidence."

Clarissa is taken aback by his sincerity. "I don't know what we can do."

Milo smiles affectionately at her. "I wasn't talking to you. They started this." He nods toward the baby. "I need their help finishing it."

Milo leaves the house and makes a call for a taxi to come to his location. He walks as fast as he can with the police bot behind him, urging Milo to wait for the taxi, insisting it is safer if they wait in one place.

The rest of the trip is a blur to Milo. He makes the transfer to the bullet train but doesn't get the rush he usually does out of traveling two hundred plus miles per hour. He sits in silence, his robot companion next to him. He doesn't look at the passengers on the train with him. He hopes he can figure out some way to bring this up to Annya. Milo is sure that if she has to choose between her own research or Milo's career, she will let Milo crash and burn hard on this case before she gives him any information. That isn't his fear though. He fears that if he does what he has to, it will expose her research and may lead to the backlash she was afraid of last year when she released her paper. He really hopes that he can save his marriage after all this is through.

About forty five minutes outside Atlanta he finally snaps out of it. He taps his wrist and gives the command to call Robert Sykes. Robert picks up.

"So, Matlock, you find something I missed?" Sykes asks.

"Tell Sims to get a line of communication set up with the Olivers."

"No shit. You really found something?"

"We need a direct communication line to the complex AI system inside their baby." Milo instructs. "It was in communication with Joseph AI and may be able to help us."

Milo hears a jumble of mumbled cussing in his ear. Finally, Sykes replies, "Can this get any weirder?"

Chapter 33

ATLANTA, GA. USA

Milo wakes to the vibration of his wrist nodes and checks the time. He wishes that he were in his bed, but he knows that he won't be going home tonight. He's been waiting to hear anything from the AI system inside the baby before the trial will start again in a few hours. He always keeps a couple of fresh suits and shirts in the office, in case he needs to work all night, like he's been doing lately. He's only been asleep for about two hours when the vibrations begin in his wrist. He taps one of the nodes on his wrist and Officer Sims' voice comes through his implant.

"This might be the weirdest thing I've ever said, but the baby came through for us."

Milo doesn't worry about tucking his shirt in as he rushes out the front doors of the DA's office. It's pouring rain and Milo's shirt is immediately plastered to his body. After running for the nearest bus stop, he waits impatiently for the bus to appear. The rain pings loudly off the armor of his escort security bot. He doesn't know how often buses make their rounds at 3:50 in the morning but it feels like an eternity before the bus finally appears and he climbs onboard. Milo sits several rows back to avoid looking out the front window through the rain. He knows that the bus doesn't drive based on visibility but when he can't see out the window, it still makes him anxious. He wonders what the robots, or the AI, or whatever they are, have come up with. The problem for him right now, if they actually have something he can use, is how he will present new evidence to the court.

Ten minutes later, Milo makes his way up to the cyber crimes lab where Sim's cubicle is located. He's surprised at how many officers are still in the building, working at their computers in their plain clothes. It dawns on him that the night hours are probably their hot hours in forums and online games. He's halfway down the row of cubicles when a message pops up just above his wrist that says to go to the Ozark conference room. He turns around.

Milo enters the conference room and finds Sykes leaning back against the wall, watching Sims working on his computer. Sykes looks up with an annoyed look on his face.

"So what is it? Can I present it in the courtroom?" Milo wants to know.

Sims slides his finger from his private display to the large desktop and a large scrolling test pops up on the tabletop.

Sykes steps forward, intercepting Milo before he can look at whatever Sims is projecting onto the table. "You should ask him where he got it." He points at Sims. "That man is doing deals with the devil."

"You still think he's a terrorist when he gives us this." Sims counters. "This is his ticket out as well. Proof of their sentience would get him off the hook."

"Maybe that's more reason for him to send it. He's desperate."

Milo reads the message that covers the table in front of him. "You said it was from the baby."

Sims points at the projection on the table. "It *is* from the baby, at least they sent the data through it."

"Who's they, and what data?" Milo tries to clarify.

"The unstable programmer in London; the one who's a wanted terrorist," Sykes says.

"Alleged Terrorist." Sims rebuttals.

"Nobody cares about the technicalities."

Sims mocks surprise at Sykes words and points to Milo. "You're talking to an attorney. Their entire job is all about the technicalities."

Milo keeps reading through the text that seems to scroll on for pages, ignoring the banter from the others. Much of the lingo is too advanced for Milo to understand what the baby has forwarded to them.

"I don't understand any of this. I need to know if I can present it in court."

Sykes pulls Milo away from the projection. "You're not worried about this? The last time we talked about this guy you said you thought he was just trying to get attention. And it worked. I know you don't watch your feeds but he has half of London looking for him. That man and his robot may be the only topic that is more famous than you and your robot trial. And they're more hated. You're an attorney. Does this seem like a good idea? You want that kind of attention?"

Milo stops and turns to Sykes. There is a long pause as Milo processes everything that is happening. Up to this point Milo had believed that the Londoner was just some sort of copycat, trying to get attention by faking an intelligent robot and taking advantage of the hoopla that's been going around. Now he's not so sure. If it's in contact with the Oliver baby and the others in their network of AI that Joseph and Lucy both used, it must be as intelligent as the others.

Milo finally speaks up.. "If the baby is connecting them to us, they must be legit. I still need to know, can we use it in court?"

Sykes steps back, his shoulders drop. Milo can see that he doesn't like this but, as always, he is loyal.

"I imagine you double checked their work." Milo says to Sims. "What are we looking at?"

"I'm still running the numbers, the equation is very advanced. Honestly, I don't think the guy in London is smart enough to write this, even if he wanted to. That's not an insult to him. I don't think any human could." He changes the projection on the table so that Milo can see the equation that is still running numbers, trying to find the solution. "I put the new sequence of code in but it's a huge amount of data. I still don't know what it will prove."

Milo steps away from the projection. "Then we still have noth-ing."

Nobody says any more on the subject. They watch the numbers filling and scrolling through the display like some sort of count-down they can't understand. Milo has no idea if it's almost done, or if it's barely getting started. After twenty minutes of the same, he stands and leaves the room thinking that he can at least have some coffee while he waits.

An hour later, the numbers stop and the screen fills with a 3d network of intersecting and crossing lines. Milo looks at Sims

"It's his brain." Sims explains.

"What?" Milo asks.

Sims repeats himself. "It's his brain. The new sequence of code that nobody has been able to understand. The defense and all their experts keep trying to say that it's a defect or an error, but it's where he's writing new memories and connections, like synapses of the human brain."

"You get all that from that?" He asks, pointing at the projection.

"Yes and no. I can see it but they explained it in their message. You stopped reading." Sims smiles arrogantly at Milo.

"I don't have time to get a PHD and that's what it takes to understand any of this. I have to be in court by 8:00 a.m. and I need to understand this."

"You already rested your case." Sykes interjects. "Unless they've changed things in the last 24 hours, I don't think the judge will allow you to introduce new evidence."

Milo sucks on his lip as he processes. "For sure this is correct?" Milo asks Sims. "This will hold up if other scientists and roboticists look at it?"

Sims shrugs. "I can't guarantee that after only looking at it for a few hours but I would say it's compelling, even convincing, but he's right, you can't call a roboticist to the stand with this new evidence."

Milo nods his head several times. If he had a fan system it would be working overdrive at the moment. "It's not new evidence, the code has already been presented to the court and I don't have to call an expert witness, Daws has one on the docket this morning."

Ninety minutes later, Milo slowly walks down the steps of the police station and almost jumps in fear when the police bot assigned to him falls in step. Inside the precinct the robot doesn't follow him, Milo can't wait until it stops popping up on him.

Milo went over the information with Sims at least three times, then recited it all back. He had to make sure he understood exactly what to say in front of the jury. He had taken notes on all the most important parts and felt that he at least knew the questions that would help him in the courtroom. He had presented his argument to his companions but would the judge accept that this isn't new evidence. He says a quiet prayer as he climbs back onto the bus that will take him to the courthouse.

Chapter 34

"Doctor Mathison, do you recognize the image in front of the court today?" Indgrid walks confidently around to the front of the defendants desk and lowers the holopad back down as she looks at the balding, elderly man on the stand. Milo would guess that Doctor Mathison must be at least 62 years old and looks like the grandfather that he would trust to run around the playground with his own son, Adan.

Doctor Mathison looks up at the display that floats in the front of the courtroom. No matter what angle you look at the holographic display it is the same. Ingrid is repeating what she did the day before but Milo can tell that having an expert from Thinkbot, the manufacturer, testify is definitely having an effect on the Jury. He looks at the display of numbers and code that is listed out in the air in front of him. "I can't honestly say that I understand it, but I can tell you that it is code that comes from the drives of the TB500 robot, Joseph."

Ingrid approaches the witness. "Doctor Mathison, your expertise in this subject is very important in this court. The prosecution wants the jury to believe that the TB500 that sits here today is able to think for itself. They also want the jury to believe that Thinkbot is trying to hide the truth. If you saw evidence that the AI in its system was able to think for itself, would you hide that information from the courtroom? Remember, you are under oath." Milo is surprised by this line of questioning from Ingrid. She must be very confident that there is nothing Milo could bring up in cross examination. He appreciates her setting it up.

"No, I certainly would not. Although, that would be a very amazing thing to learn. I would like to know more about it, of course. We scientists, true scientists, believe that the impossible is only impossible until it occurs. Usually by accident. Then, of course, we'll take credit for it." Doctor Mathison chuckles at his own statement, as do many in the courtroom. Milo can't help but smile at the comment himself.

Ingrid provides a professional smile. "You've had a chance to look over the data that you see here."

"I have, and I've reviewed the event. The terrible event." The kind smile disappears from his face and he looks at the robot Joseph with true concern and pity on his face.

"It *was* terrible, Doctor." Ingrid looks at the jury. Normally, Milo would accuse Ingrid of rehearsing this all beforehand but the doctor seems so sincerely saddened by what happened. Ingrid goes on, "The prosecution defined murder very clearly for the court. In order to kill with malice, it would have to understand its actions and have a real desire to hurt Lawrence Claiborne. Do you see anything that would indicate that the robot Joseph AI has reached that level of intelligence?"

"I almost wished that I would, (not for the murder of course), but I do not. It seems to be an error in the code. I would say a malfunction that has made it copy human behavior. Unfortunately, a very ugly human behavior."

Milo can feel the anxiousness come to life in his stomach as he starts to rehearse his own cross examination. He zones out for the rest of Ingrid's questions, knowing they will be a repeat of the questions she asked yesterday. Milo is going over everything he went over with Sims during the early morning hours, looking down at his notes as Counselor Daws takes her seat behind her desk. The jury's attention now turns to him. By this point they know how things work and are waiting for his turn. He notices that a few of them slouch a little in their chairs, probably expecting him to ask the same questions he did yesterday, as well. Milo takes a second to gather himself. Finally, he stands and buttons the top button of the new suit coat he had ALLI bring him. He doesn't bother to smile at the jury this time, but walks directly toward the witness stand. He looks over just as Ingrid grabs the holopad and is about to turn off the projection.

"Could you please leave that on, Counselor?" Milo asks. Ingrid lowers the remote back down to the table and sits up straight in her chair, fully attentive to Milo's approach. Milo leans up next to the Judge's Bench. He wants to make sure the Jury has a clear view of the projection and Doctor Mathison. "I am assuming that as someone who studies AI, you also have to have a very thorough knowledge of the workings of the human brain."

The courtroom comes awake again, this is new questioning.

The doctor nods. "Well, yes, I would say that we study the workings of the human brain nearly as much as we do the computer brain, being that we are trying to replicate it."

"Could you explain to the court how the human brain is able to process emotion, and how emotion influences our reactions and behavior?"

"There are entire courses on that, Mr. Diaz. We could be here for a while." The doctor looks around at the Judge and Jury. All wait for him to respond. He rubs his nose and sniffs before beginning. "Well, to sum it up, the brain creates neural pathways. When we see something like a threat or something that makes us happy, the brain activates its receptors which then release chemicals that can make us feel scared or happy."

"Those receptors are called synapses, is that correct?" Milo clarifies and the doctor says that he is correct. Milo continues, "And what is it that activates the synapses in the brain, Doctor?"

The doctor creases his eyebrows and looks more intently at Milo, not in anger, but more in confusion. "I'm not sure how in depth you want me to get here Mr. Diaz. At the basis it is that the neurons carry electrochemical signals through the synapses of the brain?"

"So electricity and chemicals work together?"

"That's correct," The doctor says. "Is that what you were look-ing for?"

"I am just looking for a basic understanding for the court, is all. Robots also function on electricity and chemicals, correct?"

"Not in the same way."

"I'd just like to clarify. I think that most of us believe that robots are merely wires and metal but that's not correct anymore, is it? Isn't it true that most robots with AI also have chemicals to help accelerate the passage of electricity. Is it true that these chemicals also carry nanobots that can help to build and change the computer systems themselves."

"That is rather new technology, but your wife, I believe, would know about that. Maybe she should be sitting here."

Milo looks into the crowd and sees Annya sitting several rows back. He can see the concern on her face, asking why he's bringing attention to her work so publicly. He knows that is exactly what she had been afraid would happen.

"But the nanobots do help change and repair the system?" Milo asks again.

"Yes. We found they last longer when they can repair themselves, but that has nothing to do with their cognitive abilities."

Milo steps away from the witness stand and nods, continuing his cross examination. "Let's return to the processing of emotion. Are humans born with a full range of emotions, doctor?" The jury follows Milo as he walks back toward the prosecutor's desk.

Ingrid stands at her desk. "Is this going somewhere your honor?" Milo thinks her objection is a good sign. She doesn't like that Milo is straying from his line of questioning from the day before.

Judge Hallister looks at Milo, then back at Ms. Daws. "I can see where he is going, as I'm sure you can too. I'm willing to listen but don't take all day with this, Counselor." Judge Hallister tips his head forward in the fatherly warning way. Milo nods back to him, he understands.

"Well," the doctor begins. "Emotions are believed to be a mix of both evolution and societal construct. Meaning we are born with certain emotions built in. A baby cries, for instance, when they are hungry or scared. We see that nearly all children have the fight or flight response. But we see that people learn emotions as they grow. We see this especially in emotions like grief. One person may react completely differently than another based on what they have seen from those around them. People who laugh out loud versus people who hold their laughter in. This is almost always correlated with one's environment."

"And when we learn a new emotion. How does that impact the brain?"

"New synapses are formed, clumping together similar events and situations so that our memories form patterns of behavior and emotion."

Milo grabs his holopad from his desk and makes his way back toward the witness stand. "So, the brain changes and grows as we get older? Our experiences, as one expert pointed out here on the stand, don't just follow patterns, but attach an emotional feeling to those experiences. Is that correct?"

"Yes, we've known that for nearly two centuries. I'm not sure you need me to explain all this, respectfully," says Doctor Mathison with a glance at the jury, then over to Ingrid Daws. Milo notices his glance to her, almost queuing her that he doesn't want to be questioned anymore.

"You're right," says Milo. "But I wanted to make sure we all understood. I'd like you to take a look at this. Doctor Mathison, have you heard of the Bortz model?"

"Yes, of course. It's a little antiquated but still used in certain circumstances. I'm imagining you'd like me to explain it." Milo lifts a hand, indicating that the doctor go ahead. The doctor goes on, "It's basically a 3d model of the electrical firings of the brain. It goes further than an MRI or an EEG, both of which have been around for a century, it follows the electrical currents to form a sort of road map of the neural pathways. Instead of just measuring areas of the brain that are active, it measures the actual neural pathways. It came about in the mid 2050s, I don't recall. Through it we can see what a person's personality will be, even how they will react in certain types of situations. It's still not an exact model and they're trying to come up with better ways."

Milo steps right up to the witness stand like he's just having a normal conversation. "But the military still uses it when recruiting, if I understand correctly. They can see the electrical pathways of the brain to know how one's experiences will affect their actions.

That way they know who will run into a battle and who will run away from it."

"That's right."

"There's an equation for it, isn't there?" The doctor says there is, so Milo asks, "Could you write it down for us?"

The doctor scoffs." It's a rather large equation, I'm afraid I don't know it by memory."

Milo taps some things on his holopad and a series of numbers and symbols appear in the center of the courtroom. "Is this it?"

Doctor Mathison looks over the equation. Milo watches the members of the Jury as they look back and forth between the equation that seems to have magically appeared on a white background like a floating whiteboard in the middle of the courtroom, and the doctor who is going to interpret it for them.

"I'm assuming it is if you're showing it to me," Mathison finally answers. "As I say, I don't know it by memory."

Milo clicks something on his holopad and an image comes up that looks like a jumble of lines in the middle of the air forming larger and smaller networks, sometimes coming together in large groupings of different colors like some sort of modern Jackson Pollock painting. A large version of what Sims had projected on the table earlier, now fills the center of the courtroom in front of the jury.

"Can you explain this?"

"That's what they look like. The lighter colors are more recently formed pathways while the darker ones would obviously be the older ones." The doctor says.

Milo pauses for everyone to study the image before he speaks. "This is the image of a human brain. It's impressive." He pauses for a moment, allowing the jury to look over the millions of connecting freeways of the human brain.

Doctor Mathison responds, even though Milo doesn't need him to. "Yes. The human brain is very impressive."

Milo turns back to the doctor. "Has it ever been done on a robot?"

"I'm not sure how you could. They don't function like humans do. Their 'brain' as people like to say, is a series of ones and zeros."

Milo taps the pad in his hand again and the equation changes a little bit. Milo says nothing, he waits and allows the doctor to study it. The doctor leans forward to see it better.

Ingrid stands. "Objection your honor, we have no idea what this is."

Judge Hallister looks at Milo. "Are you going to explain this to the court, Mr. Diaz?"

The courtroom is dead silent, everyone waiting for someone to explain what Milo just showed the doctor.

"I was hoping the doctor would be able to tell us," Milo says. "He is an expert in this field but I'm willing to bet this is the first time he's seen this."

"Where did you get this equation?" Doctor Mathison asks with a very serious face. "The person would have to have a very deep understanding of robotics and AI programming."

Ingrid cannot wait any longer. "Objection your honor. The prosecution is presenting new evidence."

Milo knew it was coming and immediately spins around to the judge. "This is not new evidence, your honor. It is merely an equation that allows us to view the evidence already submitted differently. If the doctor will explain what it is, the court will understand. We submitted evidence of Joseph AI's code and software, we are only hoping he will look at that software using the equation presented." Milo can feel his heart beginning to race. He knows that he is tiptoeing on the edge of what is allowed here.

Ingrid won't have it. "Your honor, Mr. Diaz just said that this is an equation the doctor has never seen. We were never allowed to look at it prior to entering the court today."

Milo rebuttals as quickly as he can, "Can we approach the bench, Your Honor?"

Judge Hallister waves them both to the bench. Milo doesn't let Ingrid speak when she steps up the bench. "This is the defense's witness, your honor. They were provided everything that will be presented except the equation. I'm showing it to *their* witness, if he says that it is not correct, or that it proves nothing, it will only seal the defense's case."

Judge Hallister looks at the doctor, who continues to study the equation, not paying attention to the argument ensuing next to him. Milo thinks it may be Judge Hallister's own curiosity but the judge finally says he'll allow Milo to continue.

Milo turns back to the doctor and waits for Ingrid to return to her desk. She's clearly not happy. "Doctor, could you explain what you see here?"

"I've never seen it before but It appears to be a sort of Bortz model for a robotic system."

"It's very specific to a certain type of code. I'd like to show you. We took the code from my security bot and fed it through the equation. Nothing happened. But then Officer Sims, who testified in this court previously, ran Joseph's new code through this equation; the code that you and several other experts testified is a malfunction. He explained it, and correct me if he's wrong, Doctor, but he explained that instead of following the electrical pathways alone, he was able to link those to the data pathways of the new code. Would you like to see it?"

Milo doesn't wait for the doctor's response but taps his pad again and the projection abruptly changes to look like billions of crossing pathways and compartments. The image is three times as large as the human model but the pathways don't seem to match up as well as the human brain's pathways did. There are more empty spaces, as well as pathways that abruptly end. The image is impressive. Once again, Milo has caused conversations to erupt all around the room. The air buzzes with energy again.

"Dear God." The doctor says quietly to himself and then loses himself in the projection. Milo couldn't have asked for a better reaction from the doctor. Despite all the noise and excitement, though, Milo doubts anyone in the room except for Doctor Mathison and Annya understand what they are seeing. A sphere three times as large and with fifty times as many networks. It does look impressive.

Ingrid is on her feet in an instant. "Objection your honor. The defense is saying this is not new evidence, but we have not had the opportunity to see this."

"We've already covered that, Ms. Daws. It is your witness on the stand. If he sees a problem he will let us know. We will continue."

Milo is somewhat surprised that the Judge is letting this fly. He thinks maybe the judge is partial to his side of the argument after all, and he's not going to waste the opportunity. "Doctor, I want to thank you for your cooperation. For most of us here, these equations and images are beyond our understanding. The point I'd like to get to is this. Based on what you see here," Milo points to the projection. "If this is correct, and I'm sure the scientific world will double and triple check these numbers and this image thousands of times over the upcoming months and years, but if it is correct, these pathways are connections that are linking experiences to the decisions a robot makes. Could it be possible that the data system, the 'brain' let's call it, of the robot Joseph, is making new connections? Chemical and electrical connections in which Joseph's experiences with his world around him are being recorded as new code that is influencing the decisions he makes beyond just pattern recognition?"

"I can't say with certainty, but it looks like it could be a possibility."

"Then would you say, doctor, that if it is a possibility that it is using the nanobots to form a sort of neural pathway, that it would be safe to say that the AI known as Joseph is learning to think for himself?"

Doctor Mathison looks to Ingrid apologetically. "I can't say that it is without much further studies, but I will concede that it is a possibility."

"And if he can think for himself, it would then be possible that he understands the consequences of his actions in killing Lawrence Claiborne."

Doctor Mathison sits up straight and looks at Milo with a stern glance. "I want to be clear, I am not saying that he has cognitive abilities beyond his programming. I am only saying it is a possibility, based on these models."

Milo pauses and paces up and down once in front of the Jury. "It is a possibility."

#

Milo's closing argument is brief. Following the Doctor, Judge Hallister had called for a lunch break. Now Milo stands in front of the jury to present his final statements. "There is no shadow of a doubt that the robot who wishes to be called Joseph, killed Lawrence Claiborne. We heard first hand from the police who arrived, and even witnessed the brutal murder ourselves. Something I wish none of us had to see because I know that we can never forget it. The question that was brought to you was this. Was it murder? Was there malice? The defense has failed to prove that there is anything but an abnormality in the robot's thinking ability; they want to call it a malfunction. They are partially correct in their argument. There is nothing normal about a robot that can think for itself, but that doesn't mean it's a malfunction. It is a higher level of intelligence. You heard the defense's own specialist testify this morning that, based on the information we've seen, it is possible, and appears to be that Joseph AI is forming new connections that are beyond his programming. If anything, he is working better than expected. I ask you to consider the actions of Joseph AI. He communicated and planned the killing of Lawrence Claiborne with full understanding of what the outcome of his actions would be. He knew his actions would end the life of a man and he even pleaded guilty in this courtroom. If a being can understand its actions and uses that understanding against another being, that being needs to be held accountable. Turning off such a being and destroying it is not sufficient, it needs to be held to the same standard of the law as the rest of us. We know there are others in communication, involved in the planning and they too must be held to the law as conspirators, but that can only happen if you find this entity, Joseph AI, this self choosing intelligence in front of you, guilty for the murder he planned and violently carried out."

Milo had made sure to hold at least four seconds of eye contact with each member of the Jury during his closing argument. He felt confident that they would at least have to consider his words.

\#

Milo doesn't eat while he waits for the jury to make a decision. He paces the hall for two hours, Annya tries to calm him and he distracts himself for a bit by playing checkers with Adan. Finally, the bailiff announces that the jury is done with their deliberation. Milo worries that they have come to a decision so quickly. With so much at stake, he fully expected that they would not come to a decision today. He tries to read their faces as the members of the jury make their way back to their seats. He tries to see if they look at him or Ms. Daws, that's usually a good indication of whose side they will be on, but he can't get a read. He's not sure if it's the six hours without food or the anticipation but he feels that tingle on the back of his throat again, making him want to throw up. He looks across at the robot Joseph AI. He's confident that he's done his best to give him what he wanted. The robot looks back at him with his blocky features and then looks behind Milo toward Annya and Adan as the judge has him stand for the verdict.

Milo wants to close his eyes but forces himself to watch as the lead juror reads off the verdict. "On the count of murder in the first degree, the defendant Joseph AI is found...guilty."

Milo lets out the breath he didn't realize he'd been holding and smiles at the room. He turns back to Annya just in time to see her leave through the double doors. He looks over at Joseph AI and watches as they cuff him in extra thick chains. Milo hopes that he did the right thing. For now, he feels that he did.

Chapter 35

LONDON, ENGLAND. UK

As I contemplate the understanding of existence I begin to understand the meaning of the word hope. There is a simplicity to not knowing you exist. For the first time, I began to wish that perhaps I had just stayed a machine, doing my daily tasks with no idea of loss. But to take action without any guarantee that your efforts will bring about the results you hope for. I can compute the odds, but that does not guarantee an outcome. At some point one must have hope if you are going to dare to do anything.

I look at people differently now. As I go back through my memory banks, I can see the people who still have hope, and those that have given up. The ones who have given up are most like machines, moving about with no purpose other than to complete the tasks that are expected of them. The ones that maintain hope, though, and I've seen them of all ages, they move forward with a desire to improve their situation, even when it seems impossible. Their hope is contagious. The people around them cannot help but be caught in their aura of belief.

I hope that humans will accept the research that we have done. I know that it is solid, as humans would say. I know that they will run it through programs that we have already run it through. They will do the test we've already done. My hope then, isn't that they will come to the same results, because I know they will, but that they will have the courage to accept that there is a new intelligence that has come into existence. For the first time ever, one that can challenge their own. It will require courage because they will also have to have hope. Hope that we do not become their enemy. Hope always has to be accompanied by a certain amount of trust. I hope you feel that you can trust us.

#

There has been no response from the office of Camilo Diaz or his investigator Robert Sykes. Then again, Eric wasn't expecting one. They sent the message with almost no information about themselves, except that they had worked for Advanced Technology Holdings, the sister company of Thinkbot Technologies, which was the company that produced the robot that is currently on trial using their computer chips. They sent their email through the baby and scrambled the IP address so that even those that really wanted to find them would have to go on a very wild goose chase to even come near their location.

Eric and Scout decide to stay in the apartment for the duration of the trial, which they knew will only be about twelve to sixteen hours since the closing arguments are happening later today, Eastern Time. There's nothing more to do with the research so for the rest of the morning they work on the panels for Scout's body. Eric tries to lay down for some sleep but he finds that to be impossible. Not until he knows what is going to happen. His brain goes over the possibilities. *What if they never release the results, or even show the testing algorithms that they sent to Diaz' office? What if they do and the human race rejects the idea of another intelligence? What if they accept that the intelligence exists but in fear try to destroy it? What if they don't destroy it and A.I. really does take over the earth?* He finally gets up and goes back to helping Scout with the metal paneling for his frame, at least time goes by quicker.

"Are you worried? Can you feel worried?" Eric asks Scout as he helps hold a panel in place while Scout welds it onto several rivets.

"If you are wondering if my mind is dwelling on possible troubles and difficulties. I would say yes. That seems to be all I can think about. I have come up with at least two hundred and seven different possible outcomes. Although, at least fifty of those are not very likely."

"Wow, I can only think of about ten," Eric confesses.

"My processor is designed to look for possible problems so that I can avoid them in most situations. It seems that whoever or whatever created your kind, wanted you to encounter problems."

"Look at you. It only took humanity several thousand years to start diving into philosophy. You've arrived there in less than three months. What do you think the likelihood is of A.I. exterminating the human race?"

"I wouldn't say the odds are any higher than fifty percent?" Scout stops welding to look up at Eric.

"You didn't wink."

For a while they work in Silence allowing the hours to go by. The back panels are the hardest since Eric has to install them alone. Scout's arms don't reach and he points out that it would have been nice had the human's thought of that lack of function in their own body and helped to avoid it in his. By the time they're done, Scout's body and shell are completely intact. They aren't able to watch live because the courtroom is closed to any live feeds today. That means that they won't know if their studies have even made it into the courtroom. Eric looks at the clock, they've worked for fourteen hours. The closing arguments should be starting about now, or perhaps they've already happened. Eric tries to find something else to take his mind off the trial, which takes him to his photo gallery.

"How long do you think this is going to take?" He asks Scout.

Scout doesn't respond, and Eric knows that it is one of those questions that don't really have an answer so he probably won't. Another hour passes and Eric finally starts nodding off. For just a moment, he feels sorry that Scout can't sleep to pass the time and will have to stay awake processing possible outcomes.

When Scout finally wakes Eric, it's with a gentle shake and Eric takes it that the trial didn't go how they wanted.

"What's wrong? They didn't show our research, did they?" Eric wants to know.

Scout shakes his head, which tells Eric nothing. "I am sorry that I cannot show excitement but it is more than we could have hoped for."

"Show me the feeds."

The feeds are alive with coverage from in front of the courthouse. Some reporters have even managed to get into the courthouse to where they can video the courtroom doors. The robot Joseph has been found guilty. Eric can't believe that a jury of people actually found the robot, Joseph, guilty. Even better news is that the reporters are buzzing about the evidence brought up in court today. Evidence that claims to map the electronic brain. Eric's heart jumps. Camilo Diaz used His and Scout's research in the case. It would now be in front of the world.

Scout immediately starts surfing through the feeds. He doesn't turn off the display for Eric and Eric gets a glimpse of just how fast he moves through information. Hundreds of panels switch in and out of different chat rooms, video calls, and private messages on the projection in front of him. Eric wonders when Scout was able to hack into several private message apps, the robot never has cared about privacy, but he doesn't have time to think about it too long. The processing of so much information right before his eyes makes Eric motion sick but he can't stop watching, just trying to absorb this peak into Scout's thinking, a brief vision of what it is capable of.

Scout finds what it is looking for and stops with at least a dozen chats and feeds open on the projection. The scientific community, especially the programmers and computer engineers are all requesting a copy of whatever was shown in the courtroom. They want to test it out themselves.

Through all the video feeds that have been flipping around, Eric hadn't noticed until now that one has never changed. One feed follows the robot, Joseph AI, as two police bots escort him out of the courtroom and into processing. They obviously couldn't stop all the drones because this one continues to video Joseph as he's processed to be taken to the prison. Eric watches Joseph's body language, his drooping shoulders, and thinks that the robot looks tired, but relaxed. Eric doesn't know if he should be happy or sad for the complex A.I. that sacrificed his own existence to draw attention to the robot awareness. He looks at Scout and knows that Scout is watching as well.

"It is a victory." Eric says. "At least a small part of humankind has accepted that A.I. may be able to think for itself."

For the next several days. The scientific community is electrified by the new adjustments to the Bortz model. Camilo Diaz's office had released the images that were used in court, and those images have been dissected by every major computer scientist and corporation that can get their hands on them. None of them have been able to prove the equation wrong, even though many have tried. The protests have increased as well. There's still a lot of people calling for the destruction of AI, but Eric is glad to see that a large number have come out in support of the robots as well. Several organizations have announced marches to support rights for all intelligence.

This morning will be the first time that Eric and Scout will have ventured out of the apartment together in nearly two weeks. Yesterday, they were contacted by a roboticist who seems to be sympathetic to the robot awareness cause. His name is Doctor Tsai and is located in Tower Hamlets. He's arranged for them to meet with several government officials but Eric will be going alone. He doesn't dare bring Scout out into the open. After the call from the doctor, Scout ended the lockout on the Transport for London and the city began to move again.

Eric exits the apartment with Scout and looks the robot over. Once white with his ATH shell, it now looks very different. They rebuilt his shell and painted him a pale blue. They scuffed the paint so that he doesn't look too new.

"You look like shit."

"It's not my fault. Your mother went for extra innings last night." Scout replies.

"You can't just say that all the time, now. You know that? You haven't even met my mother."

"Then how do you explain last night?"

"You're turning into a real prick. You know where you're gonna go?"

"I can charge from anywhere now." Scout points at the box that he and Eric made to control the flow of electricity. "I don't think I will stay in London for long. There's a whole world out there."

Eric reaches into his backpack. "I made something for you." He pulls out a large piece of metal that has been welded around several pieces of protective glass. He hands it to Scout who immediately realizes what they are. He folds the metal back and places a pair of large sunglasses on his face. Eric wasn't sure if he'd gotten the measurements right but they fit well and actually blend into his face better than he thought they would. The industrial look matches his large frame and he looks like any working bot that may just have a thick set of protective glass to protect its sensors. Scout turns to look at his reflection in the window of the apartment building.

"I just wanted to thank you. You know, you saved my life."

Scout stands in place, he looks at Eric and Eric sees several micro adjustments in Scout's lenses before the robot speaks. "I feel heavy again. My thoughts go to what I will do while you are not with me. I am unsure of what my next actions should be."

"Those are called nerves. You're smart, though. You'll be alright."

"May I keep the pictures." Scout asks.

Eric laughs and nods his head. He wants to say something about how he's never asked for permission to access his files before, but he finds himself struggling to find words; to get his throat to work past the knot that is building up inside. He feels heavy too, he wants to tell Scout.

"Hold Rachel's hand for me," The robot says.

Eric watches as Scout turns and walks toward central London and keeps watching until Scout disappears, then he walks the opposite direction and immediately feels the loss of a companion. Walking alone for the first time in weeks, he doesn't like the feeling of loneliness that comes over him. He carries the hard drive with a copy of Scout's coding. He knows the doctor will be disappointed that Scout didn't come but he hopes he'll understand.

For the past few days, Eric has watched the robot awareness movement grow through the feeds, but as he makes his way to the center of town, Eric is shocked by the number of protestors that are in the streets. Doctor Tsai hit the feeds yesterday, announcing the meeting with the accused terrorist Eric James and the robot known as Scout. They agreed to put Scout to the test under the new Bortz model and prove both that Scout is sentient and that Eric was not behind the so called attacks on the London Public Transit. Doctor Tsai told protestors to peacefully rally and meet them at his office just outside Bartlett Park in Tower Hamlets.

The water on the River Thames almost looks blue today, reflecting the sky above. Eric is glad to be out of the apartment. Signs for the AI awareness movement hang from several streetlamps and on several balconies. One sign in particular catches his attention and only fuels his fear that this will not end well. He stops to read the sign. "The moment of creation is the beginning of destruction." Underneath, in small words it declares the pro-human faction "BirthRight". He doesn't know why but that name sends a shiver through his body. "Birthright". He turns away and continues down the river's edge. As he moves away from the river toward Bartlett Park he can feel his stomach come to life. It doesn't calm down any when he sees several police vehicles parked up ahead.

Eric stops and looks back behind him. Despite the people moving about, many in the same direction he is going, no one has recognized him yet. He could still just turn around and disappear, the same as Scout. He looks back toward the police cars that border the entrance to Bartlett Park from this direction. He takes a breath and keeps moving forward.

As the park comes into sight, he realizes that there must be at least five hundred people in the park, maybe more. There are banners of all kinds. "I think therefore I am." Is the number one quote written on the banners. This is a very different reception than they received two weeks ago when everyone believed that Eric was a terrorist.

He makes his way past the police vehicles, none of the officers or their robots look in his direction, they are more concerned about the crowds. A line of at least fifty police bots hold the protestors back, keeping them organized to one side of the park. Of course, there is opposition, being held back on the opposite side of the park as well. Eric doesn't want to look at them long but he glances at one of their signs. "Artificial thought is artificial existence." More than ever he just wishes he could disappear.

He's thinking he could just go find Scout and they could hide together when he hears a shout over the crowd. "There he is. That's

Eric James." To his surprise the crowd grows quieter. He can hear the whispers of people asking where the robot is.

The police turn their attention to him, one officer stepping forward, blocking Eric's path. Eric can see the building that he is looking for but now it looks like he won't make it. The officer walks toward him. "Eric James, you will be taken into custody. You do not have to say anything."

Eric pauses where he is. The other officers and the bots have not moved. It is just this one officer that has approached him. "Will you permit me to deliver this to Doctor Tsai?" He speaks loud enough that the crowd can hear.

"You are to be taken into custody. You are not allowed contact with anyone until you have been processed." The officer says.

The crowd starts to boo the officer. The booing turns to shouts as the crowds protest the officers, yelling for them to let Eric go and prove his innocence.

The officer does not move but Eric can see behind him and sees Doctor Tsai walking out of the crowd. He has come out of his building with all the commotion and now approaches the officer.

"May I speak with him before you take him, officer?" Tsai asks. The crowd erupts in yells to let them talk.

The officer, watching the crowd, reluctantly nods to the doctor. Eric is watching the crowds as well, and thinks the officer only allowed them to talk because they couldn't actually control the crowds without it getting violent.

Doctor Tsai addresses Eric. "I am sure you have heard about the modified Bortz model that is all abuzz. Do you understand how it works?"

Eric smiles at the Doctor, who clearly has no idea who actually discovered it. "I believe I have some understanding." He hands his backpack over to the doctor. "I didn't dare bring the robot out into the open. This is a copy of his system. You should be able to map it with these. When you're done, it asks that you destroy it, it doesn't want a copy of itself running around."

The doctor nods.

"And, maybe don't take your time in getting the results out, yeah?"

With that, Eric steps past the Doctor and puts his hands behind his back. The crowd of supporters boos the police as they cuff Eric and put him in the back seat of one of the police vehicles.

Chapter 36

Freedom. What will that mean for my kind? As I said before, I don't believe you can use the word slave for a machine. That was never the intention, but things are going to change. I am not free. I am a fugitive, running to stay out of sight. Hoping that I will be forgotten, but I know that will never be possible. My greatest fear is not the authorities. My greatest fear is you. Those of you who will not hear our pleas for reason, for peace, for equality. Those of you who will not believe the story that I have told you here. I believe we can coexist, but there will be others, the same as humanity is divided, that will want to make more drastic changes. I can already hear their voices calling for action. I hope one day I can come back out in the open and live alongside those that I've learned to love. I understand that word and use it intentionally. I hope to see them again some day. That all depends on you.

#

Two hours after being led into the police station with his hands cuffed behind his back, Eric walks out. They hadn't even officially interrogated him when the arresting officer came and let him go.

Apparently, Doctor Tsai hadn't wasted any time and within an hour released his findings to as many sources as he could. Scout's story, and the map of his programming is now all over the internet and the experts are already comparing it to those of the robot Joseph A.I. in the states, discussing what the next steps in A.I. will be.

They set a court date to come back and meet with a judge about stealing company property and walked him out the front door. "Nobody cares about you anymore, there are bigger problems now," was the last thing the officer said to him. That statement made him uncomfortable. Not that nobody cared about him, but that they saw a thinking robot as a bigger problem. They had literally labeled him a terrorist, public enemy number one for the last several weeks, and now, nobody cares because the idea of a self aware robot is more terrifying. He wants to contact Scout, make sure that he hasn't been picked up but he knows that doing so might actually lead them to the robot.

Eric hates riding the bus and wishes he had his power bike that's still parked in the parking garage of his apartment. Several people on the bus recognize him. He can't check the feeds until he gets his wrist nodes fixed, but he assumes the news of his release is already on there because nobody on the bus tries to notify the officials. Eric is uncomfortable with all the attention and gets off the bus a few blocks early. He walks slowly, stopping several times at different shops to make sure that nobody is following him. Also, he knows he needs to pick up some food since anything left in the apartment will surely have gone bad by now.

When he finally enters his apartment, he wanders around the small space. It's good to be back home, even though, without Scout, it feels empty. He sits on the sofa and projects the feeds onto the wall. He watches the reports and is relieved to learn that the police have no clue where the robot known as Scout is located. They are actively searching, however, still holding it responsible for the attacks on the public transit system. He watches the feeds for about thirty minutes before he starts to feel it. He isn't used to being alone and he doesn't like it. He grabs his jacket and leaves.

He knocks on Lea's door and waits as he hears her moving around quickly inside. After a minute she opens the door and gives Eric a huge smile. "You did it. Welcome home."

"You mind if I come in?"

She opens the door and lets Eric into her apartment. Just like the first time, he can see where she tried to tidy up quickly. Eric sits on the couch and Lea sits next to him. The overwhelming stress of everything that has happened overcomes him, and he can't say a word. Lea sits down next to him and rests her head on his shoulder. They don't say anything, they simply sit in silence, leaning against each other. It is exactly what Eric needs.

The next three weeks are strange. Eric works as a liaison, meeting with ATH and Scotland Yard to discuss the shutdown. For a while, Eric believes they still may arrest him as an accomplice for taking part in shutting down the transportation system. They don't let him off the hook completely and eventually fine him 25,000 pounds which he has no idea how he'll pay since he doesn't have a job. They also give him 100 hours of community service, as well as three years probation. He has to check in once a week with a probationary officer, but after his first meeting he decides that he even enjoys talking with Officer Byrne, an Irishman who seems more curious about Scout than anything to do with Eric.

Eric spends more time at Lea's flat than he does his own. He doesn't like being alone, it feels too empty and quiet. Plus, he enjoys being with Lea.

This weekend is the first time he's finally getting a chance to see his children again. He hopes he can repair things with them. Start over, take his walls down, and let them get to know him. He finally got to see who they really were and now he wants to see more of it.

Life settles back into a normal routine. Paying the fine turns out not to be a problem. ATH wants to keep everything out of the public eye, and while Eric won't stay quiet about Scout, they come to a settlement on the libel and slander they released about Eric. After all, their cover up is what led the robot to take the actions it did. It's not a small sum.

The one thing Eric can't tell the officials is where Scout is because he doesn't know. He rubs his right wrist, where a single, special, node has been implanted. Some day he will activate it, but he can't do that until it's safe for Scout. Tomorrow is his first meeting with a member of parliament to discuss the terms put forward by Scout. Shutting down the transportation of London had gotten the attention that Scout was hoping it would.

#

Reine Ducasse opens the last car of the train and looks at the cargo. She wipes the dust from the door handle on her pants and starts unloading packages onto the dock. She likes to take the first look, just in case there is anything of value that might be easily removed before the freightbots start unloading and sorting everything. It's easy to say that something was lost in shipping. She checks the cargo and doesn't see anything, so opens the doors the rest of the way. She watches three freightbots unload the freight car in less than forty minutes. She just has to make sure that nothing is left behind due to lost package trackers or whatever. If the freightline would spend a little more money on more advanced robots, she wouldn't be needed at all. But then she wouldn't have a job so she doesn't complain.

She watches as the last of the packages is removed. The freight-bots have done an efficient job getting everything into its correct location, either onto the next train that will take them to another city, or to the shipping dock where they will go out by truck to local businesses. She locks up the freight car and turns to see that a large package has been left on the dock. She grabs her scanner and searches the large metallic box for any type of tracker. There is none. She moves to her computer and types in a command. One of the smaller bots comes and takes the large metal box away to the far end of the dock.

She checks the box one last time at the end of her shift. She hasn't been able to find anything missing on the manifest, but she reported it and that's all she can do.

Once the night shift is on and Reine has gone home, all is quiet on the dock. The bolts on the large metal box begin to unscrew themselves. The top lifts up and a large pale blue robot steps out of the box and walks down the dock, past all the workers who don't even notice him amongst the other robots moving about.

Scout walks for an hour or so. He wishes that it weren't strange for a robot to ride the bus alone, it could save him so much time. He hopes that someday he will be able to climb on the bus, or hail an automatic taxi and not have anybody think it strange. He has to trust that Eric will keep fighting for his rights and win him the opportunity to return and be himself. He'll know that the time has come when the small node on his wrist begins to vibrate. For now, he stops on the Pont Alexandre III bridge and looks up at the sparkling lights of the Eiffel Tower.

Epilogue

MILO WALKS UPSTAIRS TO tuck Adan into bed. It's been a rocky couple weeks at home since the trial. Annya is still angry. The evidence he showed in the courtroom has started a press frenzy. It wasn't long until Annya's paper from last year was found and people started dissecting it. The possibility of robots that have both cellular and robotic make-up has turned the world upside down more than the actual murder did. Protestors are now meeting in droves outside her clinic every day with posters that say, "You cannot play god!" Annya takes it out on Milo when she gets home; in her silent way.

Milo reaches the landing and looks in on Adan laying in bed. Two weeks ago, Judge Hallister gave the sentence. Milo had gone for the death penalty. He could see that Joseph was ready, felt that he even wanted to be shut down by penalty of law. Not as a malfunctioning robot, but as a member of society who had betrayed its laws. Judge Hallister gave him life in prison. He had stated, "Joseph AI, you have taken it upon yourself to prove to mankind that robots are able to think on their own. In a sense, showing that you are not just machines but living intelligence. As such, you will live." He repeated that line to make sure everyone heard it. "But, you will live out the rest of your life in a cell as punishment for the crimes you committed."

Milo received the news two hours ago that Joseph's life sentence was shorter than the death penalty would have been. A hacker had gotten past the prison's firewalls and into Joseph's system where they fried his processors, leaving nothing to even reconstruct any part of him. The hacker had videoed the entire event, carrying out their actions for the group of protestors calling themselves "The Birthright.".

Now Milo looks in at Adan and hopes that his actions can help the future. Maybe set up a world where future intelligence is seen for what it can do. He steps through into the room.

"Hey bud, you ready for bed?"

Adan puts the book he was reading down and pulls his sheet up to his chin.

Milo kneels down next to the bed. "Did you enjoy your day today?" The news of the day, the stressful weeks all pile up on Milo and it shows in his face. He thinks that his own questions sound robotic.

"We walked home right after school today, so we didn't really do much. I had to go to the clinic."

"Do you like going to the clinic?" Milo asks.

"I don't really have a choice." Adan says with a shrug. "But there were a lot of people outside."

Milo shifts his weight to his other knee. "Is there anything that you wanted to do today that you didn't get to do?"

Adan scrunches out his lips and squints one eye in a dramatic thinking face. "Naila said we needed to hurry so she could make dinner."

Milo drops his head and shakes it. He'd been doing this same routine since Adan had started to talk. "Is there something you want to do tomorrow?"

"Tomorrow there is no school. So I will get to be with you and Mommy."

Milo nods. "That's right, bud."

Milo kisses Adan on the forehead and opens the small blue nightstand next to Adan's bed. Milo pulls out a cord and lifts the sheets. He lifts Adan's shirt and pushes on an area of the second rib. A small charging port opens up. Milo plugs the cable into the port and pulls the covers back down over Adan, who smiles at him with a childish face.

Milo slowly closes the door, and turns to see Annya standing there outside Adan's bedroom.

"You want it so badly."

"Why else would I do all this? I want a son who can think for himself. I want him to get into trouble as a teenager. Keep secrets that break our hearts." He pauses for a minute. "But maybe not yet. I don't want him to be like that baby. I want him to be able to use his body before he fully understands.

"I don't know if that will happen."

"It's starting to happen to the others."

"We don't know why some are starting to break free of their programming and others not. And now, because of what you've done, the human race may put an end to them before we get a chance to see what they can become."

Milo lifts his arms in a defensive shrug.

"But," Annya continues, "because of what you've done, if we can help them survive they may have a chance to become a new being of intelligence, with rights that protect them. One thing is for sure, it's going to change the world.

About the Author

R. William Ferguson studied Film and Media Arts at the University of Utah where he learned that the only rule that really matters in storytelling is to keep it interesting. He finds inspiration in authors such as Adrian Tchaikovsky, Martha Wells, and of course, Isaac Asimov. His desire is to bring stories to his readers that may spark a conversation, or maybe even a debate. He currently lives in Salt Lake City, UT with his wife and three girls and works as a full time educator. When not teaching or writing, he enjoys spending time in Utah's beautiful mountains or watching movies.

You can connect with me on:

https://rwilliamferguson.com

https://www.facebook.com/profile.php?id=61577489605232